THE DAY HE ASKED AGAIN

HAWTHORNE HARBOR SECOND CHANCE ROMANCE, BOOK 6

ELANA JOHNSON

AEJ
CREATIVE WORKS

ISBN-13: 978-1-953506-11-5

1

David Reddington couldn't wait to get back to shore. The ocean wind felt like ice against the exposed parts of his face, and as one of the eight civilians who worked at the Port Angeles Station, he had the next three days off.

Away from the station. Away from the politics of border control and immigration and boarding boats to make sure everyone had the proper paperwork. What he really needed was a good deep sea rescue—not that he wanted anyone's life to be in danger.

Most of all, Dave just didn't want to be bored while onboard the ship he captained for the Coast Guard. A mental chuckle moved through him. *Bored on-board. Bored on-board.*

But the fact was, Dave had just turned forty, and everything about his life was boring.

"You watching the game tonight?"

Dave turned toward Ben Erwich and smiled. "Yeah," he said. "Wouldn't miss it."

"You could come over," Ben said, pushing his dark hair off his forehead before putting his hat back on. "Me and a couple of the guys are going in for pizza and drinks."

Dave thought about it for a second. He'd been invited to football games before, but he'd never gone. "I can't tonight," he said, making a quick decision. He was the captain of *Adelie*, and he wanted to keep that professional barrier between him and the crew.

It was flexible, and practically transparent, but it was still there.

"You should host it," Ben said with a grin, because he knew how much Dave hated having people over to his house. "I know my place is too small for you."

"It is not," Dave said, though the apartment Ben got with his housing allowance was pretty pitiful. Dave supposed not everyone could get permission to live twenty-five minutes away, in the town where they grew up, in a house just down the street from their parents.

But Dave had worked for over two decades for the United States Coast Guard, and he wasn't going to feel bad that he'd put in for an assignment closer to his parents and Hawthorne Harbor so he could feel like he had a home.

When he'd first started in the Guard, he'd lived on a ship, for crying out loud. He'd earned all of his honors and privileges, and he wasn't going to feel bad about them. Port Angeles didn't have barracks, so the men and women right out of basic training had no idea what it was like to live in cramped quarters and never have one single second to themselves.

True, some shared apartments, but Ben didn't.

Dave leaned against the railing, the scent of salt and seaweed sharp in his nose. "I have to record the game anyway," he said. "So no group texting where you talk about every play."

"What do you have going on tonight?"

He exhaled, but the heavy sound of it got whipped away by the wind. "Oh, there's a town meeting tonight for the Spring Fling. I'm seriously considering skipping it." He'd grown up attending the Spring Fling every April, and warmth filled him at the thought of going again this year.

He'd been back in Hawthorne Harbor for four years after a long time away, and the town festivals and traditions held just as much magic and spirit as they had when he was a kid. The Spring Fling was all about apples, and blossoms, and romance—surprisingly. But it wasn't even January yet, and the first planning meeting had been set for the event, because there were a lot of activities to coordinate.

From a bachelor auction, to a dance, to a bake-off, to guided tours of the apple orchards, someone had to make sure tourists and townspeople alike had the time of their lives come the third weekend in April.

And he knew who that someone was—Mitch Magleby. The Magleby's had their fingers in every pot in Hawthorne Harbor, but Mitch ran the community center's outreach program, and they funded and organized the Spring Fling. The community center also hosted the Festival of Trees, so Mitch was always seen around that as well.

Dave didn't care about Mitch all that much—but Mitch's daughter.... His pulse thumped erratically just thinking about Brooklynn.

And Dave had learned last year that Brooklynn volunteered on the Spring Fling committee. So maybe he'd signed up to help too. Maybe. Maybe not.

He still wasn't sure if he was even going to go to the meeting.

He let the boat and the crew on her distract him, and the time back to land passed quickly. Dave had a multitude of things to check, and lists to go through, so he began the docking prep while his seamen, petty officers, and ensigns completed their tasks and left the ship with bags over their shoulders.

They'd only been out for a couple of days, so Dave would have no problem transitioning from sea to land—at least physically.

Mentally and emotionally though, he loved the ocean. The gentle way it rocked him to sleep at night or waved hello during the day. He loved the tang of it in his mouth, and he could never figure out how humans stayed on land and worked for a living.

He felt sure he was a water creature, as it had always called to him. He'd left for the Coast Guard basic training the day after he graduated from high school, and he'd never looked back. The Guard had been a good career for him, and he'd worked his way up to Captain and gotten a post close to his family, all of whom still lived in Hawthorne Harbor.

Retirement crossed his mind again as he went through his last checklist. He could retire now and get his pension immediately. Maybe then he wouldn't be bored.

He scoffed at his thoughts. "What would you do with yourself?" he muttered under his breath. "You think you're bored now." He shook his head, finished his work, and went to his office. Now, when he had to sleep on the boat, he had his own quarters. He could handle small spaces; it was just the constant crowds that had gotten to him as an entry-level officer in the Guard all those years ago.

He joined the other men and women calling goodbye to each other, catching sight of a woman leaning against his SUV down on the end of the row. "It holds itself up," he called to Audrey Lynn, a helicopter pilot for one of the three rescue copters they had at the station.

She grinned at him as he approached. "You're done for the weekend, aren't you?" she asked.

"Yeah." Though it was only Thursday, Dave didn't have

to be back until Monday morning. And even then, it was just to check on a fishery and do some environmental protection around the hook of the inlet. "You're on all weekend, aren't you?" He opened the back door and put his backpack inside.

"She'll be there tonight," Audrey said, lifting her phone and showing him the screen.

"You asked her?" A groan started way down in his toes even as he scanned Audrey's text conversation with Brooklynn. So she'd confirmed she'd be there. He frowned at Audrey. "I'm not fourteen."

"No, that sorry gut of yours says you're forty and haven't been on a date in years."

"She won't say yes." Dave unlocked the SUV and held out the keys. "Did you want to drive?"

"Heavens, no," Audrey said, moving around the front of the vehicle to get in the passenger side. She lived in Hawthorne Harbor too, and they often carpooled if possible. Out to save the environment and all that. Plus, Audrey didn't exactly have a reliable ride.

He hoped she'd drop Brooklynn as a viable subject of conversation, but he knew better. If he didn't want to talk about his old crush on a woman who wouldn't go out with him, he'd have to ask Audrey something that would keep her talking for twenty-five minutes.

"I heard you got a new pilot," he said as he twisted the key in the ignition. "And he's somewhat of a playboy."

"Oh, please," Audrey said with an eyeroll attached.

"You should hear the women in the office talk about him. He's so handsome and so tall." She scoffed as if being handsome and tall were crimes against humanity. "All I care about is if he can hold the bird steady while people thrash around in the ocean."

"Right," Dave said, because he wasn't the only one who was single and hadn't been out with anyone in a while. "So why don't you go out with him? Get to know him better? Welcome him to Port Angeles?"

Audrey gave him a wide-eyes, horrified look. "Why would I do that?"

"Why wouldn't you?" He turned onto the highway, his plan working.

"I am the *senior* flight officer here," she said, glaring now. "I can't believe you would even *suggest* I should do such a thing." She huffed and tossed her shoulder-length hair over her shoulder. "Besides, he's like ten years younger than me."

Dave burst out laughing, because that sentence alone testified that Audrey wanted to go out with her new pilot. She wouldn't. But she wanted to.

And she spent the next twenty-five minutes detailing why she wouldn't, and defending herself that she didn't even want to.

~

That evening, Dave checked the clock every five minutes. At least it felt like he did. He needed fifteen minutes to get to the community center, and at six-forty-five, he didn't leave the house. Nor at six-fifty.

He could arrive fashionably late. It was a small town—was anyone on time?

He left his house at six-fifty-five, and he arrived at the community center to find the parking lot almost full. "What is going on here tonight?" he asked himself. He really needed a dog so when he got caught talking to himself, he could at least say he was chatting with the pooch.

A family hurried toward the entrance, their son carrying a basketball with him. Ah, rec game night. No wonder he had to park way in the back of the lot and walk through the weather to get inside.

"Uh, I'm here for the Spring Fling planning meeting?" he asked the woman at the front desk, and she directed him around the corner and down the hall. His steps grew more and more timid the closer he got. He didn't want to be the only one in the meeting.

He wasn't concerned about being late, but a tremor of anxiety hit him when he heard someone talking into a microphone just inside the appointed room. Pausing in the doorway, he scanned for two things: a place to sit and Brooklynn Perrish.

There were plenty of places to sit, as the room was about half-full. He spotted Brooklynn's blonde hair over on the left side, in the third or fourth row. She had seats on both sides of her. So while the woman up front continued to talk about the upcoming festival, Dave started toward the outside edge of the rows. No need to go right down the middle and call attention to himself.

He kept his eyes trained on Brooklynn, so much so that he wasn't watching where he was going. His foot caught on the leg of one of the metal folding chairs, sending it crashing into the one next to it.

He grabbed onto the backs of two chairs to steady himself, making more noise and drawing everyone's gaze to him. The woman up front stopped speaking.

"Hey," he said, lifting one hand when he realized he wasn't going to face-plant it right there on the carpeted floor. "Just a little late."

He rounded the corner and hurried forward, stepping over the man and woman on the end of Brooklynn's row. "Sorry," he said. "Sorry, can I get by? Sorry."

Chairs scraped as people moved, and Brooklynn's face turned a shade of pink that made Dave's heartbeat accelerate too. She was gorgeous with all those curls spilling over her shoulders, and while she shielded her eyes from him, he knew what color they were.

A deep, dark green, like the depths of the ocean when he got past the surface.

He half-sat, half-stumbled into the seat next to her, actually bumping her with his shoulder. "Sorry," he said again, looking up front. The woman had continued, but Dave had certainly made a splashy entrance.

"Hey, Brooklynn," he whispered, leaning down so his mouth was closer to her ear. "What did I miss?"

"Are you kidding me right now?" she hissed. "What are you even doing here?"

2

Brooklynn Perrish felt the weight of every eye as they continued to dart over to where David Reddington had sat down beside her. Practically on top of her, the oaf.

Even as she thought it, she regretted it. He was definitely not an oaf, and the scent of his cologne muddied her thoughts enough to mute Alecia's voice at the front of the room. When Dave was nearby, he consumed all her mental energy.

And she really hated that.

"I came to volunteer for the Spring Fling," he said in a whisper. "Isn't that why you're here?"

Yes, it was. Well, one of the reasons. Why couldn't Ginny face the front? There was nothing to see back here in the fourth row. Nothing, if Dave didn't count as the most eligible bachelor in town.

And to Brooklynn, he didn't. Oh, no, he did not.

She didn't want another relationship, especially with Dave. Surely he knew that. He'd asked her out enough times and she'd told him no over and over.

Thankfully, he didn't ask now, and Ginny finally turned all the way back to face Alecia, who was still going on about the activities the committee had planned. As if Hawthorne Harbor hadn't been hosting the Spring Fling for ninety-two years now.

She looked down at her lap, where she'd balanced a notebook before Dave had come in and interrupted everything. Yes, she'd helped organize different parts of the Fling for years now. Why did she need to take notes?

She had no idea, only that she had. Her fingers twitched, and she started scribbling furiously to catch up on what she'd missed.

Dave sat there, unconcerned about notes. He seemed to be listening, but he could've just as easily been daydreaming about fishing or whatever he did on that huge boat out at the port.

Brooklynn once again felt a tug of regret. She knew what he did on *Adelie*, and it wasn't fishing. She wasn't sure why she was so antagonistic toward him.

Oh, wait. Yes, she did.

He loved the ocean. Went out on a boat every dang day.

And that same ocean had stolen her husband from her. Snatched him from the sky and snuffed his life out.

And that rescue boat Dave manned just down the coast? Couldn't rescue Ryker.

Anger built inside her, giving way quickly to sadness and misery. When someone raised their hand to ask a question, she grew impatient. She really couldn't sit here and smell Dave's cologne all night, listening to idiotic queries about if the date could be changed.

Of course it couldn't. The Spring Fling was always the third Saturday of April. Always. The apple trees were guaranteed to bloom by then, and that was a huge part of the festival. Plus, everyone had survived tax season, and the Spring Fling had originated in town by the local accounting office at the time. Her great-grandfather had owned that firm, and the tradition had been born.

And that brought her to another reason she was seated in the fourth row of this freezing room on a January night when she'd rather be baking.

She was a Magleby, and Magleby's were expected to be involved around town. After all, her parents hadn't left town like a few others, and just because she'd been married for eight months and bore a different last name on her driver's license, she was still a Magleby, still in town, and thus, still expected to volunteer.

So she sat up straight and kept her pen moving across the page as Alecia talked. She finally finished with, "There are sheets up here to sign up for the different activities. We need as many people as we can get." She stepped away from the microphone, and the silence in the room broke as people got up and started forward.

Chatter broke out, and Brooklynn looked at Dave.

Big mistake.

For he was so handsome—*gorgeous!* her mind screamed—and she hadn't seen him in a few weeks. So she really needed a few seconds to drink in those dark, dreamy eyes, the slope of his straight nose, that strong jaw that never had a beard.

He must shave three times a day, she thought, glancing up to see his hair was getting long.

And by long, she could probably pinch it between her fingers if she tried. But she wasn't going to do that. Oh, no, she was not.

She blinked when he smiled and nodded behind her. "Do you want to go sign up?"

No, she didn't. "Yes," she said, getting to her feet. Her back groaned, as she'd had a fifty-pound dog in the grooming van that day. Her website said the limit was forty pounds, but she was a sucker and couldn't say no to a customer. Especially Nellie Ridgeway.

"You okay?" Dave asked, and Brooklynn looked back at him.

"Yes, why?"

"You seemed like you...never mind."

She pulled her hand away from her lower back, where she'd been pushing to relieve some of the ache there. She didn't need to hobble around in front of him like she was Aunt Mabel's age.

Brooklynn put some distance between them, glad when he engaged in another conversation with someone else. In fact, she lost track of Dave entirely a few minutes later, and she wondered if he'd shown up to volunteer or just sit by her.

Warmth filled her from sole to scalp, because while she hadn't accepted any of his invitations, the fact that he asked her out was flattering.

Brooklynn just wasn't sure she could ever love someone as much as she'd loved Ryker. Not only that, she didn't even go to the beach anymore. How could she be with Dave, a man whose job required him to go out on the ocean?

No, she couldn't. It was easier to reject him than to even imagine that they could be together.

She signed her name to several papers and left the community center. If she hurried home, she'd still have time to make those caramel mocha brownies. And maybe, just maybe, the sweets would quell some of the anxiety in her gut that had been plaguing her since Ryker's death three years ago.

~

The next morning, Brooklynn pulled in to the animal shelter, the plate of brownies beside her almost distracting her from the familiar SUV already in the lot.

She knew this car....

Brooklynn's fingers tightened around the wheel. She had an appointment with a corgi in twenty minutes, and she was just stopping by for a moment. Just to give Laci the brownies. Her sister had just broken up with her long-time boyfriend, and she'd texted Brooklynn that she might not survive the day if she didn't have chocolate.

So Brooklynn had plated up the cookies and left without putting makeup on. It didn't matter. Her canine customers didn't care what she looked like when she groomed them. The sky threatened to open up and dump rain on Hawthorne Harbor today anyway, and Brooklynn was considering canceling her appointments if the clients didn't have a garage or something she could use.

She normally didn't mind working out of the back of a van, but sometimes it got stuffy in there, and she almost always stood outside. But not in the rain.

"It'll take two seconds," she told herself, wondering why in the world Dave was at the animal shelter. She probably wouldn't see him anyway, as her sister worked with the vets in a separate part of the building than the adoption center.

After grabbing the brownies, she headed for the door, not enthused by the drumming of thunder overhead when she touched the door handle.

Inside, the building felt much too bright compared to outside, and she glanced to her left, expecting to see Laci standing there in her pale pink scrubs. Instead, her eyes met Dave's.

"Hey," he said, his smile warming his whole face as he stood. Surprise laced the three-letter-word. "What are you doing here?"

"My sister works here," she said, lifting the plate of brownies. Why was her heart tapping around like that? How did she make it stop? Didn't it know Brooklynn had sworn off men?

Fine, it tapped out. But Dave is a captain. Not just any old man.

He was older than her, something she actually liked. He had silver coming in around his ears, and if he kept smiling at her with those white teeth, she'd be going out with him that weekend.

"What are you doing here?" she asked, reaching for her phone in her purse and navigating on it so she wouldn't have to look at Dave's handsome face.

Gorgeous, her brain reminded her.

"Oh, I'm taking a dog for the weekend."

She lifted her eyes to his, finding him downright adorable with the way he tucked his hands in his back pockets. "A dog for the weekend?"

"Yeah, they let you take them for a few days," he said. "Get them out of here. I think they think I'll finally adopt one." He chuckled.

"So you do this a lot."

"Yeah," he said evasively.

"And you don't want a dog full-time?"

"I do, yes," he said. "I love dogs. But my job isn't very conducive to having a pet. I have to sleep on the boat sometimes."

Horror snaked right through her, leaving a cold, wet trail in its wake. "That sounds terrible," she said at the same time her brain put *dog lover* in the pro column for Dave. Why it kept reminding her how wonderful and good-looking he was, she wasn't sure.

He cocked his head and studied her with those eyes that could undo all of her defenses. Her phone buzzed, and she flinched as she looked at it.

"Laci's coming out."

"How's she doing?" he asked.

"She just broke up with her boyfriend," Brooklynn said. "Thus, the brownies."

"Is that why you made brownies?" Dave asked, just enough interest in his voice to know his question wasn't casual.

"No," Brooklynn said. "I don't date, Dave."

"Just checking." He looked toward the door Laci came through, smiling at her too.

"Dave," she said with surprise. It was no surprise that Laci knew who he was. They'd all grown up together in Hawthorne Harbor, and Brooklynn had certainly spilled many of her traitorous secrets to Laci in the middle of the night.

Laci looked from Dave to Brooklynn, and then gave him a quick hug. "It's good to see you. Are you adopting?"

"No."

"So you're following Brooklynn now." She cocked her hip and folded her arms, glaring at the man she'd just hugged.

Brooklynn wanted to crawl in a hole and curl into a ball. "Lace," she said at the same time Dave started laughing. How he could make such a joyful noise, she wasn't sure. Brooklynn hadn't felt that level of happiness in a long, long time.

Thirty-six months.

Three years.

Over one thousand days.

"No," Dave said again, still chuckling. "Though I'd love to go out with her. I know when a woman's not interested." His eyes flicked to hers for a moment. There, then gone. He ducked his head, a hint of a blush entering his face, before turning and going over to the counter.

"Here," Brooklynn said, thrusting the plate of brownies toward her sister. "That was so embarrassing. Why'd you say that?"

Laci took the plate. "I don't know. He hasn't asked you out again?"

She watched him take the leash from the adoption aide. "Not for a couple of months." She didn't mean the words to come out coated in so much sadness. Regret lanced through her. What if he never asked her out again?

He turned toward them, the light in his eyes dimming when he saw them still standing there. He took the mutt around the couch away from them, saluting her with, "I'll see you in the morning."

He'd almost moved out the doors when Brooklynn's mouth caught up to her brain. "Wait. What's in the morning?"

"The planning meeting for the bachelor auction," he said. "I guess we signed up for the same thing." And with that, he walked out, his dog for the weekend in tow.

3

Dave couldn't help stopping by the bakery in the morning on his way to the community center. Brooklynn liked to bake, he knew that. She always had. She'd had a birthday party when she turned thirteen, and it had been at the community college kitchens. Everyone had participated, and though Dave's brother's cake had been wet in the middle, it had still tasted good.

When they'd gone to their junior and senior proms together, she'd baked cookies each time. He could still smell them as he drove in his car, though this was a vastly different vehicle than what he'd driven in high school.

They hadn't had a real romance in high school. Not by his standards. They'd gone out a few times, and he'd kissed her twice. But the call of the ocean had been stronger than waiting in town for two years for her to finish high school, and Dave had left. In fact, nothing had ever called as strongly as the Coast Guard, a ship, or being out on the water.

Until now.

Now, his bones ached a bit more in the morning. Now, he wondered why he didn't retire and just teach water safety classes to kids on the weekends in the summer. None of this going out on the ocean in the winter stuff. No sleeping on ships. Or dealing with men twenty years younger than him who thought they knew more than him.

He pulled a peanut butter bar out of the bag and took a bite, the rich chocolate frosting mixing with the sweet and salty bar. A moan started in the back of his throat.

This morning, the parking lot was just as full as last night. People going in and out in exercise clothes, earbuds in, told him that the New Year's resolutions had quite worn off yet. "Give it another month," he said to himself as he parked.

He'd been up since five, and the six miles he'd put in on the beach were history. He loved running on the beach as the day woke up, though he couldn't get himself to go later in the winter and ended up running in the dark for months.

He had a headlamp and this morning, he'd had Valkerie, the cute pit bull mix he'd picked up the previous morning. She'd run and run and run, and if Dave was going to get a dog, he wanted one that could run as far as he did.

But he wasn't going to get a dog, even if it would curb his loneliness at night.

Inside the community center, he went past the front desk with, "I'm here for the Spring Fling meeting." The woman seated there barely looked up, and this time, Dave wasn't late. In fact, the only person in the room was Brooklynn Perrish.

His stomach tightened at the sight of her, of all that blonde hair he wanted to rake his fingers through. "Morning," he said, his voice perfectly pleasant and not giving away any of the raging hormones in his forty-year-old body.

"Good morning." She smiled at him, more than she'd done in the last six months.

He took the seat next to her and held out the bag. "I stopped and got you something."

"You did?" Her eyebrows went up and she looked at the bag and then him before taking it from him. The smile returned as she peered inside. "A peach bearclaw. These are my favorite." She removed the pastry from the bag and took a bite. "Mm."

Dave's whole body heated up so fast it was like someone had doused him with gasoline and tossed a lit match at his feet. "They're better in the summer, but Jean says she uses frozen peaches from last summer during the winter." Why was he talking about peaches?

"I love them," she said. "I haven't had one in a while. Thank you." She touched his hand, and a zing of electricity shot up his arm. Their eyes met, and for once, she didn't look away. And she didn't look frustrated or guarded either.

As Dave gazed at her, he realized he was seeing the real her. The one she kept hidden behind notebooks and brownies and rejections.

"Maybe—" he started just as someone said, "There you are. We're meeting in room two-oh-two. Come on."

Brooklynn broke the spell between them by looking away. "Oh, I didn't realize." She jumped to her feet and started down the aisle toward the exit.

Dave sat there and tried to get his pulse to return to normal. He couldn't believe he was four words away from asking her out. Again.

Had he not learned anything from the previous half a dozen times he'd asked and she'd said no?

She didn't date. He knew that. And yet, the invitation had been right there, so willing to come out.

He also knew *why* she didn't date, and he'd been hoping that three years would be long enough for her to move past the death of her first husband. Heck, it would be four years in June.

But Dave had no idea what it felt like to lose a loved one in a freak accident, and he couldn't judge her. Couldn't push her.

He also didn't need to open himself up to get his heart shredded, and as he got to his feet, he told himself, "You will not ask her out. You will not," over and over again as he followed her and the woman who'd interrupted him to the right room for the meeting.

Entering last again, he found himself in a room full of women, each with a notebook like Brooklynn's. His heart sank to the bottom of his boots, but he pulled up a chair to the round table, his knee practically touching Brooklynn's.

"Okay," a woman said. "Let's go around an introduce ourselves. I know most of you." Her eyes landed on Dave, and no, he didn't know her.

"I'll start," he said. "I'm Dave Reddington. I work for the Coast Guard."

The ladies went around, and he managed to remember Delaney and Michelle before the names started to blur. Delaney had almost black hair that had to come from a bottle, and she ran the meeting. He'd be fine if he could remember her name.

They talked about a theme for the bachelor auction, and it was decided that "Spring for your Fling" would be the tagline for the event. While Dave sort of hated it, all the women seemed excited about it, even Brooklynn. Honestly, the only way he'd be excited about the bachelor auction at all was if they had dozens of boxes of pizza there, and there was the possibility of eating it with Brooklynn.

"So now we need men," Delaney said, her pen poised to write. The woman on her left started naming names, and Dave could barely keep up.

When the Talker paused, Brooklynn said, "Let's add Dave to the list."

"What?" he almost shouted, horrified as Delaney started writing his name. "No, let's not add Dave to the list."

Brooklynn looked at him, her eyes wide. "Why not?"

"Why would I want to do that?"

"It's for a good cause."

"Is it? The community center does need new carpet, but come on." He nodded to Delaney's paper. "That's not my thing."

"It's just an interest list," Brooklynn said.

"I'm not interested."

Delaney and the other women switched their gazes to Brooklynn, anticipating her next argument. Dave felt a swarm of bees gathering in his chest, but he was ready to die on this hill. He would not parade in front of the single women of Hawthorne Harbor and hope one of them would bid on him. Not happening.

"What about for a maybe?" Brooklynn asked.

A growl started in the back of his throat. "*Maybe* I'll have to work that day."

"You don't work the weekends."

"Sometimes I do." Dave folded his arms, and he'd be blind if he didn't notice that all the women glanced down at his biceps and back to his eyes. "Let's move on."

"This is the last thing," Delaney said. "Then we'll split up the list and make contact with the men. We need at least twenty, you guys. Last year, we only had eleven, and it wasn't enough."

Dave wanted to say that perhaps the lack of men willing to be bid on said something. Maybe they shouldn't be doing this event as part of the Spring Fling.

"We'll just need to make it really fun this year," Michelle said, and that was another maybe Dave hadn't considered. He had no idea how it would ever be fun for a man to go out on stage and hope someone found him attractive enough to pay to go out with him.

Dave already had plenty of pressure in his life, thank you very much.

"These are your men." Delaney slid a list with five hand-printed names on it.

"I have to ask other men to do this?" He wasn't even sure how to do that.

"Which is why it would be better if you did it too," Brooklynn said with just a bit of bite in her voice. "Then you can tell them how much fun it will be and how things will work." She gave him a cocked-eyebrow *so-there* look.

He wanted to throw her sass right back in her face and then take her to lunch. Neither of those were going to happen, so he remained silent. He practically smashed his list in his fist and got up. "Are we done?"

"Yes," Delaney said. "Can you meet next Saturday?"

Dave really wanted to say no, but he nodded instead as the other women gave their assent.

"Good," Delaney said. "Try to talk to as many men as

you can this week. Then we'll have a better idea of where we are for next week."

Dave turned to leave, even Brooklynn's presence not as comforting as he usually found it. After all, she was the one trying to get him to do the auction. Why? So he could fetch the lowest amount? Or not be bid on at all? What was her goal in making him put his name on the list?

It didn't matter. He drove home in the pouring rain to Valkerie, who sat in front of the window and watched the water flow down. "Sorry, girl," he said to her as he kicked his feet up on the ottoman in front of him. "Maybe it'll clear up and we can throw a ball in the backyard."

Hours later, the weather hadn't cleared at all. In fact, it seemed like Mother Nature had parked her storm clouds right over Hawthorne Harbor and had no plans to move them. He'd watched more football and basketball games than anyone should watch in one day, and he was *bored.*

Until his phone chimed out a message from Brooklynn.

His heart caught somewhere in his throat, making breathing and reading difficult.

Hey, so I have a big favor to ask you.

A favor? He could barely type, and he had to go back and fix the word *favor* like four times before it was right.

Yeah, she messaged back. *There's this bachelor auction for the Spring Fling, and you'd be perfect for it.*

He frowned at his phone. "Who does she think she's

talking to?" She surely had his number. He'd called and texted her before lots of times. Too many times, in fact.

I might be willing to break my no-dating rule if you'll do it.

Dave's breath went right out of his body. "Oh, she's not playing nice," he said, but his lips curved up into a smile. He hated texting when he could call, so he pressed the phone button and lifted his device to his ear.

4

Brooklynn expected Dave to call, but when her phone buzzed in her hand, it still startled her. And sent another wave of electricity up into her shoulder, same as when she'd touched his arm.

Why had she done that?

Why had she sent that text?

I might be willing to break my no-dating rule if you'll do it.

That was it; she'd lost her mind.

Cinnamon barked as if to say *someone's calling you*, and Brooklyn flinched again. Her fingers fumbled over the screen, but she managed to tap the green phone icon and connect the call. "Hey," she said.

"Are you serious?" he asked, his voice still in the lower range of growly. Brooklynn had actually never seen Dave when he wasn't chipper and upbeat, and to see him get all hot under the collar about not doing the bachelor auction had practically sent her to the hospital for heart palpitations.

"Because it's not very fair to yank me around like that," he said. "I don't think it's a secret that I—"

"I'm serious," she blurted out. What she really was, was tired. Oh, so tired of trying to resist him. A corner of her heart wailed, something about Ryker and how Brooklynn couldn't be unfaithful to him.

She silenced it and straightened her back though she was alone and Dave couldn't see her. Just the thought of going out with him had her brain bouncing around, and she didn't think there was any possible way she could sleep tonight.

"When would you like to go?" he asked, his voice gentle now.

She tried to speak and ended up coughing. Why was this so hard? She was thirty-eight-years-old and had been out with plenty of men. Heck, she'd been engaged and then married. It seemed unfair that Dave Reddington made her so nervous.

Of course, she'd been on the anxious side since Ryker's death. Her mother had pushed her to go to therapy, but Brooklynn hadn't wanted to talk about the accident or her feelings or any of it.

She'd already had her little westie, and she'd simply added two more dogs to her home in an attempt to feel less lonely. Less upset. Less panicky about every little thing.

"Brooklynn?" Dave asked. "Did I lose you?"

"I'm here," she said. "Sorry, I'm...thinking."

"Okay, so I'm at work this next week, obviously. But I'm not scheduled to be on the boat overnight. I'm usually home by six or so, and we could go to dinner. Or you can wait until next weekend, and we'll go to breakfast or something."

Brooklynn didn't want to wait until next weekend, a thought that surprised her. Honestly, she'd put Dave off for the past year, and there he was, calling the moment she'd gave him any hint she might be interested.

It wasn't a secret that he was, that much was true.

"What about tomorrow?" she asked.

"Tomorrow?" he repeated, heavy shock in the word.

"Yeah," she said. "The lodge up at Olympic Park has a great brunch buffet."

"Yeah, sure," he said, a smile in the words. She imagined it lit up on his face, and with a date looming less than twenty-four hours away, Brooklynn knew she'd get no rest that night. "I'll pick you up at nine?"

"See you then," she said, and the call ended.

"Oh, my stars," she breathed, falling backward on her bed. Cinnamon, the little shorkie who had yipped at her to answer the phone came over and started licking her hand. Brooklynn stroked her with it, and that brought the other two dogs over too.

Cory, the white westie she'd had for seven years, flopped down partially on her chest, pushing her breath out of her lungs as if reminding her to breathe. "Hey, bud," she said, patting him. He was square, like a little ottoman, and she'd loved him from the very first moment she'd seen him.

She also had a yorkie named Callie, and she curled up near Brooklynn's head. "We're not sleeping here, guys," she told them. But she did love how they'd all rallied around her, almost like her girlfriends would in high school after she'd called a boy.

Not that Brooklynn ever called boys in high school. Oh, no. She wasn't painfully shy, but she certainly didn't need any extra attention on her. She'd been on the swim team, and she'd done well. Didn't break any records. Didn't win every time. But the recognition she got from her parents and her coach was enough.

"Come on," she told the dogs as she pushed Cory off her chest and sat up. "We need to figure out what to wear to brunch." And to do that, she'd need to enlist the help of a woman who'd actually been out with a man recently.

"Jules," she said when her best friend answered. "It's a code pink."

Julie gasped and then shrieked. The sound cut off suddenly and was followed by, "You better not be kidding me right now."

"I'm not. I'm going out with Dave Reddington tomorrow morning for brunch up at the park. So get over here. I'm freaking out."

Julie giggled and said, "I'm on my way," and Brooklynn

flopped back onto the bed. And maybe, just maybe, a giggle escaped from her mouth too.

"Okay, so the blue sweater is really nice," Julie said, walking around Brooklynn and tugging on the orange sweater she now wore. "But this one is perfect."

"You don't think it says fall?" Brooklynn asked, looking at herself in the mirror. A burnt orange color, the sweater was cute. It had larger looping that the blue one, and it slid off her shoulder on the right every so often, which she actually liked. "I look like a pumpkin."

"Honey, you do not look anything like a pumpkin." Julie brushed one more imaginary piece of link off Brooklynn's arm. "It's awesome. This is the one. And with those black jeans?" She purred. "He's not going to be able to keep his hands to himself."

"But I want him to keep his hands to himself."

Julie scoffed and waved her hand. "You do not. Or you wouldn't have called me." She gave Brooklynn a quick glare in the mirror. "Now, jewelry. Then we'll talk about makeup." Julie was in her element, and Brooklynn loved being with her when she got into date mode.

Brooklynn simply liked being with another human being on Saturday night. After Ryker died, she'd been so isolated, assuring everyone she was fine to get them to leave her alone. But then, she was left alone, and there were some days when she couldn't handle the pressing silence. The meals for one. Walking past the pictures of the two of them and the life they were supposed to have, and now didn't.

"I think something simple with jewelry," Julie said. "Silver to accent the rustic orange. These long teardrops are nice." She held up a pair of earrings Brooklynn had forgotten she owned. After all, the pups she spent her days with didn't care what dangled from her ears.

She nodded, and Julie handed them to her. "You're not going to wear the ring, are you?"

Brooklynn shook her head, tears springing to her eyes quickly.

"Oh, honey." Julie wrapped her arms around Brooklynn, holding her together. "It's been a long time, but are you sure you're ready for this?"

Brooklynn took a few seconds to push her emotions back down her throat. "I am, Jules." She took a deep breath. "I have to be."

"And you like Dave, right?" Julie stood back and held Brooklynn's shoulders at arm's length. "Because if I could get that man to even glance my way, I'd steal him from you. He is gorgeous, and funny, and rich."

Brooklynn pushed out a quick laugh, though he was all of those things.

"But he only has eyes for you," Julie said. "Trust me, I've tried to get him to look my way." She retreated back to the dresser while Brooklynn put in her earrings.

"I don't know how you moved on after Jim."

"Well, Jim didn't die," Julie said. "We didn't get along for a long time before the marriage ended. So it's different."

Fear struck her between the ribs. "I haven't been out with anyone in a long time," she said. "What do I even talk about? What do I do?"

Julie handed her a necklace with two hearts joined together. "Let's try this." She moved behind Brooklynn, who gathered up her copious amount of hair and held it while Julie worked the clasp on the necklace.

"First off," she said. "You don't worry so much. It's not as hard as you think. You know Dave. You like Dave. So you talk to Dave and get to know him better. That's it."

"What if he holds my hand?"

"Girl, enjoy it." Julie finished with the necklace. "And if he doesn't hold your hand, I'd be shocked."

Brooklynn looked at her hands, wondering how it would feel to have someone hold her hand. She hadn't held hands with a man in years.

"Oh, and you eat." She nodded toward the bathroom. "Let's go for a more dramatic look with the makeup since we're playing nice with the jewelry."

"I don't like how the necklace lays," Brooklynn said, fiddling with the hearts. Julie had given her this necklace after Ryker had died. "It's not right with the neck on the sweater."

"You're right. No necklace." Julie removed it and

ushered Brooklynn into the bathroom. "Dave has a brother who's married. And a nephew. Ask him about them. Ask him about his crew. Ask him about the dog he got the other day. There are all kinds of things to talk about."

Maybe for Julie. Brooklynn felt blank most of the time, and she hated it. She felt like life had turned black and white the day Ryker had died, and she existed in a comic strip. She stood there in the little box, a conversation bubble above her head, waiting for someone to come fill in what she should say, what she should think.

"Eyes closed," Julie said, and Brooklynn complied.

"You'll come over in the morning and do my makeup, right?" Brooklynn asked.

"Honey, I brought my pillow," Julie said with a laugh. "That guest bed is still made. I peeked in there when I got here."

Brooklynn smiled, a rush of gratitude and love filling her. "Thanks, Jules." She opened her eyes and looked at her best friend. "Thank you so much."

"Of course." Julie picked up the neutral palette and a makeup brush. "Now let's see what we can do."

THE NEXT MORNING, BROOKLYNN WORE THE TIGHT BLACK jeans. The orange sweater. The long, sliver teardrop earrings. The bronze and gold and glittery makeup. Julie had spent forty minutes with a flat iron and Brooklynn's hair, making sure every piece curled and waved just right.

"You are beautiful," she said with a hug only moments before the clock would strike nine. "Inside and out. And remember, he already knows it. So own it."

"Love you," Brooklynn whispered to her friend. Jules sniffed and tucked her dark hair behind her ear.

"I need to find me a man like Dave. He has a younger brother. Maybe Joey's available."

"You'd go out with a fishmonger?" Brooklynn asked.

"Have I ever been picky about who I go out with?" Julie asked with a smile.

It was true. She wasn't picky. She'd been in a couple of serious relationships since her divorce five years ago, but nothing had stuck. And she wasn't hopeless. She wasn't depressed. She didn't stay home with her three dogs and bake her anxiety into pies, cakes, and breads.

Brooklynn drew in a deep breath and paced over to the front door. Peering through the peephole, she didn't see him. "He's late."

"It's one minute after," Julie said. When Brooklynn turned around, she found her friend shaking her head and smiling as she poured herself a cup of coffee. She'd made it that morning, so it would probably taste good. Brooklynn could put flour, sugar, and chocolate together into delicious combinations, but making good coffee? She simply didn't know how to do it.

The doorbell rang, which sent all three dogs to

barking and Brooklynn's heart to pounding. She still stood at the door, only inches from Dave on the other side of it.

Julie said something, scooped up one little yapping dog, and disappeared down the hall. Brooklynn's pulse boomed in her ears, and she couldn't believe she was about to go out with another man.

And not just any man.

Dave Reddington.

5

Dave's heart took courage at the sound of barking behind the door. He'd tossed and turned all night, expecting a text from Brooklynn at any moment that told him she wouldn't go out with him.

I can't go.

I'm sick.

I made a mistake.

He'd been through every excuse in the book, and that meant he hadn't gotten much sleep. She still hadn't opened the door, which didn't help his nerves, but the dogs quieted.

And then the door swung in, revealing her stunning beauty right there in full color before him. He couldn't breathe, but somehow his mouth knew to smile. "Wow." He drank her in, feeling like he'd been in the desert for a decade without water.

She wore a pair of black jeans that accentuated the length of her legs. A pair of black ankle boots that added a couple of inches to her height. An orange sweater that reminded him of pumpkin pie and hit all her curves in all the best ways. Her hair—wow, her hair—cascaded over her shoulders and called to him to touch it. Every single piece of her was perfect, and Dave could only stand there and stare.

She was better in real life than in his fantasies, and that was saying something.

"Do you want to meet the pups?" she asked, breaking his trance.

"Yes." He moved then, right into her house, right into her personal space. He wrapped her in his arms, noticing how stiff she was—at least at first. Then she melted into him, and dang if that didn't send pulses through his whole body.

"You look great," he murmured. "I'm still sort of shocked we're doing this." They swayed slightly, and Brooklynn fit against him so well, Dave was sure she'd been made for him to hold.

She clung to him too, and everything in his life was better for those few seconds. He wasn't alone. He wasn't bored.

Brooklynn cleared her throat and backed out of his embrace. "So this is Cory. He's my westie I've had for a while."

"Oh, I love westies." Dave bent down to pick up the little dog. Cory didn't like that, as evidenced by his squirming and doleful glare. Dave put the dog down and patted the other one as Brooklynn told him it was a yorkie named Callie.

"And I have another one down the hall," she said. "Cinnamon. She's a little hyper, so I put her away."

Dave smiled and nodded, glancing around her house. The main floor was one big, open area, with a kitchen and dining room at the back and the living room to his right. "This is nice."

"My dad helped us remodel it," she said with a laugh. "You should've seen it when we bought it."

Dave noted the "us" and the "we" and he wasn't sure how he felt about them. Did she mean them literally? Had she and Ryker bought this house together? Fixed it up? And she was still here?

No wonder she'd rejected Dave over and over. A slip of trepidation moved through him. Maybe he wasn't doing the right thing. Maybe Brooklynn was nowhere near over her husband, nowhere near ready to start a new relationship.

Of course, she'd never said they'd be going out more than once, a fact Dave had spent half the night reminding himself. *This could be a one-time thing*, he told himself again as he gestured toward the door. "Should we go? Our reservation is at nine-thirty."

"You got a reservation?"

"You have to have them for the brunch," he said. "And lucky for us, the weather's bad this weekend, so a lot of people are staying home."

She stepped out onto the front porch without getting her jacket or a purse, and Dave followed her. "See? It's going to pour all day." He glanced up at the angry sky, wishing Mother Nature would play nice and give them an hour of sunshine today. Then maybe he could stroll down Main Street or through the downtown park, Brooklynn's hand in his, as they spent time together.

He reined in his thoughts on the way down the sidewalk to his SUV. She had not defined what this date was, other than brunch, and Dave was determined to let her take the lead. He opened the door for her, unable to keep his hands to himself as she passed him. He guided her with his hand on her lower back and took a deep breath of the floral accents in her hair.

Once he was behind the wheel and belted in, he said, "So, how's the mobile dog spa going?"

Work was an acceptable choice for a conversation, and Brooklynn talked about her job easily. Dave knew there'd be some not-so-easy topics, but hopefully not today.

"I can tell you love it," he said, glancing at her. Rain hit the windshield in the next moment, and his prayers for a dry drive up to the lodge went up in smoke. He focused on the road and put his wipers on.

"I do," she said, a happy note in her voice. "But enough about me."

Dave would never get enough of her. And besides, she knew what he did, where he'd gone. Maybe not every little port over the years, but honestly, there wasn't a lot to tell.

"Tell me something I don't know about you," he said before she could ask him something.

"I never finished college."

"Yeah, I never went," he said.

"No? I thought the military paid for you to go."

"They would've," he said. "But I just stayed with the Coast Guard. Did some classes and courses as I've needed to for the job. That kind of thing." He turned onto the road leading up to the lodge. "How long did you go?"

"Oh, just a year," she said. "Then I decided I'd rather do something else, and I don't need a degree in accounting to bathe dogs."

"Is that what you were studying?" For some reason, he would not have picked accounting for her.

"Heavens, no," she said. "I think that was the problem. I didn't know what to do, so I felt like I was wasting time." She folded her hands in her lap. "Of course, that's what I've been doing a lot recently." Her voice took on a haunted quality, and Dave looked at her, sensing something had changed.

Gone was the fun, vibrant Brooklynn he'd picked up a half an hour ago.

"Hey." He reached over and took her hand in his, every

skin cell vibrating with the touch. "You're not wasting time."

"Yeah, I kind of am."

"What does that mean?" Dave asked as he pulled into the parking lot on the restaurant end of the lodge. There were definitely people here for brunch, but the woman he'd talked to last night said it was not sold out.

He put the SUV in park and twisted to look at Brooklynn. She was so beautiful, it almost hurt to look at her. His fingers twitched, because he wanted to touch her, and he reminded himself how thankful he was to have this date with her at all.

He'd been out with her before. Kissed her even. But the activities of his youth seemed so far away, and they hadn't meant hardly anything to him. Regrettably. But right now, this morning, being here with her *meant* something to him.

"I guess it means I haven't really been living since Ryker died." She studied her hands, that gorgeous hair falling between them.

Dave reached over and tucked it behind her ear, drawing her attention to him. Her eyes held unshed tears, and he smiled at her. "I'm so sorry about him."

She nodded and sniffed. "Yeah, me too."

Dave stifled his sigh and looked out the windshield instead. She wasn't ready for this. No wonder she'd refused to go out with him every time he'd asked for the last year. "Should I take you home?"

"What?" She wiped her eyes and looked at him. "No, I don't want to go home."

"No?" Dave met her eye, hope filling him, making him feel lighter in his seat. "I understand if you'd rather not be here. Really."

"I don't want to be alone," she whispered, and Dave wasn't sure if that meant she liked him or was using him, but he decided on the spot that he didn't care.

He took her hand and squeezed. "You're not alone."

"Thank you," she said, straightening. "Now." She shook her hair over her shoulders, dislodging her hand from his. As he watched, she threw off the drape of depression and darkness that had covered her. "I've heard they have smoked salmon at this brunch, and I'm dying for some of that."

Dave chuckled as he flipped the hood up on his jacket. "Well, let's go get some of that." He reached for the door and added, "Stay there. I've got an umbrella in the back." He got out of the SUV, retrieved the umbrella from the back as the wind tried to blow him right off the mountain, and jogged around to her side.

He opened the umbrella and then opened the door so she could duck under it. She did, pressing right into his body and stealing his breath.

This time, he didn't freeze and go into a staring episode, but managed to get them under the roof of the restaurant and out of the rain.

"Sometimes I seriously question my life choices," she said, glancing over her shoulder.

"Yeah, no kidding," he said. "Like, why do we live here?"

"Hey, at least you got out of town for a while." She pressed one palm against his chest, the perfect flirtatious gesture that would have him grinning for weeks. "I've been living in this rain my whole life."

He chuckled as he opened the door. "Yeah, it's better weather in Southern California, that's for sure."

"Is that where you've been?" she asked, going in ahead of him.

"One of the places," he said.

"Oh, so you're a world traveler," she teased, that rare smile making an appearance. Dave felt himself teetering on the edge of a cliff, and one more touch, one more tease, one more smile would push him over and he'd be falling.

Falling in love.

"Not quite," he said with a laugh. He stepped up to the hostess podium and gave the woman there his name. "Just a US traveler. I work for the *United States* Coast Guard."

"Oh, believe me, I'm aware."

Dave detected something in her voice and turned to face her. "You are?"

"This way," the hostess said, and he reached for Brooklynn's hand so they could walk to their table together.

She let him, and Dave hoped everyone in the restaurant could see them holding hands, because it meant for this one moment, this short walk to a booth in front of the windows, that she was his.

He wanted a lot more moments than this one, but if this was all he got, Dave decided he could be happy.

They sat down, and the hostess said, "Your waitress will be Bonnie, but plates are at the end of the cold bar and the hot bar. Enjoy," before walking away.

Dave shrugged out of his wet leather jacket while Brooklynn slid into the booth. Would it be too forward to sit right beside her?

Probably.

And besides, he didn't want to sit beside her. He wanted to look at her while they talked. So he sat across from her, shoving his jacket against the wall.

"I have—" she started, but the waitress appeared with a big sigh, taking his attention.

"Would you two like anything to drink?" she asked.

He noted the nervous look in Brooklynn's eyes before he turned to the waitress. "I'll have Mountain Dew and orange juice."

Bonnie's eyebrows went up. "And for you?"

"Coffee and cream, please," she said.

Bonnie left, and Dave faced Brooklynn again. "Coffee and cream?"

"I have a confession," she said. "Two of them, actually." She leaned back in the booth. "One's serious, and one's not. Which would you like first?"

Dave wasn't sure what kind of game she was playing,

but her eyes glinted with mischief, and he really liked it. "Let's go with non-serious first. I mean, we haven't even gotten the smoked salmon yet."

She leaned forward, those dark green eyes practically sparkling like stars. "I am really bad at making coffee."

6

Dave burst out laughing, that joy-filled sound infusing Brooklynn's soul. She laughed too, something she felt like she hadn't done in a while. Surely she had, she just felt like she hadn't.

But with Dave, the perpetual darkness that plagued her seemed to be gone. Just poof. Not there anymore.

"So you order it when you go out. Hey, you do what you need to do," he said, sliding to the end of the bench. "Should we go get some food?"

"Yes, food." She joined him and headed for the cold bar first. There were shrimp and cocktail sauce, the smoked salmon she was after, and deviled eggs. All of her favorite things, though she skipped the smoked salmon for now. Dave hadn't been being literal when he said they couldn't talk about serious things until the smoked salmon, but she was going to save the second confession for a few more minutes.

If she said it at all.

Her mind whirred as she made her selections and returned to the booth. Dave followed a minute later, a sigh coming out of his mouth.

"Can I confess something too?" he asked, opening a napkin on the table beside him.

"Of course." But her heart vibrated in her chest, sending weird pulses through her veins.

"I've had a huge crush on you for years," he said, that charming smile making an appearance. The dimple in his left cheek was still there, and how he hadn't been snatched up was a complete mystery.

"That's not a confession," she said, spreading her napkin across her lap. "You've asked me out nine times in the past year. You think I didn't know you liked me?"

He shrugged one powerful shoulder. "It was one year." He put a bite of biscuit and gravy in his mouth and watched her.

Realizations hit her, and Brooklynn felt like a whispering breeze could knock her over. "How long?"

He swallowed and reached for the orange juice the waitress had brought while they'd been getting their food. "I was going to ask you out the day I got back to Hawthorne Harbor."

"But I was with Ryker."

"Right."

"And then I got married."

"Mm hm." He focused on his food then, either unable or unwilling to look at her. Guilt tripped through her, and she didn't even know why. It wasn't her fault she'd been in a relationship with Ryker when Dave had returned to town. They'd been engaged for ten months before getting married, and Dave had been in town for all of that too.

"You came to the wedding."

"I did," he said. "We're friends, Brooklynn. We've been friends for a long time. I mean, I know I left town, but we weren't really together." He lifted his eyes to hers. "Were we?"

"No," she said, her voice almost trapped in the back of her throat. "We went to a few dances together."

"Kissed a couple of times," he said, and heat shot through her body at the memories still there, shelved in the back of her mind.

"Yeah." She cleared her throat.

He continued to eat, and Brooklynn wasn't sure what else to say. She finished her shrimp before he said, "I believe there were two confessions."

"I don't even have smoked salmon yet," she said.

Dave slid out of the booth without another word and returned a few seconds later with the desired delicacy.

She tried to glare at him, but a smile played with her lips, making it impossible to convey her mock annoyance with him.

He ducked his head, an adorable move to conceal his

own smile. She still caught sight of it anyway. "I'm just...I'm wondering if this is a one-time thing or not," he said. "So I want to hear the confession, because then maybe I'll know."

Brooklynn didn't even know if this date was a one-time thing or not. Part of her wanted it to be. The other part thought it might die if she didn't see Dave every single day for the rest of her life.

"Okay," she said, drawing in a deep breath. "It starts with my horrible fear of the ocean."

Dave pulled his soda closer and unwrapped a straw, silent.

Brooklynn touched the smoked salmon, but she didn't have an appetite for it anymore. "The ocean killed Ryker." Around them, people chatted and laughed, having a great time. She felt removed from the world again, and she hated that.

She blinked, and Dave's face appeared before her in full-color. She wanted to live in full color. All the time. Every day. Every night.

With him?

He's a start, she thought, and she tried to focus on those dark eyes that seemed to see everything she was going to say anyway.

"And you work on the ocean," she said. "And I've rejected you for a year, because I can't stand the thought of falling in love with you and then losing you the way I lost Ryker."

There. She'd said it.

Now, if only Dave would say something back.

"That's a tough one," he finally said, dumping the rest of his orange juice in his soda glass now that it was half empty.

"Yeah," she said, feeling like she'd put a damper on their fun brunch date. Dave recovered quickly and moved the conversation to something else. She let him, because it was easier to talk about their families than their feelings, and Brooklynn needed easy.

Once they'd finished and he'd driven her back to her house, he walked with her all the way to her front door.

"I had a great time," he said, folding her into the strong safety of his arms. She loved the way he held her so close without being demanding that she stay.

"Me too," she said, backing up a step. "Did you get the answer to your question?"

He cocked his head and watched her. "I haven't decided yet." He touched his temple in a soft military salute, and added, "See you later, Brooklynn."

Oh, he wasn't playing fair when he said her name like that. All soft and melty and full of emotion.

"Bye," she murmured to his retreating back, and she managed to get inside the house without making a fool of herself. No, she'd done that plenty at the restaurant.

"So, how'd it go?"

The sound of Julie's voice startled Brooklynn enough

to elicit a yelp from her. She pressed her palm over her pulse and said, "You're still here."

"Duh," Julie said from the couch. "You just had your first date since Ryker's death, with the hottest man in town. I wasn't going to miss how it went."

"He's not the hottest man in town," Brooklynn said, coming around to sit beside her best friend.

Julie cocked her head and lifted only her right eyebrow as if to say, *Really? Are you blind?*

Brooklynn couldn't help it. She started giggling, because fine. Dave *was* the hottest man in town, and she'd had an amazing time with him, confessions and all.

"Hey, Mama." Brooklynn leaned down to give her mother a kiss on the forehead. She'd gotten all of her height from her dad, who was nowhere to be found in the kitchen. "Where is everyone?"

"Late," she said with a shake of her head. "Laci had to stay after work for a few minutes. Erika is out with someone and didn't want to leave. She might not come at all." She rinsed the pot she'd been washing and put it on a towel beside the sink.

"Mike's working tonight, and Scooter's picking up Tilly."

Which left Brooklynn, the oldest of the Magleby children in this small branch of the huge family tree. "Who's Erika dating?"

"John Marstrup," her mother said. "And apparently she really likes him."

"She's been out with him before," Brooklynn said in a dry tone. "She didn't like him then." She'd need to text her sister later. Erika had been through some hard stuff in the past few years, and she sometimes looked for validation in the wrong places.

Brooklynn understood. Coming from the most notable family in town wasn't easy. People looked at her for a certain standard, and the pressure to do good, always be perfect, was intense.

A moment later, her youngest brother entered the house, his daughter's shriek announcing their arrival. "Gramma! Did you see there are turkeys out by the road?" The six-year-old came into the kitchen at a run. "Turkeys!" She made a sound that was probably supposed to be a gobble, and Brooklynn laughed.

See, she laughed.

"Hey, Scoot," she said, accepting a side-hug from her brother, who'd entered the kitchen at a much slower pace.

"I know, baby," her mom said to Tilly. "I texted your daddy and told him about them. Grandpa's been out there, trying to get us one."

Tilly looked mildly horrified for a moment, and then her whole face lit up. "To eat?"

"That's right, hon. Now go into the pantry and get your

gramma some cups. The pink ones."

Tilly skipped off to get the job done, and their mother asked, "How's Heather?"

Her brother's ex-wife and Tilly's mom. "Fine," Scooter said as he sat at the bar with Brooklynn. "She's taking the medication. She did great this past weekend with Tilly."

"She's been there since Friday, right?" Brooklynn asked.

"Yeah," Scooter said, wiping his hands through his hair. "It was harder on me than I thought it would be." He looked at her with his hazel eyes, deep and dark and full of worry. "But Tilly said things were fine, and the social worker that was there had good things to report."

Their mother patted his hand. "Good. It's good for her to be with her mom too."

"I know that," Scooter said, danger in the edges of every syllable. "I'm going to go find Dad."

"Oh, he's out in the fields," their mother said. "Take a vest with you so he doesn't shoot you."

Brooklynn chuckled as her brother left the kitchen, and she thought now might be a good time to bring up Dave. No one else was here, and she wouldn't mind if Laci knew at this point in the relationship.

Relationship.

She couldn't believe she could possibly have another one of those and survive.

"Mom," she said, something in her voice drawing her mother from the butter she was stirring into the rice.

"What is it?" she asked, abandoning the task altogether.

"I went out with someone," Brooklynn said, trying the words out in her mouth as she said them.

Her mom—always the theatrical one—gasped and covered her mouth with both hands. Her wide eyes stared back at Brooklynn. "You did? When? Who?"

Her mother may not be the Magleby, but she did love a good, juicy piece of gossip. Before Brooklynn could answer her, the front door opened again.

"Mama," Laci called. "Come help me for a minute. Aunt Mabel needs—"

"I don't need help." Aunt Mabel's voice filled the foyer just outside the kitchen. "I can walk up stairs, girl."

Brooklynn got up anyway, her exchanged glance with her mother begging her not to say anything. "Hey, Aunt Mabel." She embraced her aunt, taking in a long, deep breath of the honey and lavender scent of her skin. "You've been using my soap."

"Oh, I love that stuff," Aunt Mabel said, but if Brooklynn hadn't known her, she'd have thought the older woman hated it, what with the way she scoffed and waved her wrinkled hand. "I'll tell you what I don't love." She teetered over to the kitchen table. "This rain. It's killing my arthritis."

"I'll get you some tea, Mabel," her mother said, pulling down a mug and setting the kettle on the stove. "So Brooklynn was just telling me some big news."

"Mom," Brooklynn said, but the words had already been spoken. Laci and Aunt Mabel watched her now, and a squirmy feeling moved through her stomach. "It's nothing, really."

"She went out with someone," her mom practically yelled as she filled the tea kettle with water. "She was just about to tell me who."

Brooklynn looked at Laci helplessly, but Laci only reached up and took out the elastic keeping her hair in a ponytail. The blonde tresses came down, and she raked her fingers through her hair. "I bet I know who it is."

"I do know who it is," Aunt Mabel said, her eyes closed as if she were meditating and had discovered who Brooklynn had gone to brunch with a few days ago.

"Who?" Brooklynn asked. "If you guys think you're so smart."

"David Reddington," Aunt Mabel said at the same time Laci did, except Laci said Dave, so their voices were off by a syllable.

Horror hit Brooklynn smack dab in the chest. "Fine," she said. "So you're smart."

"He had that look in his eye when he came to the shelter last week," Laci said, shrugging.

"I heard it at Duality on Monday morning," Aunt Mabel said. "I was there getting one of their fantastic pancake sausage sliders, and overheard a couple of women talking."

A couple of women talking. Brooklynn didn't know

what to think. Honestly, she should be used to being the focus of talk in Hawthorne Harbor. People she didn't know had showed up at her house and brought her dinner for a solid two months after Ryker had died. So her going out with someone new?

"I'm surprised it wasn't on the front page of the newspaper," she said dryly.

"Oh, old Bob Townsend will never allow that." Aunt Mabel shook her head. "He hasn't got a romantic bone in his body."

Brooklynn looked at Aunt Mabel, who watched her with open eyes now. "You think it's romantic?"

"Of course I do," Aunt Mabel said. "That man has had a crush on you for years."

"Yeah," Brooklynn murmured. He'd said that. She'd known he was interested in her for a year. But one was different than many, and she still hadn't worked out how she felt about being in a real relationship with him.

"Tell us about it," Laci said. "Because when I saw you on Friday, you two did not have plans to go out." She motioned to her mother that she wanted tea too, and Brooklynn got in on that too.

"It was...." Her phone went off before she could classify it, and she glanced down at where it sat on the counter.

Dave's name winked back at her before the message was whisked up and off the screen. "It was nice," she finally said. "I really like him."

"Hallelujah," Aunt Mabel said, definite sarcastic undertones to the word.

"I just...don't know if it will work out."

"No one knows that," Laci said. "I mean, look at me and Quill. We've been together for years." Her voice choked, and Brooklynn hurried to put her arm around her sister.

"I know," she said softly. "It's okay."

The conversation shifted from Brooklynn to Laci, and then to which type of tea bags her mother bought. Aunt Mabel had never *had* such delicious tea. Then her father and brother came in with one of the wild turkeys, and mayhem ensued. By the time Brooklynn remembered to look at her phone, hours had gone by.

Still, Dave's text brought a smile to her face, and she opened it while she sat in her driveway at home.

The moon is full tonight, and I love a good full moon.

He'd texted her a little bit—insignificant things like that. Things about himself, and he'd asked her a couple of questions since Sunday.

Me too, she tapped out, adding Sorry I missed this. Family dinner tonight and it was crazy.

His next text made her blood run hot and cold at the same time, which was quite discombobulating.

Wanna come over and look at the moon and tell me about it?

7

I*t's not a date*, Dave hurried to add, wishing he could just call Brooklynn. But she liked texting more than talking, and he honestly would rather have a thirty-second conversation than type everything out with his thumbs. *Just friendly.*

To his great surprise, his phone rang a few seconds after he'd seen the little READ come up next to his texts. "Hey," he said.

"So are you saying you won't hold my hand?" she asked in lieu of hello.

"I'm saying it's not raining for once, and I have popcorn and chocolate covered pretzels." He got up and wandered to the front door, peering through the screen to the world outside.

"You really know how to get me to do what you want, don't you?"

"I think you started that," he shot back.

She laughed, and the sound sent flutters right into his heart. "All right. See you in a minute. And Dave?"

"Yeah?"

"There better be something warm to drink. Just because it's not raining doesn't mean it's warm."

"Deal," he said. After hanging up he spun toward the kitchen, hoping he had some hot chocolate mix. He could make coffee too, and she wasn't good at it. So he set a pot to brew, and then started heating water in his kettle too.

He opened the cupboards, muttering, "Hot chocolate. Hot chocolate. Where would I be if I were hot chocolate?" He shifted the canister of oatmeal, and a smile burst onto his face. He grabbed the hot chocolate container and saw that it was hazelnut hot chocolate.

It would have to do.

He stuck a bag of microwave popcorn in and pulled out the tub of dark chocolate covered pretzels a friend of his from Pennsylvania had sent.

He wasn't exactly sure where he and Brooklynn were on the relationship scale. He knew if it were up to him, he'd go straight to her place after work. Bring pizza maybe. Lay on her couch while she ran her fingers through his hair and told him about her day.

Don't go too fast, he told himself as the kernels started to pop. The microwave beeped to indicate the popcorn was ready at the same time Brooklynn's voice floated through the air with a "Hello?"

"Back in the kitchen," he said. "Come on in." His heart jackhammered in his chest, and he wasn't sure why. He'd spent a couple of hours with her on Sunday. They'd held hands, and he'd hugged her.

Because of that, it was easy and natural to draw her into his arms again when she arrived in the kitchen. "Hey," he said again, his voice softer than before. "So I was just about to doctor up the popcorn. Have you ever had churro popcorn?"

"No. What's that?"

He stuck a bowl with a couple tablespoons of butter in it in the microwave. "It's cinnamon and sugar on the popcorn, like a churro."

"Sounds great." She flashed him a smile, and it sent tingles all the way to his toes. "And that coffee smells divine."

"I also have hazelnut hot chocolate and ice cream in the garage."

"You put ice cream in your hot chocolate?"

"My mother did," he said with a laugh. "It cools it down and makes it creamy. Win-win, right?"

"I like my hot drinks hot." She turned in a circle. "Where do I get a mug?"

"Oh, right there." He pointed to the cupboard above the coffee maker and pulled the butter out of the microwave. He busied himself with flavoring it, so he didn't realize that Brooklynn hadn't poured herself a cup of coffee until he turned toward her and found her frozen, both hands wrapped around the mug while she stared at it.

"Everything okay?" he asked though it was obvious that she wasn't okay.

"Where did you get this?" she asked, lifting the mug. It was multi-colored, with a black D painted on it.

"A local artist made it," he said. "My brother got it for me for Christmas last year. I guess she had a booth at the Festival of Trees." He left the popcorn on the counter though it needed to be stirred. "Why?"

"Ryker had one of these." Brooklynn finally looked up. "Obviously not exactly like this. But it was similar."

Dave took it from her, somewhat surprised she let him. He poured her a cup of coffee so he'd have something else to focus on while he spoke. "Did you get rid of his things after he died?"

"Most of them," she said.

"His coffee mug?"

She nodded, her eyes wide and afraid. "I couldn't look at it every morning." She forced a laugh that lightened the mood marginally. "But I'm terrible at making coffee, so that's a reminder of his absence every day anyway."

"Did he make the coffee?"

"Always."

"What about before you were married?"

"I managed to survive somehow."

He handed her the mug and said, "I have cream in the fridge. Sugar's right there." Dave moved back to the popcorn. "And this is ready too. I've got the heater on out back, and we should be set."

"Out back then," she said, turning toward the back door. He went first, glad she hadn't fallen apart over a mug that looked a lot like Ryker's. As soon as she left, he was throwing that mug away. Joey would understand—if he even found out. It wasn't like his younger brother came over often, especially when there was coffee to be had.

On the deck, he'd put the standing heater between the only two patio chairs he owned. In front of that, a small, circular table also waited. He put the popcorn bowl and pretzel tub there and stepped over to fiddle with the temperature dial on the heater.

"This is great," Brooklynn said. "Wow, look at that moon."

"It's the first full moon of the year," Dave said. "We call that a wolf moon. And it's a supermoon, because the moon is in its orbit closest to the earth."

"We?" Brooklynn asked in a teasing voice.

"You know, me and...me," he said with a smile.

"When did you learn so much about the moon?" She lifted her coffee to her lips and took a sip. "Oh, this is fantastic. You've got to come over in the mornings and make this for me."

Dave looked at her long enough to know she was kidding. Still.... "Shouldn't say things you don't mean," he said, turning to go back inside and get his own cup of coffee. When he returned, he said, "And we learn about the moon in the Coast Guard so we can use it to navigate."

"Fascinating." She'd taken the chair away from the door, and Dave set his coffee on the table before stepping back inside to flip off all the lights. He joined her on the deck, only a few feet between them. So maybe he was thinking about holding her hand, even if this was a friendly meeting to look at the moon.

She sighed into her chair, and he said, "I believe you have a story about your crazy family dinner."

Brooklynn looked at him, and by the light of the moon everything about her was black and white and gray. She was still the most beautiful woman he'd ever laid eyes on, and he felt himself slipping back into that trance.

"I meant what I said," she said.

He nodded, and she faced the moon again. "The story involves a wild turkey. How averse to turkeys are you?"

"I'm not averse to turkeys at all," he said.

"Good." She gave a light laugh. "Because this is funny."

"Uncle Dave!"

Dave started laughing as his three-year-old nephew came running toward him. His legs weren't long enough, and Dave thought Pierce would topple right over before he reached him. But the little boy just kept coming, and Dave swooped him off his feet and into his arms.

"Heya, buddy. What's going on?"

"I wearing big-boy underpants," he said with so much pride in his voice. "Mom says no more baby diapers."

"That's great," Dave said, giving his nephew a kiss on the cheek. "Now, where's Grandpa? I heard he's doing something with a hammer that Grandma doesn't like."

Pierce pointed toward the house, and Dave joined his brother Charlie on the front steps. "Hey, man," his brother said. "Dad's got half the wall torn down."

"Why's he doing that?" Dave asked. "Why doesn't he just call Jeremy?"

"He thinks he can do it himself."

"He's not handy," Dave said.

"Well, we all live in our own universe." Charlie flashed him a smile and turned toward the door. "I've already talked to him, but he only listens to you." A certain tang of bitterness came with the words, but Dave didn't know how to erase it.

"That's not true," he said anyway, though he'd talk to his dad, and he'd stop ripping out the wall between the living room and the kitchen, and Dave would call Jeremy on his way home.

He followed his brother inside and set Pierce down. "Go find us a ball, bud. We can throw it when I'm done with Grandpa."

"Dave, thank heaven," his mother said, appearing in the doorway that led into the kitchen. Of course, she'd obviously seen him enter, because Dave could see right through the wall.

Dave bent down and peered through the opening between the studs. "Mom, what in the world is this?" He knew what it was—how he didn't want to spend his Friday night. But he hadn't had the guts to ask Brooklynn out, and their texting since the supermoon viewing on Wednesday had been light.

He'd basically bounced the ball into her court, and she was holding onto it. So fine. He could make a house call to his parents on Friday night. That was totally normal.

"Oh, your father wants a more open floor plan. I told him to call Jeremy."

"Yeah, because I think that's a load-bearing wall."

"It is," Charlie said as he came out of the kitchen. "Mom, Jackie wants to know if we're setting the table inside or on the patio."

"It's freezing," his mother said.

"Well, she's eight months pregnant, so she's burning up." Charlie chuckled and said, "I'll get the table set."

"Where's Dad?" Dave asked.

"He's pouting in the garage because I told him he couldn't work on the wall while Pierce was here. You should see him. Stuff goes flying everywhere. I almost got hit by that hammer he swings around." She shook her head, and Dave almost laughed. He caught it just in time. But his mother could be a bit dramatic, and he was sure she hadn't almost gotten hit.

"I'll go talk to him." He ducked down again and looked through the wall. "Hey, Jackie. How long 'till dinner?"

She waved a spatula at him. "Ten minutes."

"Roger that." Dave gave his mom a quick kiss and went back out the front door. There was no direct entrance to the garage from the house, and if anything, his parents should do that upgrade. In Dave's opinion, which no one had asked for.

He keyed in the code to get the garage door up and waited while it rumbled and screeched out of the way. "Hey, Dad. Dinner's almost ready."

"Humph," his father said, not even turning toward him from the workbench along the back wall. He had every kind of tool there was, and absolutely no need for any of them.

"The wall looks...." Dave searched for the right word. "Dad, it's bad."

"I know that," he said.

Dave made it to the bench in the back. "You need a structural engineer to come clear that. You can't just start ripping down walls."

"I don't know any structural engineers."

"That's why you call Jeremy." The man owned an excellent home-building company. He did whole builds, remodels, basement finishes, all of it.

"I can do it."

"Of course you *can*," Dave said. "But Mom's concerned about the structure, and so am I. You need to have someone come look before you swing that hammer again." He picked it up, the end of it white from the plaster his father had been hitting.

"Fine," his father said.

"Great," Dave said. "So I'll be taking this with me, and you'll be calling Jeremy."

His dad finally looked at him. "I don't want to call him." His dad could be so stubborn and so proud.

Dave heaved a great big sigh, exaggerating it on purpose. "Fine, Dad. I'll call him."

"Tell him I want open concept."

"I'll tell him," Dave deadpanned, wondering when his parents had gotten so old. Seriously, what was his father thinking? He couldn't tear down walls. Dave shook his head just thinking about it.

"Given any more thought to retirement?" his dad asked, picking up a wrench and hanging it in its spot.

"A little," Dave admitted. He didn't want to admit he'd only gotten as far as thinking about it and dismissing it. Because if he thought he was bored now....

But he wasn't bored. Not since going out with Brooklynn on Sunday. She'd introduced a new, exciting element to his life, and his pulse picked up every time his phone chimed. He kept all of that to himself though, and instead listened to his father talk about how great the retired life was.

He stayed for dinner, and he called Jeremy on his way

home, just as he'd known he would. So maybe that part of his life was predictable. Boring.

But he had another meeting for the Spring Fling in the morning. Brooklynn would be there—and anything could happen then.

8

Brooklynn woke on Saturday morning to the sound of her phone ringing. She sat straight up, wondering how late she'd slept, but the clock said it was only seven-thirty.

Her heart beat rocketed around in her chest. Was something wrong? She grabbed her phone off the nightstand and flipped it over to see the call was from Delaney White.

"She can leave a message," Brooklynn said as she lay back down in bed. But she was awake now, and she wouldn't be able to go back to sleep.

The butterflies in her stomach testified that she'd be seeing Dave in just a few hours. Hanging out and munching on popcorn on Wednesday night had been great. Wonderful. Awesome. He had not held her hand, as promised, and she'd left a bit disappointed.

Then she'd decided that she couldn't see him again, at least not just the two of them. With the best coffee in the world and at his house, like she was his girlfriend. She wasn't sure why she couldn't, but she knew she liked him too much already and that scared her. So she hadn't texted him too much, and he seemed to have gotten the hint, because he didn't ask her out for Friday night.

Or Saturday night. Or for anything.

Something sharp tugged inside her, and she ignored it as she got up and stepped into the shower. She checked her messages after that, and Delaney had said they'd be meeting at the bakery instead of the community center.

That kind of information could've been sent in a text, much later than seven-thirty. Brooklynn dressed and went down the hall to make coffee. With a second thought, she decided to just heat up some milk and add chocolate powder to it. Now that she'd had Dave's coffee, she could never go back to her inferior brew.

She fed the pups, her mind mentally going through her to-do list for the day. She had the meeting this morning, and then two dog grooming appointments that afternoon. By the evening, she hoped to be in the kitchen with her baking supplies, making something delicious to spend her Saturday night with.

By the time she showed up at the bakery, she was ready for something with a lot of sugar in it. She went through the line first and got herself a lemon poppyseed muffin for breakfast, and a long doughnut with maple frosting for later.

She knew the moment Dave arrived, as did every available female in the shop. It was almost as if the chatter muted for a moment as he glanced around, that black leather jacket stretching across those broad shoulders so unfair.

So, so unfair.

He bypassed the line and came straight toward Brooklynn, who almost dropped her pastries. Thankfully, she wasn't alone, and Dave didn't lean in and embrace her the way he had at other times.

Instead, he glanced around at her, Delaney, and Michelle, and asked, "Is this where we're sitting?"

No one said anything, but Dave went around the table and slid onto the bench.

"He is so dreamy," Michelle whispered to Brooklynn, and she tossed her hair over her shoulder and went to sit next to Dave. Brooklynn watched in shock as Michelle started giggling and smiling at Dave, pushing against his chest and flirting like crazy.

Dave grinned at her and said something, which made Brooklynn's blood boil right there in her veins.

And she knew—she was not leaving this bakery without a date on the horizon. A date with Dave.

She sat down across from him, leaving the last spot for Delaney. She sat and said, "Raven can't make it this morning, so we can get started." She tapped her papers together on the table. "We need to finalize the categories for the bake-off today. And establish the theme." She glanced around at everyone. "So let's hear the ideas."

"Apples," Michelle said, and Brooklynn used every ounce of her willpower not to roll her eyes.

"We've done apples too often," Delaney said. "Let's think outside the box."

"What kind of themes do you normally do?" Dave asked.

Brooklynn opened her mouth to answer, but Michelle beat her to it with, "All kinds of things. We name a focus ingredient we want to see. We've done pumpkin, apple, pecan...." She continued rattling off the themes from the past several years, and Brooklynn thought she'd need to go see the dentist for how hard she was grinding her teeth.

Dave sat there and listened to her, nodding as if he was really listening to her. As if he cared.

Michelle finally stopped talking, and Brooklynn turned to Delaney. "What about beets?"

"Ooh, beets." Delaney wrote the word on her notebook while Brooklynn shot Michelle a *so-there* look. Michelle either missed it or didn't care, and silence descended on the table.

"Dave?" Delaney asked, and she leaned toward him. "Do you have any ideas?"

"No ideas," he said. "I know we can't do lavender, but

other than that, I don't know why we don't just let people bake what they want."

"It helps the judges choose the best one," Delaney explained. "What about banana?"

"Then you'll get fifty types of banana bread," Brooklynn said.

"Well, beets will give us a zillion different types of breads," Michelle said, and Brooklynn almost hissed at her.

She couldn't believe the toxicity of the jealousy running through her. Taking a deep breath, she glanced at Dave. He watched her too, and that only made her squirm more.

She had to get out of there. "Excuse me," she said. "I have to run to the bathroom. I'll be right back." She left her pastries on the table, so she'd have to go back. Otherwise, she thought she might just walk out the door after using the restroom.

And she didn't even have to go. But she went in the bathroom and looked at herself in the mirror. She could tell she was upset, and she wished she could get the blotchiness out of her skin. She couldn't, so she washed her hands in the coldest water possible and went back out into the bakery.

Dave pushed off the wall across from the ladies' room. "Hey."

"Hey." Brooklynn glanced down the hall to the table where they'd been sitting. "What's going on?"

"Delaney mentioned something about us bringing a baked good next week, and I freaked out and left the table." Dave gave a chuckle made of nerves. "And I don't bake, so…." He ducked his head and looked up at her, the most adorable move in the world.

"So…what?" she asked, clearly not getting what he was hinting at.

"I was wondering if you'd give me a lesson or two." His hand brushed hers, and it was no accident.

She wondered if he'd even noticed Michelle's flirting. She'd decided not to go out with him again, but her violent reaction to Michelle had her saying, "Yeah, sure. What did you have in mind?"

"What would be the easiest?"

"Chocolate chip cookies?" she guessed.

"Great, we can start there. When are you available?"

"Tonight," she said, looking him straight in the eyes. "Does that work for you?"

He grinned full-force then, and it was absolutely wonderful. "Absolutely it does."

Brooklynn didn't want to smile too widely, but she did allow her lips to curve upward. "Great. I have a couple of appointments this afternoon, so maybe like five?"

"Sure. Do I need to bring anything?"

"Just yourself." She tiptoed her fingers up the front of his shirt, not afraid to earn a few flirting points herself, and headed back to the table, ready to name every fruit in the book until Delaney picked one.

BROOKLYNN STOOD IN THE KITCHEN, HER BACK TO THE FRONT door though every cell in her body screamed at her to turn and go see if Dave had arrived yet. Of course he hadn't arrived yet, or he would've knocked. Or rang the doorbell.

She stirred the melting peanut butter and butter on the stove, her favorite no-bake cookie recipe almost done. Dave wanted to make chocolate chip cookies, but she definitely needed something sweet to snack on while they accomplished that.

She'd been in his house on Wednesday night, and it had been nice. But her nerves were firing on all cylinders to have him here for an extended period of time. Her phone chimed and she reached for it.

Julie: Have fun tonight! Relax. Flirt. Call me if you kiss him.

Brooklynn scoffed, then terror gripped her vocal chords and made them silent. Kiss him? Was that a possibility tonight? Already?

Couldn't be. She swallowed and threw her phone when the doorbell sounded. She spun, her heart pounding, and backed into the counter behind her. All she could think about was kissing Dave Reddington—a man she'd kissed before.

Not really, her mind said. Sure he'd kissed her a couple of times in high school. But he'd been a boy then, and he was definitely all man now.

He knocked, calling, "Brooklynn?" in the same breath.

She pushed off the counter and practically ran to the door, feeling much too old to be this jittery about a man. But as soon as she opened the door, Dave's presence reminded her of just how wonderful he was.

"Hey, there," he said, grinning like he showed up on her doorstep every evening. "You started without me?" He glanced over her shoulder, and she gasped.

"The no-bakes." She ran back to the stove and quickly stirred the now melted butters together. "These are just for eating while we bake," she said.

"Ah, so you have no confidence in me whatsoever." He chuckled as he joined her in the kitchen. "Probably smart."

"I have confidence in you," she said. "I mean, you're forty years old, so you've survived this long somehow."

"Forty-one," he said. "My birthday was in December."

"Forty-one then," she said. "Surely you cook for yourself."

"Small stuff," he said, inching closer. "What is this."

"No-bake cookies." She took the pan off the burner and poured in the oats and cocoa. "See, you just melt peanut butter and butter and mix all this in. Then we'll scoop it out and let it set up."

"My grandmother used to make these."

"This is Aunt Mabel's recipe from the Mansion."

Brooklynn got everything coated and she nudged him back. "I need something out of that drawer."

He didn't move at all. "Do you?"

"Dave," she said, only flirtatious undertones in her voice. "You're going to scoop these for us."

Instead of moving back, he swept his arm around her waist and pulled her close to his body. A sigh cascaded through her, and the scent of his cologne had her seriously thinking about kissing him.

Could she really kiss him that night?

"Mm," he said, breathing in the scent of her hair. "I missed you this week."

"It was a long week, wasn't it?"

"So long." He bent his head and traced the tip of his nose across her temple. "Brooklynn, I'm dying to know how you've labeled us."

She thought of the scene in the bakery, of Michelle flirting with Dave for all she was worth, of how upset it had made her. She didn't want him going out with anyone else. Or even thinking of going out with anyone else.

But she didn't know how to tell him that, especially when he pressed his lips to a spot just below her jaw. "I mean, are we friends? Is this a date? Can we go out again tomorrow?"

"Tomorrow?" she asked, the word full of air. She realized she'd lifted both arms to hold onto his powerful shoulders, and she was sure she wouldn't be able to stand on her own if he let her go.

He pulled away, but his arm stayed around her waist. His dark eyes held nothing but dangerous desire as he gazed down at her. "Just be honest with me. I feel like I need to know so I can...I don't know. Move on if I need to."

Her heart wailed, and she opened her mouth, unsure of what was about to come out. "Did you see Michelle this morning?"

"Michelle?" His eyebrows drew together. "Oh, at the meeting? Yeah...you were there."

"You didn't notice her flirting with you?"

Dave looked even more confused. "Was she?"

"Dave." Brooklynn couldn't believe he hadn't noticed. He wasn't stupid. "How could you not have seen that?"

"I saw you," he said. "And you looked mad, and then you ran off, and I followed you."

"I bet that made Michelle mad," Brooklynn said. Now that she thought about it, the flirting had gone down several notches after she'd returned from the bathroom.

"Did it?" He slipped his hand away from her, and she mourned the loss of it. "What's going on?"

Brooklynn drew in a deep breath, ready to confess everything. "She was flirting with you hard-core in the bakery. Hard. Core." Her anger rose just thinking about it. "That's why I was upset. I wasn't mad."

Dave blinked, blinked, and then understanding filled his eyes. Before he could say anything, she said, "So if someone asked me what you were to me, I'd say you were my boyfriend."

He fell back a step, clearly not expecting that. Brooklynn closed the gap between them, putting both hands on his chest and sliding them up to his collar. "So while I'm nervous, and a bit unsure, I do know one thing. I don't want you going out with Michelle or any other woman."

A smile spread Dave's lips. "Just you."

"Just me," she said. "So if you want this to be a baking lesson date, that's fine." She couldn't believe how powerful and bold she felt. With a jolt, she realized she used to be confident like this all the time.

The ocean had stolen a lot from her the day it had killed Ryker.

"How do *you* feel about that?" she asked.

"I feel great about that," he said quickly.

"Good." She tipped up onto her toes and kissed him on the cheek. "Now, let's get these scooped, and then you're going to bake me some cookies."

9

"I can't believe this is that hard," Dave said, peering at the recipe and then looking into the bowl where his cookie dough was. "This doesn't look right."

He'd followed recipes before, but something about this one eluded him.

"And you have an egg shell in there." Brooklynn giggled, a high-pitched, girly sound that drove his hormones into overdrive. Well, everything had done that since the moment she'd uttered the word *boyfriend.*

Boyfriend.

Boyfriend.

Boyfriend.

He wanted to run out of her house and scream it from the rooftops. *I'm Brooklynn Magleby's boyfriend!*

Instead, he said, "Laugh it up," with a dose of frustration coursing through him.

"I'll get it out," she said, opening a drawer in the island and taking out a spoon. "And this is so good for me."

"It is?"

"Yeah, seeing you not be perfect at something?" She nudged him with her hip. "Means you're human."

"Of course I'm human," he said darkly, still thinking about her lips against his cheek. She'd totally missed her mark, but Dave didn't want to press his luck. If she wanted to kiss him, she could.

"Well, you're pretty darn perfect," she said, fishing the egg shell out of the dough. "And this has way too much flour in it. That's the problem. How much did you put in?"

"What it said to." He jabbed at the recipe she'd laid on the counter before busying herself with feeding her three dogs. They all laid on the floor a few feet away, an invisible line she'd clearly drawn for them.

It bothered him that she thought he was perfect, and he wasn't sure why. "So how do I fix this?"

"We'll add another egg," she said.

He turned to her fridge to get the carton out. "And why do you think I'm perfect?"

She glanced at him when he joined her at the island again. "That bothers you." She wasn't asking.

"Yes, it bothers me," he admitted. "That's a high standard for someone to live up to." He cracked the egg and dropped it into the bowl. "No shells this time."

Brooklynn moved back around to the other side, where she'd been directing him if he had a question. "Oh, look. You used the half-cup for the flour. That's the problem." She indicated the used measuring cups on the counter. There was a one-cup and a half-cup.

"It says two and a half—oh." It was only two cups of flour. He put his frustration into mixing the egg into the dough, and it started to look more normal. He tipped the bowl toward her. "Better?"

"Definitely better."

"So I add the chocolate chips now."

"Yep."

He slit the bag with a knife and poured them in. "Don't think I didn't notice how you didn't answer my question." He gave her a sharp look—one he'd give to one of his junior officers when they did something stupid on-deck—and went back to mixing in the chocolate chips.

"I don't know," she said. "It's just that you're kind to everyone. Have a job. A successful career. Heck, you get up and run every morning at five o'clock. You're never late, your house was clean when I came over, you—"

"Okay," he said, cutting her off. "For the record, I cleaned just so I could invite you over. I'm never late, because the military doesn't stand for it. I run because I want to keep my job and get after my men if they don't keep up with their workouts."

"You love dogs—"

"You have three dogs, and a whole dog grooming business."

"You—"

"You're kind," Dave said over her. "You have a job, which by the way, how does that contribute toward a person's perfection score?"

She stared at him, clearly surprised that he had a problem with her thinking he was perfect. "I didn't know it was such a big deal."

"It's not," he said, his irritation subsiding as quickly as it had reared up. "I just don't think it's healthy for you to view me like that."

"Well, I was saying now I know you're *not* perfect," she said. "You just interrupted me, *and* you can't make cookies."

Dave glared for one more moment, and then he burst out laughing. The tension in the room evaporated, and he was glad when she joined her laughter to his.

"Okay, so I scoop these too?" He looked for the scooper, finding it in the sink.

"Yep. Then twelve minutes in the oven."

"Sweet." Dave could only think about what they might do during that twelve minutes and if there might be kissing involved.

He slid the tray into the oven and set the timer before turning back to her. She got up and moved into the living room, her three pups following her like shadows.

"So now what?" he asked.

"Now you come sit by me and tell me something about yourself that I don't know." She smiled at him, and he recognized this flirting when he saw it. And he liked it.

LATER THAT NIGHT, HE CLIMBED THE STEPS TO HIS HOUSE, his feet floating on clouds. No, he hadn't gotten his kiss. Brooklynn had admitted that she wasn't ready, and he was fine with it.

He really was, because he'd held her on the couch, and talked to her, and eaten cookies, and held small dogs on his lap.

It was the single best evening of his life, hands down. *Boyfriend* rang through his mind, and he paused just inside his front door and texted her.

I had the best time tonight. Sorry I freaked out about not being perfect.

He deleted off the last sentence and just sent the first.

Me too, her message came back. *And I'd love to see you tomorrow. What are you thinking?*

What was he thinking? What a dangerous question.

He wanted to kiss her—badly—but he didn't want to push her away. Frighten her. He wanted to show her his ship, but she hated the ocean. He'd love to walk with her down the beach, but again, water.

"What should we do tomorrow?" he asked the empty house. He had no idea, and that meant it was time to call for reinforcements. His youngest brother, Joey went out a lot. Maybe he'd have some non-ocean ideas for dates.

"Hey, bro," he said when Joey picked up.

"Do you know what time it is?" Joey asked. "This better be a huge emergency."

"What time is it?" Dave asked, walking into his kitchen to look at the clock on the microwave. After ten. "Oh, wow. I had no idea. Sorry."

"I'm up now." Joey sighed. "But wow, three is going to come fast."

"I'll make it quick."

"Please do," Joey said with some measure of sarcasm.

"I'm dating Brooklynn Magleby. Perrish. Whatever."

"You're dating Brooklynn?" The level of disbelief in his brother's voice sent annoyance through Dave.

"Yes," he said. "And I need some fun ideas for dates. No beach. No ocean."

"In the rain."

"Right. It's supposed to rain tomorrow too."

"So there's the movies," Joey said.

Dave rolled his eyes. "The movies?"

"Hey, it's dark in there," he said. "There's snacks. It's not a bad date."

"What else have you got?"

"The apple cider mill," he said. "They do tours on Sunday afternoons. I think there's a tasting too."

"Okay, that's interesting," he said.

"Or go up to Seattle for the day," Joey said. "Time in the car. Lunch. Walk down to some of the sights. That's fun."

Dave liked the sound of that too, but he wasn't sure

what Brooklynn was up for. "All right, thanks," he said. "Sorry I called so late."

"Yeah," Joey said. "And I guess this was an emergency. I mean, you've had a crush on Brooklynn for what? Like two years now?"

More like five, but Dave just said, "Yeah, something like that. Thanks, bro."

"Yep."

The call ended, and Dave navigated back to his texts. He suggested the cider mill and the movies to Brooklynn, and she texted back with *Movies. I'll pick it and let you know what time to come get me.*

He chuckled and shook his head. So it really was that easy. And he really did feel bad about calling his brother so late. He sighed as he opened the fridge and pulled out a can of soda. His gaze went naturally to the table where he usually stacked things, his eyes landing on the retirement packet he'd brought home that week.

He hadn't looked at it yet. Heck, making the first step and going to ask about it at all had nearly taken the whole week. But he had the packet now, and adrenaline still buzzed through him with an electric force he didn't understand.

Sitting at the table, he pulled the packet toward him and started reading.

Several minutes later, he said, "July. I have to get to July to get my full year of service."

And July felt so very far away.

"OH, YOU'RE TRYING TO DRIVE ME CRAZY," HE SAID WHEN Brooklynn answered the door the following morning. To be fair, it was almost noon, and he'd been sitting down the road a bit for a good half-hour, too antsy to stay in his house but too early to pick her up.

He whistled as he let his gaze slide down her body one more time. She wore a little black dress that screamed flirty and fun. She'd piled her hair on top of her head in a messy bun, and she wore only pink gloss on those very kissable lips.

"This is what you wear to the movies?" He swept her into his arms, getting a nose full of strawberries and flowers and chocolate. "Mm, you smell nice." He let his lips drift down to her earlobe, and he'd simply go insane if he didn't kiss her today. Right now.

"We're standing on my front porch," she said, putting pressure on his shoulders.

"Yeah, so let's go inside," he said, nudging her backward.

"The movie starts in thirty minutes, and you said you'd buy me lunch." She smirked at him, a sexy, flirty gesture that had his heart bouncing around behind his ribs.

"Fine," he said, bending down to kiss her cheek. "A promise is a promise." He secured his hand in hers as they walked toward his SUV. "Tell me how you met Ryker."

She pulled in a breath, and Dave waited. He didn't regret the question. She'd been married before; they should be able to talk about that relationship.

"Have you ever been in love?" she asked.

He looked at her, surprise pulling through him. "With a woman? No. With a ship? Yes." He grinned at her and opened the door.

She chuckled and shook her head. "Ryker was...great. I loved him a lot."

"Loved? Past tense?" He'd seen the pictures of the two of them still on her end tables in the living room.

"I still love him," she said, meeting Dave's gaze head-on. "I think I always will, Dave."

"I think you will too," he said. "I think that's normal. Natural." He wasn't sure how he felt about her still being in love with her first husband. But he supposed she had every right to be. It wasn't like they'd gotten divorced, and if Ryker were still here, Dave certainly wouldn't be taking Brooklynn to the movies right now.

He sighed and looked away. "Let's go."

She reached up and cradled his face, drawing his eyes back to hers. "The human heart has an unlimited capacity to love."

Dave had never been in love before, no. But looking into Brooklynn's eyes, he sure felt like he was falling that way. And fast.

"I sure like you," he whispered, leaning his forehead against hers.

"And I like you." She held his face in both hands now, and Dave felt something deeper than just hormones. The moment continued, and he basked in the warm glow of it.

"But if we're late to this movie, I will seriously punch you," she said, still in that soft, throaty voice.

He opened his eyes as the laughter came bubbling out of his throat. "All right, ma'am. Let's get going." He stepped back and closed her door before rounding the front of the vehicle.

As he got behind the wheel, she said, "Don't ever call me ma'am."

"Yes, ma'am," he said, flinching when she playfully punched him in the arm. They laughed together, and Brooklynn reached over and slipped her fingers between his. Dave smiled the whole way to the movie theater, because he simply couldn't believe this was his reality now.

Couldn't believe it.

Sure, he'd dreamt of it. Fantasized about it, even. But the real thing—the real conversations, the real touches, the real secret looks, were so much better than even his imagination had conjured up.

As they hurried toward their theater, their hands full of food, Dave prayed they wouldn't be late and miss the beginning.

But when someone said, "Brooklynn?" with a heavy dose of shock in his voice, Dave's hopes and prayers dried up.

"Robbie," she said, her voice just as shocked. Dave looked at her to find her eyes wide and all her nervous energy back. She met his eye, her gaze skittering away in the next moment.

"Dave," she said calmly, but he could still hear the tremor beneath his name. "This is Robbie Perrish. Ryker's brother."

Dave almost dropped his hot dog combo meal, barely remembering he couldn't shake the man's hand and hold food, a drink, and a bucket of popcorn at the same time. "Hey," he managed to say.

"Robbie, this is Dave," Brooklynn said. "My new boyfriend."

Robbie's shock morphed into fury almost instantly, and Dave had no idea what to say or do. "Hey," he said again, watching the storms pass through Robbie's eyes.

He finally turned back to Brooklynn, as if he'd sized up Dave and found him lacking. "Can I talk to you alone for a moment?" he asked. He stalked away before waiting for her to answer.

"We're going to be late," Dave said, not liking the way Robbie made him feel guilty and made Brooklynn transform back into the anxious version of herself.

"I know." Brooklynn stepped over to a closed concessions counter and set down her food. "I'll be right back."

Dave watched her walk away, hoping what she'd said was true and that she'd really be right back. But he had his doubts.

10

Brooklynn's insides quaked like gelatin as she followed Robbie. He looked so much like Ryker. So much. Too much.

He finally spun back, and she almost crashed into him on her next step. "You're *dating* him?"

She lifted her chin, looking the other man right in the eyes. "Ryker's dead, Robbie. Not sure if you knew that."

Robbie's eyes stormed, and he was so, so angry. Brooklynn cared; she didn't want to hurt him. A lot of people had suffered when Ryker had died.

"So yes," she said. "I'm dating Dave. He's the first man I've been out with in three years, and I'm...I'm ready to move on."

"You know who he is, right?" Robbie asked, glancing behind her to where Dave presumably still stood.

"Yes, he's David Reddington."

"You can't even walk down the beach," Robbie said. "He works for the Coast Guard."

"I'm aware," Brooklynn said. And no, she didn't like Dave's job. But she sure did like him. "Is that all? Our movie is about to start, and I don't want to miss the beginning."

"I just don't want you to get hurt again," he said. "You've already been through so much."

Brooklynn had a hard time keeping her scoff in her mouth, but she did it. "Thank you for your concern. I know what I'm doing." She gave him a quick smile that held no joy and turned around.

You've already been through so much. As if Robbie had been there to help. None of Ryker's family had come over after his death. Not even once. So why Robbie cared now was beyond Brooklynn's understanding.

"Ready?" Dave asked, his eyes full of concern. "You okay?"

She picked up her food and drink. "I'm great. Let's hurry so we don't miss the beginning."

He nodded her toward the right theater, and she went inside. The previews had already started, but they found their seats and settled in. She ate her chicken bacon ranch wrap and stole some of Dave's French fries. They shared the popcorn, and only a few minutes into the movie, he lifted the armrest between them and brought her into his side.

She sighed, the comfort running through her something she'd been missing for three long years. He pressed his lips to her temple and asked, "Will you tell me about him after the movie?"

"Yes," she whispered, snuggling deeper into Dave's body and hoping she could make this Sunday afternoon movie a weekly occurrence.

THE FOLLOWING EVENING, BROOKLYNN HAD BEEN HOME FOR five minutes when her doorbell rang. She glanced toward it while Cinnamon, Cory, and Callie started yapping, the sounds layering over one another.

"Hush," she said, but they didn't listen to her at all.

She hadn't showered yet, and she was considering ordering delivery for dinner so she didn't have to leave the house again that night. But when she opened the door and saw Dave standing there in his Coast Guard uniform, she wanted to parade him all over town.

Brooklynn couldn't even breathe as she drank in his dark blue suit jacket with all those colored squares, that white hat perched perfectly on his head. And that grin. Oh, that grin should be illegal.

"Thought we could go to dinner," he said, reaching for her hand. He was one of the handsiest men she'd ever met, and she really liked it.

"I'm exhausted," she said. "I had two huge dogs today, and one of them was terrified of everything." She stepped back, tugging on his hand to get him to come with her. "Come in. Let's order something."

"Pizza?" he asked.

"If you want," she said, "But you can get anything delivered these days."

"Explain," he said, and she wondered if that was how he ordered his men around on the ship.

"It's called Grub to Go," she said, swiping on her phone. "It's an app, and it'll tell us how long until the food comes. I need to shower, but now that you're here, you can answer the door." She handed him the phone. "And you can order for me."

Something wonderful twinkled in his eyes. "Yeah, this is going to change my life." He looked at her phone. "I can get a sandwich from The Anchor delivered?"

"Yep," she said. "And they'll text when they're coming, when they've picked up, all of it."

"This is...wow." He tapped and swiped. "We can get hot dogs from Coneys?"

"Not hot dogs," she said, starting down the hall to her bedroom.

"Not hot dogs?"

"Something *good*," she called over her shoulder, laughing when he said, "Hot dogs are good."

She locked the door behind her and sighed. She'd texted Dave a little bit today, and they'd spent almost all day together yesterday. After the movie, they'd wound up walking down Main Street, holding hands where anyone could see and talking. She'd told him about Robbie, and the Perrish's and how they'd essentially cut her out of their lives the moment Ryker died.

She hadn't even known what she'd done. His death was an accident, and she wasn't even there. Dave had listened to it all and then said, "I'm so sorry, sweetheart. No one deserves to be treated like that."

His words had healed something inside her she hadn't even known was still bleeding.

After she showered and dressed, she went down the hall, still trying to towel out as much of the water from her hair as she could. "So is this going to become a thing?" she asked.

Dave looked up from his phone, and he looked so natural sitting at her kitchen counter. "What?"

"You coming over after work." She nodded to his sexy uniform jacket hanging over the back of the couch. "You didn't even go home and change first." He'd also loosened his tie, and wow, he was just so handsome.

"I was excited to see you," he said with a smile. "And it can become a thing if you want it to."

The thought of seeing him every evening practically sent her heart into an attack, and she was glad he couldn't see her most vital organ. "What did you get for dinner?"

"Is that going to determine if I can come over tomorrow?"

"Maybe I'd like to come to your place," she said.

"My door's always open for you, sweetheart," he said, and Brooklynn knew he meant it.

Her phone went off, and he glanced at it on the counter beside him. "Food's almost here."

"What did you get?" she asked again, her stomach grumbling for something to eat.

"You'll see." He got up and moved toward the front door, as if he needed to be waiting for the delivery guy. All three of her dogs followed him, so he'd charmed them as completely as he had her.

"You don't have to stand on the porch," she said as he opened the door. "Don't let Callie out. She likes to bolt."

He bent and swept the little dog into his arms. "It's pouring out here."

As soon as he'd spoken, Brooklynn could hear the crash of the raindrops against the roof, the sidewalk outside. "Come back in," she said, stepping over to him and wrapping her hands around her upper arm. He turned and looked at her, the spark between them flaring into something huge in less than a breath.

Headlights cut through the deluge of water outside, and he said, "They're here."

She took Callie from him and nudged the other dogs back. Cinnamon growled deep in her throat, as if her twelve pounds could warn anyone away from the house.

"Grub to Go," the guy said from the porch, and Dave took the bag from him and came back inside.

The logo on the outside was a dead giveaway, and Brooklynn's breath caught in her throat.

"I hope you like fried chicken," Dave said, continuing into the kitchen. He didn't seem to notice how still she'd gone, and she told herself to move.

But she felt rooted to the ground, even when Callie squirmed to get down. She almost dropped the dog, and she ended up bending slightly before tossing her to the ground.

"You don't like fried chicken," Dave said, and Brooklynn tore her eyes from the red rooster head with the yellow beak logo.

She swallowed and tried to speak, but her voice didn't work.

"What?" Dave asked, leaving the chicken on the counter and coming toward her. "Are you allergic or something?"

She shook her head, the numbness starting to wear off. "That was—" She cleared her throat. "That was Ryker's favorite place to eat. We went there on our first date. Royal Rooster."

Dave paused, and his face transformed into one of pure horror. "I didn't know."

"I know you didn't." She nodded like everything was fine, but inside, she felt like someone had stuffed fireworks in her chest and lit them all at the same time. Her eyes burned, and she didn't want to cry about this. Not in front of Dave. Not about *this*.

"Hey," Dave said in a gentle voice. He came forward and put both hands on her arms and rubbed them. "It's fine. I can see it's triggered something for you. I'm sorry. I didn't know."

"It's not your fault," she said. "I'm fine."

"Honey, you're crying."

She hadn't even felt the tears tracking down her face. She crumpled into him, stealing strength from the safety of his arms. He held her tight until her emotions passed, and she stepped out of his arms and wiped her face.

"I'm okay," she said. "I am."

Dave retreated a few steps, and he looked unhappy and upset, which was rare for him. Brooklynn hated that things had changed so quickly, that she hadn't been able to contain her memories and her emotions over a stupid chicken logo on a paper bag.

"I...don't know what to do," Dave said, the helplessness in his voice so heavy. So heavy.

"You don't need to do anything," Brooklynn said, wishing she could rewind time just five minutes and give a better reaction. "Let's eat."

"Brooklynn." He stepped in front of her, blocking her access to the kitchen and the fried chicken. He hadn't said her name often, but she sure liked how it sounded in his voice.

"I'm fine," she said.

"Well, I'm not fine," he said. "First it was that coffee mug, which I threw away, by the way." He exhaled and ran his hand over his short hair. "But I might need a cheat sheet of things we can and can't eat. Or places we can't go. Or whatever."

"There is no cheat sheet. I can eat at Royal Rooster."

He gave her a hard look she didn't like. But she couldn't glare back, and she ended up dipping her head. "I'm sorry," she said. "I just...had a bad reaction." And it had been completely involuntary.

"Will everything remind you of him?"

"I don't know," she said honestly, hoping he wouldn't think a relationship with her would be too hard. But in this moment, even she thought it was too hard, and the ache behind her eyes felt endless.

"I think I'll go," Dave said, and panic coursed through Brooklynn.

"Go?" She hated the alarm in the word, sure it was etched on her face too.

"Brooklynn, I'm not sure...I don't know what to do."

"You don't need to do anything," she said, stepping around him to get into the kitchen. She reached into the bag and pulled out the box of fried chicken. "Honestly, Dave, I'm okay."

When he didn't move and continued to wear a dark look on that beautiful face, she stopped trying to distract him with food. "Okay, look. Yes, I reacted badly. I know that, but I couldn't...it just happened. I don't know what will make it happen again. Could be something one day that's fine the next." She threw her hands up in frustration. "I don't know what to do either. But I know I don't want you to leave." Tears pricked her eyes again. "The only thing that would make this worse would be if I had to do it alone."

"Okay," he said, stepping over to the counter. "I just...I want you to be happy, Brooklynn."

"I *am* happy," she said. "And you can't make everything better by throwing away a mug, and I can't pretend I didn't have a life before Ryker died."

"I'm not expecting you to pretend anything," he said. "I know you had a life before. It just seems like—well, with Robbie not reacting well, and you crying over the fried chicken. I don't know." He shook his head. "It feels hard tonight."

"We can do hard things," she said.

"Do you have a saying for everything?" He chuckled and shook his head, reaching into the bag and pulling out the container of mashed potatoes. "First it was the human heart had an unlimited capacity to love, and now this."

"Guess you'll have to stick around and find out," Brooklynn said with a smile, glad when Dave smiled back, loaded a plate with food, and sat down at her kitchen table.

Now she just needed to figure out how to move forward without breaking down. If she couldn't, she felt certain she'd lose Dave, and she couldn't bear to go back to being alone.

11

Dave didn't go to Brooklynn's the next night. Or the next. A week of weekdays passed, and they only talked through texting. He really didn't want to spend another Friday night alone, so he called her and asked her to dinner.

"I'd love to," she said. "I have a late appointment tonight, so it'll have to be later."

"How much later?"

"Probably eight?" she guessed.

"No problem," he said. "Anywhere specific you want to go?"

"Somewhere with great dessert," she said, a smile in her voice. Dave worried all day about where to take her for dinner. Would it trigger another episode like the one on Monday night? Was she really ready to be in a relationship with him?

He didn't know the answer to any of his questions, but he wanted to spend his time with her, so he tried to set aside his doubts and worries and focus on the task at hand.

The problem was, the *Adelie* wasn't doing much today. Patrolling the shoreline and looking for sections of the shore that needed some environmental help. It was utterly boring, and everyone on the ship did their jobs, so he didn't have much to do himself.

He left the cabin where the controls were and went out on deck when he saw Ben and Jake through the glass. "Hey, boys," he said to his friends.

"Captain," they said in unison, their salutes identical too. Dave wasn't bothered by the formality. He'd spent enough years in the military to be used to it.

"Heard the captain got himself a girl," Jake said, passing a sandwich to Ben. "You want one, Captain?"

"Sure." Dave took a sandwich too, not even trying to deny that he had a girlfriend.

"Yeah?" Ben asked. "Who is it?"

"A girl I knew growing up," he said, unwrapping his lunch.

"Oh, he likes her," Ben teased. "Look at his ears turn red."

Dave had no idea if that was true or not, so he simply rolled his eyes. "I'm not fifteen," he said. "I'm allowed to date."

"Yeah, you just never do," Jake said with a laugh. "And

I'm pretty bummed, by the way. I lost fifty bucks because it wasn't Audrey."

"Oh, jeez," Dave said. "Me and the helicopter pilot? Please. They have egos as big as the sun."

"Uh, Captain," Ben said, his grin so wide it could've split his face. "So do you."

"I do not," Dave said. "I *have* to be commanding. It's not like I'm really that arrogant." He scanned the shoreline, finding nothing out of the ordinary. He seriously hated the environmental scoping assignments, and retirement once more crossed his mind.

He did love the swell of the waves though. The scent of the fresh air out on the water. The way the very wind seemed to have conversations with itself.

Thankfully, the conversation moved to something else, and Dave enjoyed his time with his friends.

"Captain," someone called behind him, and Dave turned to find his executive officer waving to him from the cockpit. He headed toward Mitchell without saying goodbye to his friends. Mitch wore a look on his face Dave had seen before—they had a new job to do.

"What's up?" Dave asked as he joined Mitch inside the cockpit and out of the wind.

"We just got notice of a boat coming over from Victoria Island they want us to inspect."

"Board?"

"Yes." He tilted the tablet toward Dave, who took in the boat's features.

"All right. You have the coordinates." All correspondence came with precise coordinates, and Mitch got their eighty-seven-foot long boat going in the right direction. "Speed, twenty knots," he reported, and Dave repeated it back to him.

The sky looked darker than it should have at just after noon, and Dave hoped it wasn't a sign for what was to come. "Let the crew know," he said, and Mitch picked up the radio to inform the other nine people aboard about their new directive from the port.

Dave read the report on the tablet, realizing that he'd have to inspect the boat for weapons, drugs, and illegal immigrants. He'd need to see paperwork, check the engine room, make sure all the controls worked on the boat, count the lifejackets, all of it. That way, he'd have access to all the compartments to find anything, should it be there.

In his twenty-two years with the Coast Guard, he'd boarded plenty of boats. Since becoming Captain five years ago, he sometimes sent his First Officer, and sometimes went himself. In this situation, he'd go, and he'd take three people with him. It was one more than usual, but the port had flagged this as a potential threat.

"Get me Ben, Jake, and Fi," he said, and Mitch got the job done.

"You're taking Fiona?" he asked.

"She'll be great with the boaters," he said, though he didn't owe Mitch an explanation. Though, Fi had gotten herself in a bit of trouble back at port, and Dave had said he'd take her on his crew. Everyone else was male, and she'd fit in just fine in the few months since joining the crew of the *Adelie*.

Ben arrived first, and Dave waited until everyone had joined them in the cockpit before he fully explained what they'd be doing.

"We're ten minutes out," Mitch said, and Dave acknowledged that he'd heard him.

"Ben, I want you and I to go inspect together. There could be refugees or illegal immigrants on board, and I don't need to be alone if I encounter them." He turned to Fiona, a petite brunette who had plenty of firepower packed in her small frame. "Fi, I want you to stay with the boaters. Make this sound routine. We're just making sure everyone's safe coming over from the island, that kind of thing."

"Yes, sir," she said.

"Jake, you'll keep their boat secure." He didn't need to explain further. Jake had plenty of experience in boarding boats, as he'd worked out of San Diego before traveling north along the Pacific Coast.

"It's just routine," Dave said, though something told him to make sure Mitch called in every few minutes. "Should take thirty minutes. Everyone ready?"

"Yes, sir," they chorused, and Dave nodded. "Let's get our jackets on then." He turned back to Mitch and waited until the others had stepped outside. "Mitch, I want you to call in every five minutes."

"Got a bad feeling?"

Dave looked over his shoulder at the sky outside. "Yeah, something like that." He knocked twice on Mitch's controls and said, "Report to port the moment we board too."

"Yes, sir," Mitch said, his eyes round and watchful.

Dave turned away from him and exited the cockpit to get his own lifejacket on. He grabbed the boarding checklist from the wall and said, "Fi, tell me the first thing I should look at."

"The engine room," she said quickly. "Unless you know where certain holds are and suspect there might be drugs or weapons."

"We don't have the schematics for this boat."

"Then the engine room," she said. "First aid station. Life jackets. Paperwork. We ask them questions and keep them calm when we get to weapons and drugs."

"Alarms," Jake added. "Fire extinguishers."

"Good," Dave said, leading the way to the boarding area. "There she is." He spotted the boat in question on the horizon, and the radio on his hip beeped.

"They've been hailed captain. They've responded that we can board."

"Good." So there wouldn't be any problems there. He didn't need an open-ocean showdown today, and the ominous feeling pressing into his shoulders dissipated.

"Jake, you lead out," he said as they approached the boat. Jake was one of two Boarding Officers on the *Adelie*, and he had loads of experience with inspections and enforcing the law on the ocean.

"Yes, sir," Jake said, stepping to the railing and lifting his hand to the three men on deck. "Ho, there," he called. "United States Coast Guard, requesting to board your boat."

Dave watched as the two men behind the first exchanged a glance, and he nudged Fi by moving his elbow a couple of inches. "The guy in front is in charge," he muttered. "Keep your eye on him."

"The other two are nervous," she whispered back.

"Keep them calm."

Jake told them they were performing a routine inspection and they'd need to see their paperwork. "Any weapons on-board?" he asked as he swung from the *Adelie* onto the boat in question.

"We have two handguns," the first man said. "In a safe in the office."

"Okay." Jake nodded and looked back to Dave. "I'll secure the boat. First Class Officer Downs will stay with you. Anyone else that should come up?"

"Just the three of us," the man said, and Dave didn't like how the guy behind him looked toward the steps.

"I'm the Boarding Officer," Jake continued, nonplussed. "My Captain, Captain David Reddington is coming on-board to complete the inspection. He'll be assisted by Senior Chief Petty Officer Erwich."

With everyone on board, Dave shook hands and got to work. "How many lifejackets are on board?"

"Six," the first man said.

The inspection continued, and a measure of relief coursed through him when he went below-deck and got away from the men. He opened every cupboard and cabinet, every closet, every door. He didn't find anyone or anything out of the ordinary. They blew the horn and checked for fire extinguishers.

He completed the entire checklist, and all he could find was that there wasn't a carbon monoxide detector in one room and the placard above the garbage was missing. So he had Jake write them up for that, and he asked, "Where are you guys headed?" while Jake checked the paperwork.

"Fishing vessel," Jake said. "They told Officer Downs they were going to Hawthorne Harbor Bay."

Dave's heard skipped a beat. That wasn't far from where he lived. "What kind of fish?"

"Oysters," the man said. "Crab."

Made sense. They wouldn't be the only ones fishing for crab in Hawthorne Harbor Bay. Dave wasn't sure what his bad feeling was about, because there was no one else on this boat, and no drugs that he'd seen. Of course, a trained dog might be able to sniff out something he couldn't, but the Coast Guard didn't employ dogs on the *Adelie*.

"Two violations," he said, handing the list to Jake so he could fill out the report and get the guy to sign it. He explained what they were to the men while Jake filled out the paperwork. The man signed it, and Jake gave him the yellow copy.

Once they were all back on board the *Adelie* and sailing away, Dave finally relaxed. "Something shady about them," he said to Ben, and Ben agreed.

"But we saw nothing," Ben said. "So at least they aren't smuggling over teenagers for a sex trafficking ring."

"This time," Dave said.

"Paperwork checked out," Jake said. "Called it in and everything."

"All right," Dave said, sighing. "Good job, guys." He nodded to Fi, and she saluted him back.

Dave wasn't sure why he still felt unsettled, and as the afternoon wore on and they completed a couple more boardings of commercial fishing vessels for a company operating out of Port Angeles that had had several violations over the past year, nothing happened.

All in all, it was a better afternoon than morning, but nothing of consequence happened. So maybe his nerves had everything to do with Brooklynn, and nothing to do with his job.

But at least with her, he wasn't bored.

"This place is nice," Brooklynn said, glancing around. "I haven't been here in so long."

"Me either," Dave said, keeping his hand in hers as they edged toward the hostess stand. He said there were two of them, and they got taken back immediately, as the night life in Hawthorne Harbor wasn't exactly thriving.

They sat and their waiter brought water, but Dave needed a whole lot more than that. He ordered his caffeinated soda, and Brooklynn ordered raspberry lemonade. Then she looked up at the waiter with a playful edge in her eyes. "And I want dessert first," she said, smiling. She pointed down to her menu, which he hadn't even noticed was open to the treats. "This chocolate lasagna cake."

"With ice cream or without?"

Brooklynn looked at Dave, who grinned at her and gestured for her to decide.

"With," she said, and the waiter left.

"You eat dessert first?" he asked, intrigued by her more and more every time he saw her. Tonight, she wore a pair of gray slacks and a blouse the color of the lavender that flooded Hawthorne Harbor in July. She was elegant and beautiful, and he felt like the luckiest man in the world.

"I'm always too full after dinner," she said. "Then you can't even enjoy it." She grinned at him and put her elbows on the table. "So, how was the ship today?"

"Great," he said. "It didn't start raining until we were almost done."

"Tell me about your boat," she said, and Dave cocked his head.

"You really want to know?"

"Yes," she said. "I...." She looked thoughtful for a few moments, and Dave let her have the time she needed to organize her thoughts. "I need to get over my fear of the ocean if we're going to be together."

"You do?" he asked. "Why's that?"

"You work on the ocean."

"Yeah, but you don't have to come out on the boat with me."

"Yeah, but I have to kiss you good-bye every morning, and I don't want to then spend the rest of the day in pure panic mode, hoping you'll come back." Brooklynn tucked her hair behind her ear. "At least, I don't want to live like that."

Dave allowed the conversation to stay serious, though all he could think about was kissing her every morning. Having her in his house with him. Or him in hers. Whatever. He just wanted to be with her, wherever she was. "So what's your plan for that?"

"I'm doing some group therapy," she said. "I just got an appointment for next week. And, I don't know." She shrugged. "I thought if I knew what your job was, then I wouldn't have to worry so much."

"So you worry about me. Now?"

"Yes," she said quietly.

"And you want to kiss me in the morning." He grinned at her, hoping to lighten the mood. After the day he'd had, he didn't want tonight to be serious.

She giggled and shook her head, looking down at the menu. "What are you going to get?"

"Oh, I see how it is." He laughed too, choosing something quickly when the waiter reappeared with Brooklynn's chocolate lasagna cake and taking their orders.

He picked up the second spoon that had come with the dessert. "Before I came back to Hawthorne Harbor, I worked on an icebreaker on the Great Lakes."

"An icebreaker?" She paused with her spoonful of cake and ice cream halfway to her mouth. "That sounds dangerous—and exciting."

"It was both of those things," he said. "Sometimes I regret leaving."

"Oh?"

"Yeah, the weather's better here, if you can believe it. And I love being closer to my family, and you—obviously. But the job on the *Adelie* is boring."

"You think your job is boring." She looked at him like she couldn't believe he was telling the truth.

"I don't *think* it," he said. "It is."

She put her treat in her mouth, and Dave had a hard time functioning as he watched her pretty pink lips move. He had to kiss her soon, or he'd combust. He felt sure of it.

"Unbelievable," she finally said. "And here I am, worrying about you."

He reached out and touched her hand. "There's nothing to worry about."

"I guess not."

"I mean, you could get bitten by a dog. I literally don't even think about it."

"Thanks," she said in a dry tone, and rolled her eyes.

"Trust me," he said as he scooped up more cake. "I'm thinking about you all day long. Just not that you'll get a dog bite." He grinned at her and popped the chocolate deliciousness in his mouth. "More like how much longer I can last without kissing you."

Her eyes flashed with dark fire, and Dave wanted to get seared by it. Badly. "Well, maybe not much longer," she teased.

"Is that so?" he asked. "Are you going to give me a timeframe?"

She took a bite of ice cream with fudge swirled through it. "Nope." She shook her head, that flirtatious smile on her face. "It'll be a surprise."

Dave smiled back at her, feeling like someone had filled his blood with carbonation. "Can't wait."

12

Brooklynn hadn't had a date for Valentine's Day in years. The February before Ryker had died, he'd been out of town and she'd made herself a batch of red velvet cupcakes and gone to her parents' house.

But tonight, Dave was coming to get her and they were going to Bell Hill for dinner and dancing. He'd apparently bought a ticket to a community event up there the local dance studio was putting on.

"There will be food and music," he'd told her earlier in the week when he'd asked her out. "It looks like it'll be fun at least. If we're hungry because the food is bad, we can stop anywhere you want."

She'd readily agreed, because she didn't care what she did with Dave. They'd been spending many evenings together, sometimes just at her house, and sometimes at his. If it wasn't raining, they walked down the pier and got him his beloved hot dog. She loved the pork nachos at a nearby place, and she'd become grateful for the walking and standing her job required as she ate out more and more.

She still hadn't kissed him, and she knew he was dying a slow death. He had not brought it up again, not even to say, "I hope I get my surprise tonight."

"Tonight," Brooklynn told herself as she slipped into the dark green dress she'd bought with Julie the previous evening. The dress shop had just gotten in a new selection as most women didn't wait until the night before Valentine's Day to get their shopping done. But Brooklynn hadn't dated in a while, and her wardrobe was sorely lacking for nice dinners and fancy dates.

She put the necklace with her first wedding band around her neck and tucked it under the collar of the dress. She'd worn it a few times when she'd gone out with Dave, and he'd never mentioned it. She hadn't either, but she felt like her whole heart was with her when she wore it. And she wanted to be complete when she was with Dave.

Her group therapy had gone well. She was with several other people who had severe fears, and the first few sessions had been a discussion of who they were and why they were afraid of what they were.

Two other people had lost family members to accidents, one to a snake bite, and one in a mountain biking accident in Olympia Park. She'd become fast friends with them, and when her phone chimed, it was from Darcy, the woman whose brother who had passed away five years ago because he wasn't wearing a helmet and fell down part of a mountain.

Have fun with Dave tonight!

Brooklynn had told her about Dave and his job, and Darcy had encouraged her to keep dating him. Brooklynn didn't exactly want to break up with him—the very thought gave her anxiety. But his job also caused a great deal of unrest within her.

Thanks, she texted back. What are you and Ty doing?

Staying in. He got Thai and I picked a movie.

It sounded like heaven to Brooklynn, and she wondered if she and Dave would ever just stay in on holidays. She hoped so. And she hoped they'd go out too. She realized in that moment that she was thinking long-term with him, and she waited for the fear to hit her right behind the lungs.

But it didn't.

A smile touched her lips as tears formed in her eyes. No, she wasn't ever going to stop loving Ryker. But maybe her heart was now open to love someone else as much as she'd once loved him.

She slipped on her shoes and went into the bathroom to make sure her hair wasn't a frizzy mess. She'd just tamed her curls when Dave rang the doorbell. That got her heart working hard, and she hushed her pups as they yipped and ran ahead of her as if a dangerous man stood on the doorstep.

"It's just Dave," she said to Cinnamon, who led the pack despite being the smallest.

"Just Dave?" he echoed when she opened the door. But he wore a playful smile that said he was kidding, as well as the most handsome black suit, with a bouquet of red roses in his hand.

"Hey, you," she said, grinning at him for all she was worth. She felt sixteen again, especially now that she'd realized that she wasn't afraid of a future with Dave.

"Hey, yourself." He swept right into her house, taking her easily into his arms. She'd been waiting for lightning to strike or some major strong feeling to overwhelm her before she kissed Dave. The right time. Something.

But giggling and looking up at him, she realized she had to *make* the right time. She lifted up in her heels, whispered "Surprise," and pressed her lips to his. Heat exploded through her, and when he growled low in his throat and brought her closer, she was really glad he had such a great hold on her body.

He kissed her, and Brooklynn had never been kissed with as much emotion and passion as Dave had in his touch. Her head swam, and she felt herself falling, falling, falling, the way she'd only done once before in her life.

She kissed him back, hoping she was conveying everything she felt for him too. By the time he finally pulled away, she couldn't breathe properly, and she felt like she'd just wrestled with a fifty-pound dog to get him to hold still so she could clip around his eyes.

He pressed his forehead to hers and swayed with her. "Happy Valentine's Day," he whispered. "I had flowers, but I'm not sure where they went." He made no move to try to find them. He lowered his head and skated his lips along her throat, making her shiver. "We should probably go. The dinner starts in half an hour."

"Mm," she said, enjoying the warmth from his body as it melded with hers.

He did pull completely back then, and he stooped to pick up the roses he'd dropped. "Here they are." He looked at her over the top of the petals, and Brooklynn's breath caught in her chest.

"You're so handsome," she said, taking the flowers. "Thank you. Do I have time to put them in water?"

"If you want," he said, coming in and closing the door behind him. He bent down to pat her dogs while she got out a vase and filled it with water. She arranged the roses, smiling at them as happiness burst through her.

"All right," she said, taking her coat off the back of the couch and letting him help her into it. He wrapped his arms around her from behind and pushed her hair back so he could kiss her ear. "Ready?" she asked.

"Ready." He turned her in his arms and kissed her again, and Brooklynn decided this was definitely the best Valentine's Day she'd ever had.

A COUPLE OF HOURS LATER, THE DINNER HAD CONCLUDED but the dancing was still going strong. Brooklynn's feet hurt in her heels, and when Dave caught her adjusting the straps for the third time, he said, "Let's get out of here."

"Yeah?" she asked. "I'm fine."

"Well, I want a hamburger," he said with a smile. Dinner had been nice, actually. Chicken cordon blue with mashed potatoes and green bean casserole. The dance students were currently giving ballroom lessons to couples, and Brooklynn had enjoyed the teen who'd helped her and Dave learn to twirl and dip.

"Oh, I'll take one of those," Brooklynn said, linking her arm through his as they headed for the coat closet and then slipped out into the night. Every move he made was perfection, from how he helped her into her coat to how he took her hand firmly yet gently in his.

He guided her with his hand on her back while she got in the SUV, and then he leaned into the car after her. "That was really fun, right?"

"Totally," she said, seeing some apprehension in his gorgeous eyes. She leaned toward him, glad when he closed the distance between them and kissed her. She held onto his face, completely enamored with the taste of him, the smell of him, the feel of his mouth against hers.

Someone honked, and Dave pulled back, moving smoothly out of the doorway and closing the door behind him. He walked around the front of the car and got behind the wheel. "So where to?"

"You said you wanted a hamburger."

"I do, but there's at least a dozen choices for that."

"You pick."

He glanced at her, and he was probably thinking she'd have another break-down if he chose wrong. So she said, "I love Tricky's," she said. "And they have sweet potato fries they serve with maple syrup."

"Are you serious?" he asked.

"You've never had them?"

"I have not."

"Well, prepare to have your mind blown."

He chuckled, reached over and took her hand, and lifted her wrist to his lips. "Have I told you today that I really like you?"

"Not today." She leaned her head back and smiled, her eyes drifting closed.

"Tired?"

"No," she answered. "Just happy to be here with you."

A few seconds passed as he pointed the SUV back toward Hawthorne Harbor. "Up for talking about something serious?"

Brooklynn straightened and opened her eyes. "Depends."

"I knew you'd say that." He let go of her hand and turned down the radio. "It's about a family," he said. "I've been thinking about it a lot the past couple of weeks. I'm not sure why."

Kids. "Oh," she said.

"You don't want kids?" He seemed surprised.

"It's not that I don't," she said. "Ryker and I—he...." She didn't know how to answer that wouldn't make her former husband seem like a non-serious playboy. "He didn't want them right away, and I said that was fine."

"Okay," Dave said, and she'd seen him shut down this way before. Usually when he didn't know what to do or say. She'd really like to see him in action on his ship, because he probably always knew what to do and exactly what to say.

"I'm thirty-eight," she said next. "If I want to have a baby of my own, that would need to happen pretty soon."

"Yeah?" Dave asked, and it was obvious he was oblivious to women's issues.

"Yes," she said with a smile. "Women can't have kids forever, Dave."

"I know that." He cut a glance at her and focused on the dark road in front of them again. "So how soon?"

Brooklynn felt backed into a corner, and she shrugged, the idea of having a baby forming fully in her mind. "Soon."

He didn't say anything else, and the drive back to Hawthorne Harbor seemed to take no time at all, both of them inside their own minds. He pulled up to the Tricky's drive-through and ordered their food, and they went back to her house to eat.

He loosened that tie and discarded his jacket like he'd done with his Coast Guard uniform a time or two before, and Brooklynn stood and watched how comfortable he was in her house.

"Would you move in with me?" she asked, and he froze.

He looked at her with wide eyes and swallowed before he spoke. "You want to live together?"

Brooklynn suddenly realized how her question had sounded, and her face heated. "I meant after we're married."

If anything, his eyes grew larger and his mouth actually dropped open. "Married?"

"Stop it," she said, finally tearing her eyes from his and opening their food bags. "You're the one who just brought up *babies*," she said. "Pretty sure we need to get married before that can happen." She cocked her eyebrows at him and cocked her head. "Unless you'd like my mother to die of a heart attack before she gets to meet her second grandchild."

"Well, yeah," Dave said, approaching the kitchen. "I was just seeing if you wanted kids. You didn't seem super keen on it."

"I'm *keen* on it," she said. "I just...hadn't thought about it in a while." She pulled out his burger and slid it to him.

"And I was just seeing if you thought you'd move in here, or if I'd move in with you."

"Your place is way nicer," he said.

"And yours is much bigger," she said. "And closer to the edge of town, so it's not as crowded."

"Your place does not feel crowded," he said, sitting and unwrapping his burger.

"Harder to get to the highway to get to Port Angeles."

"It's five minutes."

"So you have strong feelings about living here."

"No," he said. "I'm just saying—I have no feelings. I don't care."

Brooklynn wished he'd have a stronger opinion. She bit into her gypsy burger, the bacon and caramelized onions making a party with the juicy beef in her mouth. She glanced down at her dogs, all lined up like the three blind mice. Except, of course, they weren't blind, and they could see that hamburger, *please share, thank you very much.*

"I don't want to live here," she said, her voice barely loud enough for her own ears to hear. She took a bite of her burger and looked at Dave.

He stared at her again, this time clearly to tease her. Sure enough, in the next moment, he laughed, the tension in the house breaking with the jovial sound of it. Leaving his burger on the counter, he got up and came around to where she stood.

He took her into his arms, forcing her to stop eating

too, and gazed down at her. "Wherever you want is fine," he said. "We could get a new place."

Instead of answering, she kissed him, not quite sure what she was feeling and not knowing how to articulate it. "Mm," he said against her lips. "You taste really good."

She laughed and swatted him back. "Stop it. I'm not your hamburger."

"No, but yours tastes *good*." He grinned at her again, and Brooklynn couldn't help laughing. For the first time, her laughter sounded as joyful as his did, and that only made Brooklynn happier than she already was.

13

Dave tugged lightly on the leash, the boxer he'd just picked up from the animal shelter not quite sure he wanted to go home with him for the weekend. "Come on, bud. I'll let you sleep in the bed."

As if the dog could understand English, he finally jumped into the back of Dave's SUV. "Good boy, Tantor." He scrubbed the dog behind his ears, and by the time he got in the driver's seat, the dog sat in the passenger seat. "Yep, you get to ride up front too." Dave rolled the window down, glad the rain had started to lessen slightly now that March had dawned.

"Now, my girlfriend doesn't like it when dogs jump on her," he said as he started driving back to his place. Brooklynn had promised him dinner at his home that night, and his mouth watered just thinking about her cooking.

And the woman.

Oh, the woman.

The woman had made her way right into his heart, and he'd fallen way beyond a crush. He told her every time he saw her how much he liked her, but he'd never quite made it to *I love you.*

He honestly wasn't sure what love looked like or felt like. He knew he loved seeing Brooklynn, and talking to her, and the time he had to spend at work with others had become a chore.

He thought of the retirement packet he'd shoved in a drawer a few weeks ago. He hadn't brought it up with Brooklynn, though they'd talked about pretty much everything else. Kids, marriage, their future.

Dave wondered if she'd say yes if he asked her to marry him tonight. The idea felt false in his mind, and he dismissed it. She wasn't ready—and he wasn't even sure he was in love with her.

"Here we are," he said, turning the corner and seeing a black truck parked in his driveway. "And hey, Charlie's here too, and so is Pierce. He'll love you." He pulled in beside his brother and made the boxer sit before he could get out of the SUV.

Charlie met him on the porch, his face full of anxiety. "There you are. Why didn't you answer your phone?"

"It didn't ring," he said, pausing to look at his brother. "What's going on?"

"Jackie's in labor," he said. "You said I could bring Pierce here when that happened."

Surprise punched Dave in the face. "Oh, my heck. Yeah, of course. Go."

"I wasn't sure if I should leave him with Brooklynn, but she said it was fine."

"So you've only been here a minute."

"Yeah, just pulled up. He's got his overnight bag, and Mom said she can take him during the day tomorrow if you need a break. The house is torn apart, but she said they could go to the mall or something."

"Go, Charlie," Dave said. "We'll feed him and keep him alive for the weekend." He grinned as his brother did, and Dave gave him a quick hug. "Tell Jackie we love her."

"Will do." Charlie practically ran down the steps to his truck, and the engine roaring to life startled Tantor, who whined and pulled toward the front door.

"Yeah, let's go in," he said, thinking he should've warned Brooklynn about Pierce being part of their lives for a few days. He pushed through the door to find the smell of something frying.

"Hey," he called, taking a moment to lock the door behind him. "Something smells good."

"Uncle Dave!" Pierce came darting out of the kitchen, a wide smile on his face. He ran toward Dave, who lifted him high into the air, both of them laughing.

"I get to sleep here," Pierce said. "Two nights, Daddy said." He held up two chubby fingers and looked at them. "But I three."

"Yes," Dave said. "You're three. Did you meet Brooklynn?"

"Yeah," Pierce said, looking toward the kitchen. "Her gave me a cookie."

"Oh-ho," Dave said, chuckling. She knew how to get right into the heart of a child, and Dave carried Pierce in one hand and led Tantor with the other. They all went into the kitchen together, where Brooklynn stood at the stove, a spatula in her hand.

"Hey," she said over her shoulder. She looked back at the pan, but then her attention flew back to his. She stared at him, and he'd seen that look in her eyes before. When she'd drank him in on her front porch while he wore his officer's uniform. Before she'd kissed him on Valentine's Day. His mind blanked at the other times, because the same desire coursing through her expression was attacking his body too.

"I got a boxer," he said somewhat robotically. "Until Monday morning." He set Pierce down and unclipped the leash from the dog's collar. "And Pierce will be here with us until then, too. Probably."

With us.

And he'd used *we* outside with Charlie too. It felt nice to be part of an *us* and a *we*, and he grinned at Brooklynn as he walked closer. "Fried potatoes." He pressed a kiss to her temple. She knew how to get into his heart too—with carbs. "And you gave Pierce a cookie, and he thinks you're super awesome because of it."

She laughed, nudging him away from her with her hip. "Get out the ketchup. These are done, and we're ready to eat."

He did as she asked and set the ketchup on the counter with the other things she'd already gotten out. Salt and pepper. Plates—she'd already adjusted to three instead of two. Silverware. Glasses, with one plastic cup for Pierce.

Dave pulled a couple of bowls from the cupboard and filled one with water and went out to his garage to get dog food. Tantor walked around and sniffed everything in sight, but at least he wasn't cowering in the corner. And he hadn't jumped on Pierce or Brooklynn yet.

Maybe if he and Brooklynn got married, he could get a dog. He'd have someone to take care of it when he had to sleep on the ship, and if they got a new place together, they could look for something with a big yard. After all, she came with three pups of her own, and his would be a fourth.

"This is a Magleby favorite," she said. "It's nothing special. Just meatballs in brown gravy." She took the lid off the pot and the salty scent of beef hit him.

"Smells great."

"Fried potatoes," she said needlessly. "And my grandmother always made us eat something green." She glowed when she spoke of her family, and Dave wondered when he'd get introduced to Hawthorne Harbor's royal family. "So I made creamed peas."

Dave looked at the peas swimming in thick cream. "I didn't know you could do that. I've heard of it with corn."

"Well, corn's not green." Brooklynn picked up a plate. "And I'm starving, so let's get started." She looked over to Pierce. "You hungry, Pierce? Want a meatball?" She went about talking to him, getting him every little thing he wanted, and making sure the gravy from the meatballs didn't touch the potatoes.

Dave stood back and watched her, marveling at this female presence in his home and life. She'd completely changed everything, in the best way possible.

"Are you going to eat?" she asked, her plate full as she walked over to the table where she'd gotten Pierce all set up.

"Yes," Dave said, grabbing the last plate. "So you met Charlie."

"Yes," Brooklynn said. "Briefly. He seemed a bit panicked. And surprised to see me here."

"He knows we're together," Dave said, loading meatballs and potatoes on his plate. He took plenty of creamed peas too and went to the table. "Does your family know about me?" He chose to turn back to the counter for the salt and pepper instead of watching her for her reaction. After all, he didn't want to be disappointed if she hadn't even said anything about him yet.

Her silence told him all he needed to know anyway. "I'll take that as a no." He sat across from her and shook the salt over all of his food. His mother would pounce all over him for not tasting it first, but Brooklynn didn't say anything.

"I told my mother and sister when you asked me out," she said. "And this town is not quiet with the rumors. My aunt Mabel heard about us at Duality the day after our Sunday brunch."

"But you didn't tell them we're dat*ing*." He cut a meatball in half and stabbed it with his fork before looking at her. "You just told them I'd asked you out." He put the food in his mouth and chose to watch her this time.

"No, I told them after we'd been out," she said, lifting her chin. "But I suppose it's time for you to meet them."

Dave regretted his challenging tone. "If you think so," he said. "I'm fine, sweetheart. I just want you to be ready."

"We could go for Sunday dinner this weekend," she said, squirting ketchup on her potatoes. "I'll tell my mother, and say I have a surprise for everyone else."

Dave swallowed. "And will they be surprised?"

"I doubt it," she said. "You don't spend much time in town, but I'm telling you. Our relationship is *not* a secret."

"You don't think so?" Dave scooped up some peas, noticing that Pierce had gravy all over his face and most of his food was gone already.

"I know so," Brooklynn said with a laugh. "I had a dog today from a regular client. A single woman. She asked me all kinds of questions about you." She popped her meatball into her mouth, a sparkle in her eyes.

Dave shook his head, a smile on his face. "I don't believe that."

"She wants Joey's number."

Dave paused before a laugh flew from his mouth. Pierce looked at him as if the child had just now realized he wasn't alone in the room. "Joey doesn't date," Dave said.

"Yeah, well, neither did I," Brooklynn said, giggling. "I'll call my mom after dinner."

"Bwookwynn," Pierce said, not quite getting the name right. "More meatballs?"

"I'll get them," Dave said, jumping up and grabbing his nephew's plate. He put two more meatballs on Pierce's plate and slid it back in front of him. He sat down, thinking his job done.

Then Brooklynn reached over and started cutting the big meatballs into smaller chunks, and Dave knew—he was in love with her.

14

Brooklynn pointed to her right. "Turn up there."

"Believe it or not, I know where your parents live," Dave said, seemingly nonplussed about this formal meeting. "I mean, they're Magleby's."

"I know," Brooklynn said. "I'm a little nervous."

"Yeah?" He reached over and took her hand in his. "Why?"

"I don't know," she said. "And don't say you don't believe me." In her therapy group, it was okay to say *I don't know*. The group leader might ask questions, but she could pass on answering them if she wanted to. Dave pushed her for answers, and most of the time, she did know why she felt a certain way. But tonight, she didn't.

Absently, she reached up and fingered the diamond ring she wore on a chain around her neck.

"I wasn't going to say that," he said, glancing at her. "Is that a new necklace?"

"No." She dropped her hand back to her lap, glad he had to focus on making the turn. "It's…." Could she tell him, moments before they arrived for her family dinner? Would it upset him?

"It's what?" he asked, her hesitance clearly telling him the necklace was important.

"It's my old wedding band," she said, the words bursting out of her mouth. "Oh, look, they're all out on the porch." Both of her parents stood on the porch, as did Erika and Laci.

Dave said nothing as he pulled up to the house and unbuckled his seat belt. "We'll talk about the wedding band later." He got out before she could respond, and dread filled her stomach like lead.

"Hey, Mom," she said as she got out. "Dad." She went around the front of the SUV. "I think you guys know David Reddington."

"Of course," her mother said, always playing the perfect part. She hugged Dave hello, and he turned on the charm. He really was magnificent and commanding, and as he followed her parents inside, Erika fanned herself.

"Dang, girl," she said. "He is *hot*."

"Erika," Laci admonished, but Brooklynn just laughed. So maybe it was nervous laughter. Maybe all she could think about was their little talk about her wedding band.

"Well, I can't bring John home now," she said.

"Are you still dating him?" Brooklynn asked as she went into the house.

"Don't sound so surprised."

"I'm not surprised," Brooklynn said, though she was. Since her failed engagement five years ago, Erika hadn't stayed with the same man for more than a few months. "I was just asking."

"Scoot's talking to him," Laci muttered, and Brooklynn focused on the kitchen. Sure enough, her brother had Dave almost against the wall, talking to him.

She hurried over to Dave. "You met my brother Scooter."

"Yeah," Dave said, relief in his expression. "He was telling me about a skateboard he built."

"Scoot," Brooklynn warned. "He's not investing in your skateboard."

"Come on, Brookie," he said with a grin.

"Did Tilly come?" she asked, looking around for her niece and knowing her question would annoy her brother.

"She's with her mom." Scoot glared at Brooklynn, but she didn't care.

"Where's Mike?"

"Late," her mother said, interrupting them. "But the food's ready, so let's sit down, and he'll join us when he gets here."

Brooklynn didn't want to do that. It wasn't hard to wait,

but her mother had things scheduled down to the minute. She stepped over to the table that had been set with the nice plates and silverware, as if this were Thanksgiving dinner.

Embarrassment squirreled through her, especially when her mom said, "So Dave. How are you and Brooklynn getting along?"

"Mom," Brooklynn said. "We get along fine, otherwise he wouldn't be here."

"Must be serious," her mom said, clearly not picking up on the frustrated tone in Brooklynn's voice. "I mean, you've only ever brought home one man in the past, and you married him."

A hush fell over the table, and Brooklynn glared at her mother.

"We've talked about marriage," Dave said, and Brooklynn's gaze whipped to his. She wanted to wave her arms and shake her head, anything to get him to stop right there. He looked at her, clearly confused. "But...it's a ways off."

"It is?" her mom asked. "Why's that?"

Horror snaked through Brooklynn, and she realized this dinner was a very bad idea. Her mother always asked too many questions, and it was a miracle she and Scooter had managed to get spouses in the first place.

"Wilma, I think you better stop talking," her dad said, and Brooklynn tried to convey her gratitude to him from across the table.

"Why?" She looked around and realized no one had started eating. "What are you waiting for? Eat, eat."

All of the Magleby's reached for the item nearest them, Brooklynn included, at the same time the front door opened. "Hey," Mike said. "Sorry I'm—you couldn't even wait ten minutes?"

"The pork chops were hot," her mom said as if that explained everything. Mike ground his teeth together, and her dad got up to go talk to him. They came over to the table just a few seconds later, and Brooklynn met her brother's eye.

"This is David Reddington," she said. "My boyfriend."

"They've talked about marriage," her mom said, and Brooklynn's groan wasn't the loudest one at the table.

"Enough, Mom," Laci said. "So Dave, Brooklynn says you work for the Coast Guard? Tell us about that."

"Yeah," he said, exchanging at glance with Brooklynn. "Been with them for twenty-two years. I captain the *Adelie* out of Port Angeles."

She noticed the way her dad nodded, as if he approved of Dave's job. It was certainly better than Ryker's, who'd worked as the assistant manager of the grocery store. Brooklynn hadn't cared much what he did, but her father had said she'd always have to work. With Dave, though, Brooklynn wouldn't have to work. Surely he made quite a bit of money being as high up as he was.

She'd missed part of the conversation as she thought

about Ryker, because Mike said, "Eighty-seven feet long? That's huge."

"We're a law enforcement and rescue ship," he said. "Helicopters can land on the stern."

"Do you carry a gun?" he asked next, and Brooklynn's gaze flew to Dave's. She hadn't realized he was *law enforcement*.

"Yeah," Dave said. "We're the country's maritime law enforcement."

"You have a gun?" Brooklynn asked, her anxiety tripling.

"Yes," he said calmly, glancing around the table and coming back to her. "We're part of Homeland Security. We deal with illegal immigrants, smugglers, terrorist threats —" He cut off, his eyes going wide. "I mean, they do in some parts of the ocean. Up here, we mostly deal with fisheries and environmental issues." He gave a light laugh that Brooklynn saw right through.

"That's so cool," Mike said, and Brooklynn wanted to punch him. At least she didn't feel like crying. Just hitting something really hard and then running away.

The conversation moved to the Spring Fling, but Brooklynn ignored any attempt to draw her into the discussion. She gave one-word answers and ate as fast as she could.

Oh, yes. This dinner was a huge mistake.

~

By the time they finally escaped, Brooklynn felt like she'd been through World War III. Maybe without all the shooting, but definitely parts of her had died.

"I'm so sorry," she said as he drove away from the house.

"It was fine," he said, but Brooklynn knew in this instance, *fine* even from a man was not okay.

"My mom can be a little intense."

"I don't care about your mom," he said, almost in a bark.

Brooklynn flinched. "Well...okay."

"I didn't mean it like that." He sighed, the fight leaving those boxy shoulders, and pulled to a stop at the end of the lane where it met the highway. "I just—you wear your wedding band around your neck? All the time?" He looked at her with desperation in those beautiful eyes, and so much hurt her heart wailed.

She didn't want to hurt him. "It's just like a memento."

"No, it's like a keepsake," he said. "Something that means so much to you that you need it with you always." His gaze fell to her collarbone and rebounded to her eyes. "I just feel stupid." He turned, pressing on the accelerator a little too roughly.

"Why do you feel stupid?"

"I don't want to name all the reasons," he said darkly.

Anger flared in Brooklynn too. "Well, you didn't tell me you were basically a cop on a boat."

"I work for the *Coast Guard*," he said. "I didn't realize I had to be so specific."

"Smugglers? Terrorists? Yeah, you should've been more specific." She hated how out of control she felt, but she couldn't imagine marrying this man and sending him off to work—*armed!* With a *gun*—each morning and expecting him to come home whole.

And he wanted kids. A family. What if he died?

And she absolutely could not plan another funeral for her husband. She wouldn't.

She shook her head, her emotions teeming against the back of her tongue. She didn't have to defend the way she felt. Not to him. Not to anyone. Maybe her group therapist would want her to be concise in what she articulated, but right now, she wasn't in her group.

She pulled out her phone and sent a quick text to Darcy. Dave carries a gun on his ship. I don't know what to do. I can't get involved with another man who'll die on me.

She wasn't sure if she was being irrational or not. All she knew was something had broken inside her the day Ryker had died. She'd developed irrational fears and anxiety.

Her therapy had been helping. Encouraging her to move past an irrational dislike of the ocean and boats and the beach. Everything surrounding the ocean, from sailing to wake boarding, to parasailing—which was what had killed Ryker.

No, she told herself. *Ryker killed Ryker.*

That was something she'd learned. Parasailing hadn't done anything. The ocean hadn't done anything. The mountain hadn't killed Darcy's brother.

Accidents happen. Mistakes are made. Decisions too. And sometimes things go wrong.

Dave pulled into her driveway and got out to walk her to the door, their usual routine. In fact, she'd expected him to come in and they'd have a long chat about her family and how things had gone.

He opened her door, and she looked at him. "I hate that you're not happy." But what she really hated was that she was the cause of his turmoil.

"And I hate that you're not," he said, reaching for her hand and helping her out of the SUV. He didn't hold onto her hand as they walked up the sidewalk.

"I'm so much better," she said.

"Yeah," he agreed as they climbed the steps. "But Brooklynn." He blew his breath out and looked away, out over her front lawn, his jaw tight and the muscle jumping.

When he finally looked at her, his expression was made of marble. "I don't think you're ready."

"Ready for what?"

"For us," he said, his voice breaking slightly as he emphasized the last word.

"Are you breaking up with me?" she asked, her voice bordering on hysterical.

"No," he said, folding her into his arms. "No, of course not."

Brooklynn clung to him, so close to breaking wide open again. Her shoulders shook, and Dave whispered, "Don't cry, sweetheart."

But Brooklynn couldn't help it.

She cried.

15

Dave opened Brooklynn's door with one hand while he kept her close with the other. He got her inside and down the hall to her bedroom. She curled into herself and he curled himself around her, stroking her hair and letting her cry.

When she finally quieted, Dave asked, "What can I do?"

"Nothing," she said.

He felt...he didn't know what. Stupid, for sure. How could he have thought she'd moved past her first husband? She kissed him like she was falling for him as fast as he had for her. They'd spent so much time together over the past couple of months, and she'd started out anxious and guarded, and now she was happy and carefree.

Well, she usually was.

She'd told him about multiple therapy sessions, and she always had a good story or two about the dogs she'd groomed that day. And yet, she harbored darkness inside her he didn't comprehend. He had a feeling he never would.

"Once," he said. "I was stationed on the East Coast, up by the Statue of Liberty. We'd patrol the ocean out there, and there's a lot of boat traffic in and out of the bay where the National Monument is."

She stilled in his arms, and he wasn't sure if he should keep talking or not. But he decided to keep going. "An unfamiliar boat came on our radar, and we prepared to board it. That's something we do all the time. It's routine. We make sure there are enough lifejackets and that all the safety equipment is working properly. Well, anyway, this boat wouldn't give us permission to board."

"Do you need permission?" she asked.

"No," he said. "We just give polite notification, ask anyway. So we boarded the boat, and it was clear there were multiple violations. They tried to say they were a deep sea fishing boat, but there were no instruments for that. No equipment. My gut told me there was something wrong, and I've learned to listen to that instinct."

And right now, it was telling him that Brooklynn needed more time. More therapy.

Dave didn't want to be a jerk, but he needed things too. He deserved to have all of her, not just the parts Ryker had broken and left behind. Not just the parts she was willing to fix. Frustration mingled inside him, and he didn't continue his story.

Brooklynn didn't ask either, so they lay there in silence until he said, "I should go." He slipped away from her, wanting her to get up and walk him to the door. Kiss him good-night. At least call him back.

She didn't do any of those things. Just said, "Okay. I'll talk to you later."

Dave went down the hall to the kitchen and let her dogs out the back door so they could take care of their business. That done, and the pups back inside, he locked the door and went out the front, locking that one behind him too.

As he walked away, his gut told him it was the last time, and all he could do was hope it was wrong.

Someone rang Dave's doorbell at six-thirty the following morning, making the law enforcement persona he could be emerge. He straightened from where he'd been clipping the leash to Tantor's collar. "Who could that be?" he asked the dog.

Tantor didn't whine or even move toward the door. He'd done so well this weekend, and Dave didn't want to take him back to the shelter. But every time he went, the dog he'd taken last time wasn't there anymore. Starlee said they'd been getting adopted, so he knew Tantor would be okay.

Knocking reverberated through the house, and Brooklynn called, "Dave? It's Brooklynn."

That got him moving toward the door, and he practically yanked it off the hinges to get it open faster. She stood there in a jeans and a jacket, clutching a bakery bag in one hand and carrying two cups of coffee in the other.

"Come in," he said, opening the screen door and taking the coffee from her. "Sorry, I was a bit startled someone would ring my doorbell so early."

"I wasn't sure what time you went to work," she said, stepping past him and into the house. "And I didn't want to miss you." She bypassed the living room and went into the kitchen to set down the bakery bag.

Tantor followed her, and Dave couldn't help but do the same. She acted like nothing had happened last night, but something had. Something big.

"I can't stay long," he said. "I have to be in Port Angeles in an hour, and I have to stop and drop off Tantor first."

She turned toward him, a shaky smile on her face. "I'm sorry." Her voice sounded close to breaking, but it held. "Last night was a disaster, and it's my fault."

"How is it your fault?" By his recollection, he'd brought up the fact that they'd talked about marriage.

She reached into her pocket and held out her fist to him. Dave looked at it and then back into her eyes. "What's going on?"

“Take this, please,” she said, shaking her fist slightly.

Dave extended his hand out too, and she dropped something into his palm. It was her former wedding ring, held by that silver chain he’d seen her wear often.

Often.

“Brooklynn,” he said quietly. “I can’t take this.”

“I don’t want it,” she said, her voice strong. He watched her transform from the shaky woman to the powerful one who knew what she wanted. “I thought it helped me feel more normal, but it doesn’t. The only thing that does that —the *person* who does that—is you.” She stepped closer to him, and Dave’s heart grew wings and started to lift with hope again.

“I thought I needed that ring so I could be more complete, but I realized last night as soon as you left, that you make me feel more like myself than I have in years. Not that ring.” She didn’t even glance at it.

She fiddled with the buttons on his shirt, sending sparks through his whole body. She had no idea what she did to him, and Dave wasn’t going to tell her until they were married. Maybe not even then.

“I sure do like you,” she whispered, an echo of words he’d said to her so many times over the past few months.

His first instinct was to kiss her and tell her everything would be all right, but he hesitated. “What do you want me to do with this?” he asked, keeping his hands between them, the ring still glinting in the light coming through the windows.

"I don't care what you do with it," she said.

"Then you take it."

"I'll throw it away."

"Then maybe that's what needs to happen." He watched as an inch of anxiety entered her expression. She didn't want to depend on it anymore, he understood that. But he also suspected she wouldn't really throw it away.

"Okay," he said. "I'll keep it." He shoved the necklace in his pocket, and she stepped into him so he'd had nowhere to put his hands but around her.

"I'm sorry," she said again, just before kissing him. She moved in a slow, careful way, almost like she was trying to explore his mouth and make sure she found every part of it.

He certainly didn't mind, and he kissed her back in the same slow, round way. She sighed and leaned her head against his chest. "So we're okay?"

"I didn't know we couldn't talk about our relationship at dinner," he said. "And I certainly didn't know you thought I just went out on a boat and sailed around the bay."

"I guess I don't know what you do," she said, stepping back. "And Dave, I need to know."

Of course she did. "All right," he said. "Maybe we can talk about it tonight?" He glanced at the clock. As much as he'd like to stay here and tell her everything about the last twenty-two years of his life, he had to get to the port—and that was *after* he picked up Audrey.

"Tonight's fine," she said. "My house? No, I'll come here. Our romantic weekend sort of took a backseat when we got Pierce."

"I thought it was fun," Dave said.

"It was," Brooklynn said, stepping over to the bakery bag. "But I wanted romantic. And then my family dinner killed everything."

Dave snaked his arms around her and pulled her into his chest. "Not everything." He swept her hair to the side and kissed the back of her neck and along her shoulder to her ear.

She giggled, and the things that had cracked last night seemed glued back together. Tighter than ever.

"I brought apple turnovers," she said. "The trees should be blooming soon."

He took the treat from her and picked up one of the to-go cups of coffee. "Thanks, sweetheart. Can you really take Tantor back to the shelter?"

"I really can. My first client isn't until ten today."

"Thank you." He kissed her quickly, swiped his keys from the counter, and headed for the garage. "Then I'm going to go. I'll see you tonight."

"Bye," she called from behind him, and he left her in his house while he went to work.

He paid attention to every detail of the day, and none of them were dangerous. They were on patrol that day, which meant they monitored the sea traffic the same way the police would monitor street traffic.

They boarded six boats, from casual fishermen to a family going boating to a big ship coming into port to deliver supplies.

Dave loved his job; he did. But the gun on his hip had never felt so heavy, and while his faith in his relationship with Brooklynn had been restored by her early-morning visit, he still wasn't convinced she would ever be ready to stand next to him and say, "I do."

"So what's the point?" he asked himself as Mitch hailed another boat to do another routine boarding.

16

Brooklynn canceled all her clients for the day and instead, curled into the pillows on Dave's couch and sipped her coffee. It disappeared pretty quickly, and she left the house to take Tantor back to the shelter. On her way back to Dave's, she went through the drive-through at Brewed for fresh coffee, and she nursed that now, hoping to make it last until noon.

She wasn't sure why she didn't want to leave, only that she didn't. She wasn't melancholy, but her thoughts felt frenzied in her mind. Unable to focus on any one thing, she picked up her phone and called Darcy.

"Hey," the other woman said. "Can I call you back in two minutes? I'm almost under the dryer."

"Sure," Brooklynn said. Darcy hadn't answered her text from last night, and she felt distant and removed from everyone and everything.

It was a lot longer than two minutes, but Darcy did call back. "What's up?" she asked, a soft whirring in the background.

Brooklynn sighed. "I was just wondering if you had time for lunch today."

"Probably a bit later," Darcy said, her voice chipper. "Maybe like one or so. I'm getting my hair bleached and colored today, and it takes *forever*."

"One should work," Brooklynn said. "I'm thinking of inviting Julie too. Is that okay with you?"

"Of course," Darcy said. "I'd love to meet her."

Brooklynn talked about Julie all the time to Darcy, but she hadn't mentioned Darcy to Julie. Yet. She hadn't wanted her best friend to feel like Brooklynn didn't need her anymore.

"She might not be able to," Brooklynn said. "She works in a law office, and they have some busy days."

"Whatever," Darcy said, and Brooklynn wished she could be as carefree about things. She reminded herself that Darcy had lost a brother, not a spouse. And no one came along and tried to be a replacement for her brother.

A replacement.

Horror struck her heart, making it sing like a gong. No wonder she hadn't been able to move past Ryker and make something serious with Dave work. She'd been thinking of him as a replacement all this time.

She said she'd text Darcy about the final details of lunch later, and she put in a call to her group therapist.

"Brooklynn," Dr. Jackson said. "How are you?"

"I'm wondering if you have any time for a private session today?" she asked in a rush, hoping to get the words out before she lost her bravery.

"I'm with a client right now," the doctor said. "But I could squeeze you in for a few minutes in about a half an hour."

"I'll be there." Brooklynn hung up and got off the couch. Dave's house was as comfortable as hers now, and that fact didn't elude her as she drove into downtown and parked at Dr. Jackson's building. She was early, but she didn't care. She checked in, and she sat in the waiting room, trying to sort through her thoughts and feelings.

Why was that so dang hard?

"Brooklynn," the receptionist said. "He's ready for you."

She jumped to her feet and followed the woman down the hall, nervous energy zipping through her like an electric current.

"Right in here," she said, gesturing toward an open office.

Brooklynn went in, her heart beat flapping a bit in her chest. "I've never done a private therapy session," she said to Dr. Jackson, who stood from an armchair to greet her.

"It's just like group," he said, shaking her hand. "Except there's no group." He smiled at her, and she sat in the other armchair as if they'd have tea together and talk about the upcoming Spring Fling.

"So tell me," he said kindly, his wrinkles appearing around his wise eyes as he smiled. "What brings you to your first private session?"

"My boyfriend," she said, quickly realizing that no, Dave wasn't the reason she was there. "I mean, me. How I feel about my boyfriend."

"And how do you feel about your boyfriend?" Dr. Jackson had no notebook to write in, nothing to look at. Only her.

"He's the first man I've dated since Ryker's death," she said, twisting her fingers around themselves nervously. "And I like him so much. But he doesn't think I'm ready."

"Why would he think that?"

She told him about the dinner, the necklace, their conversation that morning. Dr. Jackson listened and only asked two clarifying questions before letting her continue.

"And I don't know," Brooklynn said, unable to get herself to call Dave a replacement. "I just feel like if I can't figure this out, I'm going to lose him."

"And you don't want to lose him?" Dr. Jackson asked.

Brooklynn shook her head, tears gathering in her eyes.

"Grief and loss take time to overcome," Dr. Jackson said. "Your fear is your biggest obstacle. Do you fear being unfaithful to Ryker?"

"Sometimes," she said. "In the beginning. But now... no, I don't feel like I'm being unfaithful to him by dating Dave."

"Can you name your fears surrounding Dave?"

"That I'm not good enough for him." She held up one finger. "That he'll die on the ocean, the same way Ryker did." Another finger. "And that I'm trying to replace Ryker with Dave, and he deserves more than that."

Three fingers.

Three fears.

Dr. Jackson watched her for a few seconds. "You have incredible self-esteem," he finally said. "So I'm not sure why you're worried you aren't good enough for him."

"He's a Captain in the United States Coast Guard, and I groom dogs for a living."

"This isn't about your occupations," Dr. Jackson said. "Dig deeper."

Brooklynn didn't want to dig. Digging hurt. "His house is nicer than mine. He makes a lot more money than I do."

"Mm hm," Dr. Jackson said. "Keep going."

"He's happy, and I feel like I have happy moments, but really, I'm just getting by."

"And there's the real reason. You think that your supposed unhappiness will bring him down."

Brooklynn looked away. She'd never focused down on why she felt inadequate to be with Dave. In fact, she wasn't sure she'd even been able to pinpoint that she felt like she wasn't good enough for him until she'd said it.

"What makes you happy?" Dr. Jackson asked.

"Dave," she said immediately. "Dogs. The apple orchards. My family, though sometimes I want to strangle them."

They both laughed, and Brooklynn felt her heart take courage.

"I'm afraid our time is up," Dr. Jackson said. "This was a quick session, because you didn't have an appointment." He stood and started for the door. "But I'd love to see you again, privately. In group too, if you'd like. But I think you'll make better progress if we can talk about your specific needs each week for a little while."

"I'll make an appointment," she said.

"As many as you want," he said with a smile, and Brooklynn left his office, at least some of her feelings sorted out. Unknotted. Free for her to examine and then do something about.

"So we have twenty men for the bachelor auction," she said later that day, her Cobb salad in front of her almost gone. Darcy looked at Julie, who had been able to sneak away for forty-five minutes.

"You should do it," Darcy said.

"I've done the bachelor auction before," Julie said, glancing at Brooklynn. "Remember Finn?"

"Oh, you can't count Finn," Brooklynn said with a laugh. Lunch with her friends was what Dr. Jackson should've ordered, because Brooklynn felt a million times better already.

"Oh, I'm counting Finn," Julie said, spearing another

piece of asparagus from her salad. "And it was a disaster." She leaned toward Darcy. "He was a lawyer in a rival firm. Thank the stars he moved, or I never would've been able to show my face at work again."

"Well," Brooklynn said, a new sparkle in her whole soul. "You don't have to kiss men on the first date."

"You do when you buy them for only one date," Julie shot back quickly, a smile following it. Everyone laughed, and a rush of happiness filled Brooklynn.

"What else do you need to finish for the Spring Fling?" Darcy asked, keeping the conversation away from Dave.

Brooklynn sighed. "Not much. We've had the event schedule up online and at the community center for a while. The bake-off has a theme and Michelle Dennesy got all the judges, so that should go smoothly."

"Are you going to enter again?" Julie looked at Darcy. "She's a great baker."

"Is she?" Darcy looked at Brooklynn. "You never said that."

It was strange bringing together two completely different parts of her life. Two different people. But they'd been getting along. "Yeah," she said. "Stress reliever." She looked back at Julie. "I don't think I'm going to enter. I haven't spent much time baking since I started dating Dave."

"Oooh, finally, we can talk about Dave." Julie's eyes sparkled like stars. "How's it going with him?"

Brooklynn glanced at Darcy. "We had a rough night last night. But we're working through some things."

Darcy said nothing about the text, and Brooklynn was glad.

"What things?" Julie asked, concern lighting her eyes now.

"I just found out he's armed on the ship," Brooklynn said, darting another look at Darcy. "It scared me. I...need some time to figure out how to not worry about him so much."

"So things are serious," Julie said.

"We've talked about serious things," Brooklynn admitted. "And honestly, I think he'd ask me to marry him right now. But—"

"You think so?" Darcy asked.

"Does he know about the wedding ring?" Julie asked.

Brooklynn looked back and forth between them, unsure which question to answer.

"Do you love him too?" Darcy asked next, and the words hit Brooklynn like a load of bricks.

"Too?"

"You just said you thought he'd ask you to marry him right now. Which means you know he loves you. Has he said he loves you?" Darcy's fork hung in midair, where her hand had frozen.

Brooklynn shook her head. "He hasn't said that." She could just feel it. She'd been loved before, and she definitely felt loved by Dave. The way he'd crawled into bed with her last night, held her close to his heartbeat, stayed until she'd quieted.

He definitely loved her, whether he'd said it or not.

She looked at Julie. "I told him about the wedding ring last night. I gave it to him this morning."

"Oh, wow." Julie leaned back into the booth, her eyes wide. "So you *are* in love with him."

Brooklynn shook her head. "No." She swept her gaze around the crowded café, where most of the customers were women out with their friends or businessmen and women taking a quick lunch break.

"No, I mean—" She looked at Darcy and then Julie.

Julie smiled and nodded, tears filling her eyes.

"Yes," Brooklynn whispered. "Yes, I'm in love with him."

17

Dave pulled up to his house and waited for the garage door to go all the way up. Brooklynn's car sat in the driveway, and it made his heart thump in a whole new way. First, he was a little nervous to see her. Second, he was a lot excited to see her. He always wanted to find her car in his driveway after work.

Of course, today had been a horrible day on the boat, with fog and rain and general unrest out on the water with low visibility. He'd thought a lot about retiring, actually, and with the way his bones ached, it was sounding better and better.

He eased his SUV into the garage and got out of the car with a groan and a sigh. "You sound like an old man," he muttered to himself. He felt like an old man—until he pushed through the door and into his house, where soft music played and Brooklynn sat on the couch with all three of her dogs.

"Well, look at you," he said with a smile, taking off his Coast Guard jacket and hanging it on the hook by the door. "It's so good to see you." He started toward her, glad when she got up and received him into her arms. "It's been a terrible day."

"Yeah?" She swayed with him, and Dave took a slow breath in and let it out. "Well, I ordered pizza. It'll be here in a few minutes."

"Pizza is my love language," he whispered, bending down to kiss her.

They were interrupted by the doorbell, which set off all three dogs. They ran toward the offender, yipping and skidding on the hard floor. Two of them stood up on their hind legs and pawed at the door as if they'd attack whoever was on the other side, if only they could get to them.

"Better go rescue the pizza delivery guy from your hounds," he teased, and Brooklynn went to do just that. She picked up both yappers while Dave answered the door.

Except it wasn't the pizza delivery guy—it was Bethany Ryan. "Oh," he said, startled by the sudden appearance of a woman he hadn't seen in a year. "Bethany." He glanced over his shoulder to Brooklynn. "What are you doing here?"

Brooklynn came to his side, and he slipped his hand

into hers, hoping his former seaman wasn't going to cause a problem. Wouldn't that just be the cherry on top of a terrible day?

Her eyes slid down Brooklynn's body and went back to Dave. "I…was just stopping by to say hi."

Confusion riddled through him, especially when she backed up and said, "I can see you're busy. I'll see you later." She scampered down the steps and disappeared out of the halo of his porch light, the darkness swallowing her.

Something told him to go after her, so he said, "Be right back, sweetheart," and started after Bethany. At the bottom of the steps, his eyes adjusted to the dim lighting, and he saw her cutting across his lawn to her car parked on the street.

"Bethany," he called, starting across the lawn. Boy, it was cold out here, and the water on the grass seeped through his shoes. "Wait up a minute."

She yanked open her car door, which threw light onto her face. *Something is definitely wrong*, his gut screamed at him. But it has been wrong a lot lately—first with that boat they'd boarded and found nothing, and second when he'd walked away from Brooklynn's, thinking everything was over.

He went around the front of the car too, pausing with the door between them. "You look upset," he said. "What's wrong?"

"No one wants to be told by their ex-boss that they look upset."

"Well, you do," he barked. "Now, why did you come here tonight? I know it wasn't to say hi." He'd had to file paperwork to get her off his crew last year, and their professional relationship had not ended well. She'd been transferred to the Seattle Base, and last he'd heard, she was doing fine.

She sighed and looked away, the light illuminating her clenched jaw now. "No, I didn't stop by to say hi."

"Yeah, because I never gave you my home address. Which means you used the Coast Guard database and came here for something." Headlights cut a path through the darkness, and he watched as a car with the pizza delivery light on top pulled into his driveway. He glanced to the porch, where Brooklynn stood, sans dogs, her arms folded as she watched his conversation.

Bethany's eyes met his. "I'm in trouble, Captain."

Dave's heart squeezed, and he reached for her. "Come in and tell us about it," he said. "We have food and dogs." He put a smile on his face, glad when she edged around the car door and closed it.

He didn't touch her, but gestured toward his porch. "Give me a couple words for what kind of trouble before we get back to the house." He wasn't sure if this was military trouble, legal trouble, or personal trouble, and he'd have to explain who Bethany was to Brooklynn, who signed for the pizza and managed to watch them at the same time.

"Personal issues," Bethany muttered. "My boyfriend's been hitting me."

Dave's fists clenched then, and he opted to go down the sidewalk to the driveway so he wouldn't have to cross that soaking wet grass again. "Where is he now?"

"I'm not sure," Bethany muttered, a definite hint of embarrassment in the words. "I left, and I told him I wasn't coming back this time. But I don't have anywhere else to go, and he won't think to come down here to find me."

"But you have to report to your ship tomorrow morning, right?" he asked.

"I'm off tomorrow," she said. "I've put in for a transfer, but it's still a few weeks away."

"So what's your plan?" Dave asked, because surely she had one. She might be in trouble, but her brain worked, and Bethany had been one of his best problem solvers. If only she'd have been able to follow orders, he might've kept her.

She slid him a look out of the corner of her eye, and Dave didn't like it. Not one little bit. "Bethany," he warned as they climbed the steps. They followed Brooklynn into the house, and Dave closed and locked the door behind them, unsure if he was willing to deal with her tonight. He and Brooklynn needed some time to talk, and Bethany being here was a problem.

One look at Brooklynn's face confirmed it. He had to get rid of her.

"Brooklynn," he said. "This is Bethany Ryan. She used to work for me on the *Adelie*." He nodded to Brooklynn. "Beth, this is my girlfriend, Brooklynn."

"Nice to meet you, ma'am," Bethany said, reaching to shake Brooklynn's hand.

"Oh, she doesn't like it when you call her ma'am," Dave said with a forced chuckle. Neither woman said anything, and the smell of the pizza was making Dave's stomach claw itself out.

He opened one of the boxes and took out a slice. "Tell us what's going on," he said, making eye contact with Brooklynn. He hoped his expression said, *I'm working on it. Sorry.*

She explained about her boyfriend, and she showed them a few bruises along her arms. Brooklynn didn't eat, and her eyes stormed with every minute that Bethany spoke. She looked at Dave, who had consumed half a pizza, and back to Bethany. "Dave, could you excuse us for a minute?"

Fear gripped his stomach and squeezed, making those four pieces of pizza regrettable. "Uh...."

"It's fine," Brooklynn said. "I just think Bethany...I just need a minute with her. Maybe we could go in your spare bedroom?" Her eyebrows went up, but she didn't wait for him to confirm. She got up from the table and marched away, Bethany going with her. Whatever silent conversation they'd had while he wolfed down pizza, he wasn't sure. He knew he didn't even really want to know.

Five minutes later, Brooklynn said, "I'm taking her to the hospital, and then a hotel. She'll be safe there until tomorrow, and then we're going to file a report with the police and the Coast Guard."

Dave stood in his own kitchen, dumbfounded, as Brooklynn put on her coat. "Really?" he asked.

"I'll meet you out front," Brooklynn said to Bethany, who moved toward the front door. Brooklynn stepped over to Dave and kissed his cheek. "She has bruises and scars all over her back and shoulders. This is more than a few knocks against the ship railings on her arms. This is serious abuse."

"You don't have to put her in a hotel. She's not your problem."

"I know," Brooklynn said. "But she came to you for help, Dave. And we're going to help her."

"Let me come with you," he said, nervous about her being alone with Bethany for some reason.

"She specifically requested that you not come," she said, lowering her voice. "I think she may have been sexually abused as well." She cradled his face in her hand. "I'll be fine, and I have my phone."

Dave felt helpless, and he sighed. "But I wanted tonight to be...us. We need to talk about my job."

"And we will." She smiled at him softly. "I'll be back in

a couple of hours. Don't eat all the pizza." And with that, she was gone.

Cinnamon whined, and Dave knew exactly how the little dog felt. He lay down on the couch and lifted all three dogs on top of him, letting them nestle on his chest and down by his knees. "At least you guys are still here," he murmured to them as he closed his eyes and prayed for sleep to erase this awful day from his memory.

He woke when the pups started barking. His head hurt, and his jaw felt tight. He normally slept with a mouthguard to prevent the unconscious grinding of his teeth, but he hadn't put it in before laying down on the couch.

"Go see who's here," he mumbled to the dogs, and they jumped off him and sprinted for the front door. A moment later, Brooklynn came through it, and she looked exhausted.

Dave was too, but he got himself off the couch and over to greet her. "What time is it?"

"Only eight-thirty," she said, bending to pick up Cory. She stroked the westie as she walked toward the couch. "I need a drink."

"I'll get it." Dave hurried into the kitchen and opened the fridge. "Water or soda?"

"Soda."

He grabbed two cans and took them to her in the living room, where she'd sat on the couch. "Is she okay?"

"She's in a hotel for the night," she said. "I checked in under my name." She popped the top of her soda and drank it, gulp after gulp. It was one of the sexiest things Dave had seen her do, and he grinned at her.

"Wow," he said.

"Yeah, we've been talking to a lot of people. The hospital had to call the cops. They said it's procedure when someone comes in with that many injuries."

"I feel so bad."

"Can you imagine if you'd let her walk away?" Brooklynn shook her head. "She's scared, and embarrassed, and broke."

"How can she be broke? She has a job."

"Her boyfriend takes all her money."

Dave shook his head. "How does someone get in a situation like that?"

"It's slow and subtle," Brooklynn said. "And then you're in too deep." She finished her soda and curled into his side, yawning. "Hospital food is gross."

He laughed and offered to get her some pizza. She said yes, and he heated up a couple of slices before taking them to her. She ate and cuddled into him again. "So tell me what makes a terrible day on the job."

"The weather," he said. "I can't wait for all this rain and fog to stop."

"So when I send you off to work in the morning, the weather is my biggest concern?"

"Honestly? Usually." He leaned back against the couch and closed his eyes. "It makes everything harder. Harder to determine what people are doing on their boats. Harder to board. Harder to traffic the commercial fisheries."

"So that's what you do. Watch people on their boats and board them."

"When we're on patrol, yes, that's what we do. We work with fisheries too. We make sure the environmental laws are being upheld—like you can't dump waste in certain parts of the bay. That kind of thing."

"How many people are on your boat?"

"Eleven."

"Bethany said she used to be one of them."

"She did."

"What happened?"

"She had a problem following my orders," he said. "And it caused unity problems on-board. I filed her transfer myself, citing a difference of opinions as the reason we couldn't get along."

"Hmm." Brooklynn finished eating and cuddled into him again. "She had nothing but good things to say about you. She said she was stupid when she was on your ship, and she wishes she could come back."

"Yeah, that's not going to happen," he said. "She

caused a problem with everyone on board. She literally couldn't get along with anyone."

"Well, she had a boyfriend in Seattle."

"It's honestly surprising."

"I liked her."

"You like everyone," he said, smiling and placing a kiss on the top of her head. "It's something I love about you."

"Mm," she said, snuggling deeper into his side. "I think you should give her a second chance."

"Brooklynn," he said, a hint of warning in his voice. "That's not how the military works. I can't just take her from her post in Seattle, and besides, my ship's full."

"You sound just like her." She gave a small laugh. "I'm just saying, she's in a tough spot, and if you can help her, you should."

"Noted," he said.

"Is that how you talk to your crew?" she asked, pushing off him and looking into his face, plenty of teasing in her expression. "Noted. Make it so. Yes, sir."

"They call *me* sir," he said, grinning. "You should try it sometime."

"Oh-ho," she said, chortling. "I don't think so."

He laughed too, and the moment between them felt lighthearted and wonderful. She sobered, and so did he, and she said, "Dave, I sure like it when you come home to me."

Not knowing what to say, he kissed her instead, because he sure liked coming home to her too. He liked that she'd taken charge in a difficult situation, for a woman she didn't know. He liked nearly everything about Brooklynn, and he kissed her like he did so she'd know.

Because he still couldn't get himself to say those three little words.

Not yet, he told himself. He didn't need to yet.

18

Brooklynn continued her private therapy appointments and her group therapy meetings. Things between her and Dave seemed to get better and better each day. Bethany filed her complaints and got an immediate transfer to a new cutter in the San Diego area.

Every night, Dave told her a little more about his job. Stories from the past or whatever had happened that day. He never really seemed to be in any danger or do much of anything that felt dangerous to Brooklynn.

April dawned, and with it, the apple trees started to blossom. It was her favorite time of year, and she begged Dave to take her out into the orchards, so they could hold hands and kiss under the flowering tree branches.

"There's a whole town that does a huge carnival with the apple blossoms," she told him when he insisted they wait until the trees were in full bloom. "We should go."

"You said it was five hours away," he said without looking up from the paperwork he'd brought home with him that night. "I'm not driving five hours for what I can see here in a couple of weeks."

"It's not until the end of the month anyway," Brooklynn said, going over to the kitchen table where he worked. "What are you doing? Can we go get a treat?"

He pulled a folder over the papers and got up from the table. "I thought you were going to make us something."

"The prelims for the bake-off are tonight," she said. "Let's go taste with the judges."

"Can we do that?"

"Of course," she said, grabbing her purse. "We organized this thing. We can taste a few cookies." She grinned at him, glad it didn't get dark quite so early anymore. She'd been working on building her self-confidence when it came to Dave, and she liked that she could get him to do what she wanted, when he just wanted to stay home.

He drove them over to the community center, where past the front desk and down the hall, she knew right where the bake-off entries had been dropped off by five o'clock. The entrants had the opportunity to bring in their proposed entries two weeks before the event in order to get feedback on their creations.

It wasn't required, which was how Brooklynn knew they could have as many treats as they wanted.

"Holy brown cows," Dave said when they stepped into the room. "Look at all of this."

"Hello, Roberta," Brooklynn said as she strode over to the only judge in the room. "How's it going?"

"Good," Roberta said. "I'm almost done, and the other four have already finished."

"So this is all free?" Brooklynn asked.

"Help yourself," Roberta said, consulting her clipboard and reaching for a piece of dark bread.

They'd chosen coffee as the focus ingredient for this year, and she couldn't wait to taste the chocolate and coffee pairings. She picked up a cookie that had a dark batter, as well as three different kinds of chocolate chips, and bit into it.

"Oh, this has butterscotch," she said, the tanginess of it exploding across her tongue. "I was not expecting that." But it was delicious, and she ate the whole thing.

"You have to try this," Dave said a few paces away from her. "It's so good." He lifted another spoonful of what looked like tiramisu to his mouth. He nodded and pointed with his spoon to the dish. "Mm."

Brooklynn laughed at him and joined him to try the tiramisu. The pudding was smooth and the coffee and chocolate tasted divine with the cookies. "Mm," she said, moaning. "This is going to win."

"It's fantastic," Dave said, stepping down to a cheesecake. "This looks promising too."

They spent the next several minutes sampling items and saying if they were tasty or not. Brooklynn liked everything she put in her mouth, but nothing quite as well as the caramel macchiato ice cream. Even melted, it was delicious.

"But it won't win," she said.

"Why not?" Dave asked, tucking his hand in hers. "And are we going home now?"

"Because it's a *bake*-off," she said. "And even if they had to cook something for that ice cream, they didn't have to bake." She glanced up at him. "Can we stop somewhere for food? Then you can go back to your secret paperwork."

"It's not a secret," he said.

"You never let me see what it is." Brooklynn noted that Dave didn't jump to say what he'd spent so much time reading and marking.

"Doesn't mean it's a secret," he said. But he didn't say what it was, and Brooklynn felt awkward asking again. So she let him move the conversation to something else, buy her a cranberry turkey sandwich, and take her back to his place.

FINALLY, THE FIRST DAY OF THE SPRING FLING CELEBRATION arrived. Dave had put in for the day off, and he'd gotten it.

"What happens to a ship without her Captain?" Brooklynn asked him when he picked her up for breakfast. The weather had cleared the last few days, and the apple trees were glorious with their pink and white blossoms.

"Someone else fills in," he said. "Hopefully, it'll be a boring day." He opened her door and helped her in, something he did every single time without fail. Brooklynn had enjoyed the last month with him, and she hadn't made the mistake of taking him home to meet her parents again.

He hadn't taken her to meet his either, and she stewed about it while he crossed over to his side of the car.

"Do you think I should meet your parents?" she asked.

He looked at her, surprise in his eyes. "You want to?"

"Well, it's normal, right? I mean, you met mine, and you already knew them."

Dave reached for her hand and lifted her wrist to his lips. "I'd love to take you home to meet them," he said. "I just—I'm never quite sure where you are, and if you're ready."

A pang of regret pinched in her chest, but she managed to put a smile on her face. "I'm not going to break again," she said. "It's okay to ask me."

"I know," he said, but she wasn't sure he did. He never asked how her therapy sessions had gone, and she had been relatively tight-lipped about them too. "I just figured you'd talk to me about what you're comfortable talking to me about. I don't want to have to ask all the time or feel like I'm making you tell me something you don't want to."

Brooklynn looked at the side of his face, knowing he could feel the weight of her eyes and was choosing not to look at her. "I think I'm doing really good," she said, which did draw his attention. "I'm still working on overcoming my fear, but every day you go out on the ship and come home okay helps."

"All right." He drew in a deep breath and twisted the key in the ignition. "Let's go eat, and then we're going to go see some apple blossoms."

She giggled, because she knew he was just going along for her. They'd both grown up in the area, and Washington was famous for its apples.

Over omelets and bacon, he talked about his siblings, and with her right there, they set up a family dinner with his parents so they could officially meet Brooklynn in her official capacity as his girlfriend.

The parking lot at the orchards was overflowing, with cars parked down the street. "This is as good as we're going to get," Dave said, pulling into a spot barely big enough for his SUV. They got out and walked down the road to the huge red barn signaling the entrance to the orchards.

Much like the Lavender Festival, which had huge lavender fields just for tourists, this particular orchard was owned by the Magleby's and associated with the Spring Fling each year. Yes, there were apples grown here. But during the Spring Fling, the orchard was purely for touring.

Cider and apple tarts waited for customers in a booth just inside the barn, and Brooklynn grabbed a map of the orchard and said, "I wonder where the kissing spot is this year."

"That's not a real thing," Dave said.

Oh, but it was. She searched the map, a giddy feeling in her gut. "Yep. Right there." She pointed and tilted the map toward him. "See?"

He squinted at it, and she giggled. "Your old man eyes can't see that?" She moved it closer as he continued to peer at it. "See?"

Dave took the map and tilted it, and she laughed. "I see it," he said. "That's where you want to go, is it?"

"Definitely." She linked her arm through his and took the map back. "Didn't you ever bring a girl out here in high school?"

"Just to kiss her? No." He shook his head. "Not my style."

Brooklynn smiled up into the sky, some clouds starting to roll in. "Yeah, me either. I always wanted to though."

"Well, for you, I might have. You should've said."

"And what would that have sounded like? 'Hey, Dave, want to take me out to the orchards and kiss me?' Talk about desperate."

"Isn't that what you just did?"

Brooklynn paused, shock traveling through her. "I guess I'm desperate."

He chuckled and let a few people go past them. "Baby,

if you want to kiss me, you can just do it." He closed his eyes and puckered his lips.

"Stop it," she said, laughing and pushing against his chest. He laughed with her, tucked her into his side, and they continued walking under the canopies of blossoms.

"Did your life turn out the way you wanted it to?" Brooklynn asked, unsure of where the question had come from.

"I think so," he said. "So far."

"You always wanted to be in the Coast Guard."

"I always did." He bent and picked up a fallen blossom. "What about you? Are you where you want to be in your life?"

"I think so," she repeated back to him. "I love my job. Have three great dogs. A great boyfriend."

"Just great?"

"Handsome?" she guessed. "Wait. Hot. A hot boyfriend."

He sent his laughter into the sky then, and she simply smiled at the sound of it. "I'm much too old to be called hot," he said. "And your birthday is coming up."

"Another couple of months," she said, trying not to dwell on the fact that she'd be one year closer to forty. And if she wanted even one baby of her own, she'd have to tie the knot quickly and get the deed done soon after that.

She pushed away the pressure of becoming a mother. She couldn't deal with it and everything else she was already in therapy for. There were other ways to build a family, and she needed to make sure she was physically, mentally, and emotionally ready to become a wife again before she could even come to the mother bridge.

He navigated them through the trees without using the map, somehow getting them to the kissing spot anyway. "So, here we are," he said, stepping away from her but not letting go of her hand. "Do you want a selfie? Is that what the kids are doing these days?"

"A kissing selfie," she said. "Yeah, I think we can pass on that." She tugged on his hand, her love for him growing and expanding right there under the party-cloudy sky and apple blossoms.

He came closer, and she stepped into his embrace easily. She wanted to tell him she loved him; the words crowded behind her tongue, clogging her throat.

She gazed up at him, her fear disappearing in the tenderness of his gaze. "Dave?" she asked.

"Yeah?"

"I'm in love with you."

He blinked, grinned, and chuckled. "Is that so?"

"Yeah," she said, smiling too. "That's so."

"That's awesome," he said. "Because I love you too." He kissed her, and everything in Brooklynn's world filled with sunshine and the scent of apple blossoms.

19

Dave enjoyed kissing Brooklynn when he knew she loved him. And he loved her. The feeling was quite indescribable actually, and he let the sweet scent of apple blossoms fill his senses.

She giggled and broke their connection, and Dave simply held onto her and let the seconds go by one by one. A breeze kicked up, and he whispered, "Should we go? Did you get your apple blossom fix?"

"Yeah," she said, stepping back and putting her hand in his. "You up for more coffee-flavored treats?"

"Oh, I don't know," Dave said, though the memory of that tiramisu sure did call to him. "Maybe ask me when I haven't just eaten a huge breakfast."

She smiled and laid her cheek against his bicep, and Dave hoped they'd always feel so comfortable with one another. No, she didn't tell him a lot about her therapy, but he didn't mind so much.

Her mood had definitely improved over the past month as she'd started seeing Dr. Jackson privately, and he was glad she could get the help she needed. He certainly didn't know how to give it to her, and the last thing he wanted was to see her cry the way she had that night at her house.

By the time they'd navigated through the orchard and back to the SUV, the wind had blown in gray clouds. His thoughts wandered down the road to Port Angeles, and he wondered what the conditions were like out on the ocean.

Not your problem, he told himself as he buckled his seat belt. "So what next?" he asked.

"Let's go see if the dance committee needs our help with the decorating."

"You just want to get in that community center and eat the treats."

"Maybe."

He shook his head, the sky above him threatening to open and douse Hawthorne Harbor in rain. That wouldn't be good for the tours of the apple orchards, and it was a good thing they hadn't postponed their journey to the kissing spot. They might not have gotten the chance later.

The first drops of rain hit the windshield as he pulled into the community center, and he drove through the circle to let Brooklynn out. "I'll park and be in soon," he said. She nodded, ducked out of the car, and ran for the entrance.

After parking, he flipped his collar up and walked as quickly as he could toward the doors. When the thunder cracked overhead, he started running. His time on the beach paid off, because he made it to safety before the sky broke open.

He held the door for several others hurrying inside, and once he was inside, he pulled out his phone to make sure the ringer was on. His gut writhed, and he had a bad feeling about his crew out on the *Adelie.*

"Brooklynn," he said, spying her up ahead. She turned, and the throng of people who'd come inside flowed around her as they dispersed to different activities. "I need to call in."

"But it's your day off." A panicked look crossed her face. "And what? You're going to go to work? Out on the ship in this weather?"

"I don't know," he said, pulling up the number of the commanding officer who ran the whole port. "I just know I need to check in. Give me a minute, would you?"

She nodded, just once, and he walked away from her while the line rang. "David," his CO said. "Everything okay?"

"The weather's turned," Dave said. "I'm just wondering how things are there. Something told me I needed to call in."

"Things are fine," Brian said. "We're bringing in the

Swordfish. No need to be out there for fishery inspection when they're all shut down too."

"Good call," Dave said. "Okay, well, let me know if the status changes."

"We'll be fine," Brian said. "Enjoy your day off."

Dave hung up and turned to find Brooklynn chatting with another woman. He approached, and she twisted toward him and grabbed onto his arm. "Dave, this is my friend Darcy. You know, the woman from my group therapy."

"Oh, Darcy, of course." Dave stepped forward and hugged her, because yes, Brooklynn had spoken of her often. "Are you here alone?"

"Oh, no," Darcy said, hooking her thumb over her shoulder. "My sister and mother are around here somewhere."

"Everything okay in port?" Brooklynn asked, and she sounded so much like a member of the crew there.

"Yeah," he said. "They're bringing in a non-essential ship. Other than that, the CO says everything is fine."

"Good."

"Well, I better go," Darcy said, smiling at Brooklynn. "My mom's convinced her coffee caramel cake is going to win, and I want to be with her to console her."

"You don't think it will?" Brooklynn asked.

"Honey, the caramel was like brittle. I doubt the judges were even able to taste it." She laughed, and Dave liked her energy. Brooklynn hugged her, and Darcy left.

"I like her," Dave said, watching her weave through the crowd.

"Yeah, she's great," Brooklynn agreed. "Should we go see if they have anything to do here?"

"I wonder what they'll do with all the outdoor activities," he said.

"Shut them down," Brooklynn said, a hint of sadness in her voice. "I mean, you can't move the orchards indoors."

"The food trucks won't like this weather either."

"They set up tents one year," Brooklynn said. "But it was so windy, that they ended up closing everything."

"They might have to do that today," Dave said, letting Brooklynn lead him toward the gym where the actual fling part of the Spring Fling would be held that evening. The dance. He'd come as a teenager a few times, but he hadn't been back since returning to town.

The woman he wanted to dance with had been unavailable, and Dave hadn't seen the point. They went into the gym, Brooklynn heading toward a woman standing in the middle of the huge space with a clipboard in her hand.

The lights flickered once, twice, three times, and then they went out. A cry of surprise tinged with fear went up, and Dave froze. His hand pulled against Brooklynn's, and he brought her back to his side.

"Does this place have generators?" he asked.

"I don't think so," she said. "My dad's never said anything about generators."

"Stay calm," a woman called. "Let's get to the doors."

"Wait," Dave said. There were windows way up high near the ceiling, and it took several seconds for his eyes to adjust. The door did let in a rectangle of light, because the lobby had a lot of windows and doors as well.

A sense of foreboding came over him as he and Brooklynn retraced their steps. It wouldn't stay warm in here without power. And there wasn't much to eat beside the bake-off items. How long would the power be out?

THERE WAS A DEFINITE FEELING OF PANIC IN THE LOBBY, AS more and more people continued to pack into the space.

"Maybe we should go," he said to Brooklynn, keeping a tight hold on her hand. The water sluiced down the glass outside, and that didn't look like a viable option either. "I'll go get the car."

"Can you believe this?" Darcy asked, and Brooklynn kept hold of his hand as she shook her head. So maybe she didn't want him to go get the car. He honestly wasn't sure what there was to do at the community center if there was no light and no heat.

"Everyone," a booming voice said, causing the nervous chatter to quiet.

"That's my dad," Brooklynn said, straining up on her tiptoes to try to find him.

"We're going to put a movie on in the small gym. We've got ushers with flashlights if you'll come this way."

He went with Brooklynn though he wanted to leave. Several people braved the weather and left the community center, but he and Brooklynn allowed themselves to be herded into the small gym.

Her father started the movie, one of those kid's animated ones, and returned a few minutes later with a huge bag of popcorn that people started passing around.

Dave's nerves felt like they'd been tangled in the garbage disposal. He didn't want to sit here and watch this movie.

His phone rang, a clear, loud sound that echoed through the gym. He answered it quickly so it would stop ringing, and stood up to leave so he could talk freely.

"David Reddington," he said, because he'd caught Brian's name on the screen briefly.

"Dave, I need you here. How hard would it be to get here?"

Hard, he thought. "I can do it."

"How soon?"

"What's going on?"

"We've got three civilian boats stalled and taking on water in the storm. The *Adelie* is on her way to assist, and I've got Audrey getting her bird in the air. I want you on the *Swordfish* in forty minutes."

"Forty minutes?" He almost choked. "Sir, I live twenty-five minutes away." He turned back to the gym, wondering if he could really leave Brooklynn here.

"You're the best sea captain we have," he said.

"Surely Captain Hiller can take the *Swordfish* back out," Dave said, but he was already moving toward the exit. He paused and turned back to see Brooklynn coming toward him.

"Hiller is ill," Brian said. "Get here as fast as you can, Captain. That's an order."

Dave hung up, his resolve hardening. "I have to get to port," he said. "They've got a rescue mission underway." He leaned down to kiss her quickly. "I'll call you as soon as I can." He started to turn, but she grabbed onto his arm —hard.

"Dave," she said, her eyes filling with tears. "Please don't go."

"I have orders," he said.

"I have a bad feeling," she said, lifting her chin and containing her tears so they didn't streak down her face. "Please, don't go. I love you, and I can't...I can't bear the thought of you out there in that storm, on a boat. Please."

Dave looked into her eyes, torn right down the middle. He hadn't told her that he'd been reading about retirement. Filling out the paperwork. Making sure all of his investments were up-to-date and in order. She'd sort of asked, weeks ago, but he'd said nothing.

He was wasting time he didn't have. Time the people stranded out in the ocean probably didn't have.

"Can you get a ride home with Darcy?" he asked. "Or your dad?"

"Dave," she said, still pleading with him.

"I love you," he said, pressing another kiss to her forehead before turning and jogging out of the building.

THE DRIVE TO PORT ANGELES WAS TERRIFYING, AND DAVE kept a steady stream of prayer going the entire way. He pulled up to the dock, parking illegally and jumping out of the SUV. Brian met him wearing full rain gear, and that was when Dave really knew the grave situation they were in .

"The boat's ready," he said, handing Dave a thick, plastic container and walking with him toward the *Swordfish*. "Give me your keys, and I'll have someone move your car."

Dave handed over the keys. "I'm not in my uniform."

"We have one for you on the ship," he said. "Your exec has the coordinates, and I've got Matt getting his helicopter ready."

"Can he fly in this?"

"Audrey's been out there," Brian said. "She says it's okay. Difficult, but okay."

Dave didn't know how that was possible, but he nodded. "Is she back?"

"Yeah, she's refueling and taking the mandatory break."

"All right." He went up the gangplank to the ship while Brian stayed on the docks. Once on the boat, everything got packed up, and they set off. He stepped into the cockpit and shed his soaked jacket.

"Get me up to speed," he said to the man standing there. He missed his boat. He missed his crew.

But there were people out there who needed help, and that was what Dave had trained his whole life to do—help people.

As the man talked about the drifting boats and their calls for help, Dave changed into the officer's uniform provided for him, his mind whirring around the situation —and Brooklynn. He'd promised her he'd call, but he didn't have time right now. It would be a miracle if his phone even had service in this soupy weather.

"How far out are we?" he asked.

"Fifteen minutes."

"And we're at full speed?"

"We're at full speed for these conditions, sir."

He nodded and looked at the plastic file. "And what's your name?"

"Brandon Lillith, sir."

"All right, Officer Lillith. Let's get there, get everyone to safety, and get home." He picked up the radio. "I can talk to the whole crew on this?"

Officer Lillith nodded, and Dave pressed the button, completely unsure of what to say to assure these people he would do exactly as he'd said. Get them out there. Get everyone to safety. Get everyone home, safe and sound.

But he had to do it. He had to get back to Brooklynn as fast as possible.

20

Brooklynn watched Dave walk out into the rain with all the confidence of a man who could battle the ocean and win. But she'd known another man like that, and he'd lost.

Her soul raged the same way the storm did, and she spun away from the rain assaulting the glass doors. She would not let her tears run down her face the way the water did the windows. Oh, no, she would not.

She held her head high and went back into the small gym to find her father. He could spare twenty minutes to take her home. He must've seen her and Dave leave, because he sat on the end of the bleachers right beside the door. He stood almost as soon as she'd entered, and by the time her eyes adjusted to the dark, he wrapped her in a hug.

"Dad," she said, very close to snapping into a thousand pieces. "Can you drive me home?"

"Sure, baby," he whispered. "Let's go." He didn't ask any questions, something Brooklynn appreciated in that moment. They dashed through the driving rain to his truck, which was about a million years old. It still started and the heater still blew, so he refused to get another one.

"Where did Dave go?" he asked once he'd fiddled with all the dials and pulled out of the parking space.

"He got called out on a rescue mission." She stared numbly out her window, her arms cinched tightly across her stomach.

Her dad didn't take the turn he needed to in order to deliver her back to her pups and her bad coffee and the silence in her house. She didn't say anything, and they continued toward her childhood home on the edge of town.

"Your mother's home," he said. "She'll keep you company. I have to get back and make sure everything's okay with the Fling."

"I know, Dad." Brooklynn swung her attention toward him. "Thank you."

"He's a good captain," her dad said, and that only made Brooklynn's fury and frustration swirl dangerously together. She'd never seen a tornado in real life, but she felt as if she had one clashing with her lungs.

Her teeth hurt she pressed them so hard against one

another. She looked away, glad when he turned onto the lane that led past all the trees and to the house.

Dave hadn't hesitated for long when she'd begged him not to go. What would he ignore next time?

There won't be a next time, she thought. Her heart shrank at the idea of not having another day with him. Another kiss. Another embrace. At the same time, she didn't think she was strong enough to weather storms like this.

"There you go," her dad said, pulling up to the house. She'd still have to run through the rain for several steps to get under the eaves of the porch, but it was as close as he could get her.

"Thanks, Dad," she said, glad when none of her irritation bled into the words. Her parents had been nothing but supportive all these years, and as she got out of the truck she saw a light flip on and the front door open. Her mother was there, waiting to receive her with open arms and hopefully something with a lot of chocolate in it.

She barely heard her father's rumbly truck pull away because of all the rain. Her mother beckoned to her from the front door, but Brooklynn stood just outside the envelope of safety and let the rain soak her.

Tilting her head back, she looked up into the sky, feeling the very heavens weeping and wailing around her.

Please, she thought, unable to form much more of a prayer than that.

"Brooklynn," her mom called, and she had the distinct feeling it wasn't the first time. "You'll freeze to death."

But the rain wasn't really that cold. Or maybe she was just so numb that it didn't feel too icy. No matter what, she turned slowly in a full circle, her mind spinning at a much faster rate than her body.

She felt removed from the earth, from reality, and she hated it. Something Dr. Jackson had said in their last group session flowed through her mind.

We all make decisions, he'd said. Sometimes they impact others, and sometimes they're more contained.

She had a decision to make.

Reality came zooming back, and she shivered when she realized the rain had soaked her clothes to the skin. She dashed up the steps and into her mother's arms, her tears mingling with the rain on her face.

An hour later, she emerged from her old bedroom, wearing a ratty pair of sweatpants and her brother's too-big sweatshirt. The scent of chocolate chip cookies hung in the air, and she padded into the kitchen to find her mother there, pulling out the last tray of baked goods.

"There you are," she said, setting the tray on the stove-top. "I was just about to come looking for you." She looked at Brooklynn with concern radiating from her eyes.

Brooklynn tried to smile, but it felt wrong on her face. If anything, the day outside seemed darker, more ominous, and she tore her eyes from the windows. "These look good."

"Coffee or hot chocolate?"

"Hot chocolate." She was already keyed up, and she didn't need the extra stimulant. A sigh leaked from her mouth as she sat at the kitchen table and let her mother bring her sugar and chocolate.

She sat beside her and patted her hand. "It's going to be okay."

"You don't know that," Brooklynn said, more acid in her tone than she liked. She didn't touch her cookie or her mug, though the steam rising from it comforted her the slightest bit. "No one can know that, Mom."

"Did he say he'd call?"

"As soon as he could." Brooklynn folded her arms, the only thing she could think to do to keep all her vital parts where they should be. She felt like her skin was trying to claw itself off, and her foot started tapping.

It had certainly been long enough for him to drive to the port. Surely, he'd call before he set sail. The minutes ticked by, and her mother ate enough chocolate chip cookies for both of them.

Dave didn't call.

Her worry ate through her as time marched forward. The door opened, and her father came blustering in. "Whoo-ee," he said. "It is coming down out there." He swept the kitchen, where she and her mother sat at the table. "Heard from Dave?"

"No," her mother said, getting up. "I'll start dinner. What do you want, Brookie?"

"I'm not hungry," Brooklynn said. She couldn't imagine putting anything in her mouth right now.

"You have to eat," she said.

Her father removed his hat and coat, the water dripping onto the floor beneath the hooks where he hung them. Brooklynn couldn't even imagine what the weather would be like on the ocean.

Her mother set a pot filled with water on the stove, ignoring Brooklynn completely. Fine. Didn't matter. Let her make dinner.

Just the fact that it was dinnertime was upsetting.

Her brain wouldn't seem to shut off, and she hated the track it was currently on. She needed to break up with Dave. Then it wouldn't be her job to worry about where he was and if he was coming back.

She could groom the canines around town, make her banana bread at night, and take her little dogs for a walk in good weather.

She could be lonely. Desperate. And single forever. Never kiss Dave again.

Her heart didn't like the sound of that, though her brain really didn't want to be this agitated ever again. She'd already been through a vigil on the beach once. She couldn't do it again.

As darkness fell, the scent of garlic and steak filled the house. Brooklynn couldn't stand the thought of Dave on a boat on the ocean—in the dark.

Everything was harder at night.

She exploded to her feet. "I'm going to Port Angeles." She reached for her coat.

"Do you think that's wise?" her dad asked.

"Dinner's ready," her mom said.

She faced her dad. "Can I borrow your truck, please?" Brooklynn held out her hand as if her father would drop the keys in her palm.

"Brooklynn," her dad said, standing up from the spot he'd taken on the couch.

"Dad, I can't sit here."

"It's still raining outside," he said. "The roads could be icy."

She'd stood in the rain, and it wasn't that cold. Of course, it had been a few hours—why hadn't Dave called yet?—so maybe the temperature had dropped.

"Dad, that truck will never go off the road." Brooklynn lifted her chin.

He glanced into the kitchen and back to Brooklynn.

"Mitch," her mother said, but her dad dug in his pocket and handed the keys to Brooklynn.

"Thanks, Dad." She hugged him quickly and put her coat on. "I'll call you when I get there."

"If you don't, I'll call you," her dad said. "Be careful."

Brooklynn didn't feel much better once she was

behind the wheel of the truck, but at least she hadn't had to dash through the rain to get to it. She kept the windshield wipers going at double speed and both hands right on the wheel where they were supposed to be.

Tension pulled through every muscle in her body, but she made it to Port Angeles in forty minutes. She dialed her dad, and he answered with, "You're okay?"

"I just pulled into town," she said, unsure of where to go next. "I'm going to go see what I can find out." She could see the ocean frothing in front of her, and she turned down the street that ran along the coast. "There's a ferry station here."

"Keep going," he said. "It's out by the bird refuge."

"Bird refuge?" Why hadn't she asked more questions about where Dave worked? She had no idea where to go to find him. "Oh, there's a sign." She continued down the road, and it seemed to like she'd drive right off the edge of the world and into the water. "I'll call you later, Dad."

"Thirty minutes," her dad said, and she agreed.

After hanging up, she swallowed, glad the road turned and started arcing north. The bird refuge came into view, and she kept going. Finally, finally, it looked like a station up ahead, and that had to be the Coast Guard station.

Waves crashed on both sides, and she saw a boat dock on her right as she came up to the station. A man wearing a bright yellow poncho over his Coast Guard uniform walked down the road, his head bent against the weather.

This was the absolute edge of the planet, and she wondered how in the world Dave drove up here every day.

"We're closed, ma'am," the officer said. "You can't go in."

She didn't want to go in. Did she? "I'm just looking for information," she said. "My boyfriend—" Her voice stopped working, cracking and breaking on the word. The man peered at her through the rain.

"Ma'am?"

"David Reddington," she blurted. "Captain David Reddington. Do you know if his ship is back in?"

"All the ships but one are back in, ma'am," he yelled. "Which one was he on?"

"I don't know," she said.

"Just a minute." He stepped back over to his station and ducked inside. She could just make out his silhouette as he picked up the phone.

Her nerves remained agitated, but at least she was doing something. She didn't dare look right, though, because the ocean foamed right there, and she couldn't bear the thought of a wave crashing over her, sweeping the truck right off the map.

The man approached again. "He's on the *Swordfish*, ma'am. They're fifteen minutes from port. The CO is sending someone to talk to you."

Talk to her. Like, alert her of Dave's death? That he was hurt?

"Do I wait here?" she asked.

He turned and pointed almost immediately to her right. "Pull in to that little lot there. I'll take you into the building to wait for her."

Brooklynn nodded and moved her truck where he told her to. She flipped up her hood and dashed through the rain to the little blue building where he stood waiting for her.

"A woman named Audrey is coming," he said. "She's one of the helicopter pilots who works rescue missions with the ships."

"Thank you," Brooklynn said, glad this building had heat, because it had grown cold in the hours since Dave had left. She hadn't waited fifteen minutes before the door opened again. This time, a waterlogged woman walked through it, and she looked about how like Brooklynn felt. Ragged. Tired.

"You must be Brooklynn." She put a smile on her face and shook Brooklynn's hand.

"Yes."

"I'm Audrey Lynn. I was out on the rescue mission just before Captain Reddington arrived."

"Oh." Brooklynn's hopes fell. "So you don't know how he's doing."

"The *Swordfish* had to be deployed because the *Adelie* couldn't handle the weather much longer. I came in with her, and another pilot and crew went out in our place."

"Dave's captaining that."

"Yes, ma'am."

"Do you know how he is? That guy said the ship was only fifteen minutes out."

"They're limping back."

"Limping?"

"Towing a couple of boats. We got all the people saved, and it's just taking longer than normal, because of the extra load. That's all." She smiled, but it didn't exactly radiate happiness.

"So Dave's okay." Brooklynn didn't dare let the relief spread through her until she knew for certain.

"He's sustained some minor injuries, as have most of us," she said.

"Injuries?"

"I believe the executive officer's report was a separated shoulder."

That relief she'd been holding in for so long finally rushed through her making, her shoulders sag. She could handle a separated shoulder.

"He'll be at least another hour after he pulls in to port," she said. "Paperwork and debriefing."

"Can I wait here for him?" she asked, debating about whether she should stay or go. He didn't need to know she'd driven to Port Angeles to inquire after him. No one needed to know.

"I'm headed out, but I can get word to him." Audrey's eyebrows went up, clearly asking Brooklynn what she wanted to do.

"How well do you know Dave?" Brooklynn asked.

"Pretty well," she said. "I live in Hawthorne Harbor too. We drive over together sometimes."

"Oh." Brooklynn didn't know that. Dave had never said anything. "Should I stay or go?" she asked, trying to push aside her feelings. Now that she wasn't consumed with worry, she could feel other things, and she didn't like the jealously coursing through her.

If Dave was interested in Audrey, he could've been with her all these years. He wasn't.

"That's up to you, ma'am," Audrey said.

Brooklynn really didn't want to be called ma'am one more time. "I'll wait here. If you could let him know?"

"Yes, ma'am."

Brooklynn clenched her jaw, nodded, and turned away from the military pilot. She opened the door and left, and Brooklynn darted over to the door to watch her walk across the street to the hut and talk to the man there. Then she got in a car and drove away, toward the bird refuge.

Now Brooklynn just had to wait for Dave.

21

Dave couldn't wait to get back to the station. He needed to get out of this rain and somewhere warm again. He could barely feel his fingers, but he stayed in position, wanting everyone on board to know their captain was in control.

But he knew he couldn't control the ocean. The weather. Any of it. His impatience kept his fingers clenched into fists, and he refused to look away from their destination. The lights on the tip of the land where he launched from each day finally came into view, and they docked a few minutes later.

It had taken twice as long to get back as it had to get out there, and the rescue had used up all the fuel in another helicopter. But hey, Audrey's pretty boy pilot friend had performed great. They hadn't lost any civilians, and all the divers were accounted for as well.

His shoulder ached where he'd wrenched it, and he knew Officer Lillith had called in medical for him. That would take forever. And then he'd have to debrief and fill out paperwork. Make sure all the civilians had rides to somewhere safe.

And then...then he could call Brooklynn, if the hour wasn't too late.

"Captain," Officer Lillith said, and Dave turned toward him. "We're disembarking."

"I'll sweep the ship," Dave said, watching as officers worked to secure the two boats the *Swordfish* had towed in. They'd been heavily damaged, but they could be salvaged. And if it were him, he'd rather have a damaged boat he could fix than one at the bottom of the ocean.

He made sure all passengers were cleared from the ship before he went down to the dock himself. Two men stood there, waiting for him. "Captain, we received word that your arm is injured."

"I popped my shoulder out," he said. "We can go inside to look at it." They followed him, and then Dave let them remove his poncho and his jacket. He did what they asked, wishing he could dictate his reports while they fiddled around with his arm.

"I'm going to put it in a sling," one of them said. "You'll need to go over to the hospital to get it reset."

"Fine," Dave said. "Do either of you have a phone I could borrow?"

"CO Pendelton is waiting for you," one said.

So no phone. "Thank you," he said, saluting them and walking away. Might as well get his interview with the commanding officer over with.

More than an hour later, his shoulder still hurt but it was back in its rightful place. His interview was done, as was his paperwork. A headache pounded behind his eyes, and he should stay at the station that night. Those who didn't live in town were. Ben had offered for Dave to crash at his place.

But he'd lost his phone in the rescue, and he needed to call Brooklynn. More than that, he needed to *see* her. Reassure her that he was fine, that it would take more than a storm and a couple of sinking boats to take him out of the game.

"Sir," someone said behind him, and he turned to find the CO's secretary approaching.

"Yeah?"

"There's a Brooklynn Perrish waiting for you at the gate."

His heart leapt into his throat and stuck. "What? How long has she been there?"

"I'm not sure, sir. I was just to tell you when you left." He saluted and walked away, leaving Dave to hurry to his SUV and get behind the wheel. A small building sat near the gate, but he didn't see her car there. Perhaps she'd been waiting too long and had left.

He pulled in beside a red truck, giving it a sidelong glance. "I know that truck...." So she was still here. Anticipation coursed through him now. She'd see he was fine. That no one else had come to the station in a panic to find out about their loved ones.

He opened the door and found her sitting on the couch, her head in her hands. "Brooklynn," he said, and she flinched.

It took a moment or two for her eyes to focus, and then she jumped to her feet. "Dave." She hurried toward him and he went to her too, taking her into his arms. "You're all right."

He suppressed most of the groan that came from lifting his arm the wrong way and held onto her when she tried to step back.

"Oh, you're hurt."

"I'm fine," he said.

"Audrey said you'd separated your shoulder."

Surprise filled him. "You spoke to Audrey?"

"Yes." She stepped back. "She came to tell me what was happening."

Dave wasn't sure how to feel. Everything mixed inside him, and he simply blinked at Brooklynn. "I'm fine."

"You separated your shoulder," she said as if it was a life-threatening injury.

"I saved seven people and two boats," he said. "All of the crew is fine. Everyone did their jobs spectacularly today."

She recoiled from him, a bit of shock in her expression now.

"I'm sorry." Dave sighed. "I just...you didn't need to come."

"You didn't call."

"I lost my phone." He wasn't going to tell her it had gone overboard. That would only add fuel to her nerves. "I'm tired and hungry. You want to grab something to eat?"

"I have my father's truck."

"Yeah, I saw it out there." Now they'd have to drive separate cars home. What was she going to do? Follow him to make sure he didn't slide off the road? He didn't like the venomous thought and pushed it away.

She was sensitive, that was all. She'd lost someone she loved in an accident on the ocean. He tried to see things from her perspective, and he wondered if he'd always have to do that when she didn't give him the same luxury.

He turned toward the door. "Let's get back to town before we eat. There's nothing good here anyway." And then he could figure out how to get over his frustration with her during the drive.

On the way back to town, he looked more in his rearview mirror than he did the road in front of him. Miracles definitely still happened, because it was due to one that he arrived home in one piece.

He pulled into the garage and went inside, his flesh still chilled despite the seat warmer he'd run for thirty minutes. His stomach growled, but he didn't want to go out. Brooklynn pulled in after him, and he left the garage door open so she could come in behind him.

Usually pretty clean, Dave ignored his tendencies and dropped his coat on the floor and kicked his boots off next. Brooklynn came in, and he said, "I don't feel like going out. I'm cold, and I'm going to hop in the shower."

"I'll order something," she said. "Or dig through your fridge."

"You won't find anything in there," he said. "Don't you need to get home and take care of your dogs?"

"They're fine," she said, moving ahead of him into the kitchen.

Dave didn't say anything else as he followed her and turned down the hall that led to his master bedroom. With the door locked, he undressed and stepped into the shower. "Am I just delaying the inevitable?" he said into the hot spray, his muscles starting to relax.

The following day was Sunday, and he rarely reported to the port on Sundays. But Brian had asked him to come back and go through the rescue footage from the surveillance videos, and Dave had agreed.

But Dave didn't want to make that drive to the tip of the United States again. He thought of his retirement packet and wondered if time had started to go backward. July seemed like it would never arrive.

Once warm, he washed and got out of the shower. Dressed in his comfiest clothes, he finally went out to the kitchen and living room, which melded together into one big room at the back of the house.

Brooklynn lounged on the couch with her feet tucked

under her, and Dave had to admit he sure did like her there.

"Smells good," he said, spying the white containers on the counter.

"I got Chinese," she said needlessly, as Dave was already opening the distinct boxes. He got down two plates and served himself some food before asking her what she wanted.

She got up and came over to the island too. "Are you upset with me?" she asked, spooning some ham fried rice onto her plate.

Dave didn't want to lie, but he didn't want to argue with her tonight either. "I don't know," he said.

"I wish that were a no," she said.

"You didn't need to come to the station," he said, trying to use his most delicate voice.

She nodded, quick little movements of her head. "Did I embarrass you?"

"No," he said. "It's just...I was fine."

"But I didn't know that." She looked at him, her dark eyes blazing like fire. "You said you'd call."

This was the exact conversation he didn't want to have. He turned away from her and pulled the bottle of painkiller from the cabinet above the microwave. After filling a glass with water, he downed four of them and took his food to the other side of the island. He didn't have to defend himself. It wouldn't have mattered if he'd called before leaving on the *Swordfish*, or the moment he'd returned. It was what happened in between that really mattered, and he couldn't put her on speakerphone for the whole rescue.

Brooklynn sat next to him, and they ate in tense silence. The moment she finished, she stood and put her plate in the sink. "Dave, I'm sorry I came to the station. I was worried."

"I know," he said.

A couple seconds of silence drew his attention to her. She drew in a deep breath as she wore that strong, determined look that usually got his hormones going into overdrive.

"I don't think this is going to work out," she said, and though Dave had realized a moment ago what she was going to say, each word punched him right in the gut.

"Because I didn't call?" he asked when he really wanted to apologize and beg her to reconsider. Would she do that? Could she?

"It's not just that," she said. "It's...everything." She turned away from him and collected her coat from where she'd laid it over the back of the chair at the built-in desk. "Best of luck to you."

"Brooklynn," he called after her. She didn't come back, and he went after her. "Wait a second."

She opened the front door and stepped outside, letting a blast of wind in behind her. Dave wasn't wearing shoes, but he followed her anyway. "Hey," he said, finding her at the top of the steps, staring out into the rain. "Come on. It can't be everything between us."

She shook her head, her chin trembling. "It is. Your job. Your whole career. That you didn't even consider my reservations. And yes, that you didn't call."

"Nothing happened," he said. His gut had been wrong a few times over the past couple of months too. Maybe her personal fears and worries had colored her perspective.

"This time," she whispered. "I have to go. My dogs need to go out."

"Brooklynn," he called after her as she went down the steps. She didn't look back once, and Dave felt his heart drive away with the woman he'd loved for so long.

A WEEK WENT BY, AND DAVE MADE THE JOURNEY TO THE station every day. Every night, he came home to an empty house, despite his texts asking if he could stop by her house. His invitations for her to grab some food and meet at his place likewise only met with silence.

He didn't want to give up, but he didn't need her calling the Chief of Police and reporting him as a stalker. He'd seen her in action on behalf of Bethany's rights, and Dave didn't want to anger Brooklynn further.

She'd taught him about Grub to Go, and on Saturday, he sent her favorite ham sandwich from The Anchor to her house. Still, he got nothing in response. Not even a thank you.

The following week, like a lovesick sixteen-year-old, Dave drove slowly by her house one day after work. Her big dog spa van sat in the driveway, so she hadn't left town. Maybe she'd lost her phone. Maybe it had fallen overboard while she took sailing lessons.

Dave scoffed, because while Brooklynn had been religiously attending her therapy appointments, she still seemed deathly frightened of the ocean.

He ran along the beach every morning at five o'clock, his mind revolving around Brooklynn. Maybe he should just go by her house and wait until she came home. Force her to talk to him.

He'd thought he'd been unhappy before, when he'd moved back to Hawthorne Harbor and found her with a boyfriend and then a fiancé. But now? Now, he knew misery and loneliness on a whole new level.

With his second Friday night alone suffocating him, he left his house and went to his parents'. He'd have to tell them at some point that he and Brooklynn had broken up, though he'd be surprised if they didn't know already. Brooklynn had told him that the gossip mill in town operated better than the cider mill, and he believed her.

He'd believed everything she'd told him, and foolishness pinched behind his lungs when he thought of how she'd said she loved him.

Had she been lying then? Was his job really too big to be overcome by love?

"Hey," he said upon entering the house. "Wow, that wall looks great." He could see right into the kitchen, and while the entire load-bearing wall hadn't been able to come down, a large part had, opening up the house significantly.

"Dave," his mother said from her place at the counter. She got up, limping for the first few steps toward him. "What are you doing here?"

He gave his mother a hug, holding onto her for a few extra seconds, giving away his loneliness if she hadn't already known.

"What's on your mind?" she asked, stepping back. "I didn't make dinner tonight, but we have some leftovers in the fridge."

"I can heat them up," he said. "If you don't mind."

"Not at all. Your dad won't eat that beef and broccoli."

Dave would, and he slid the plastic container in the microwave before turning to her. "Brooklynn broke up with me."

His mother nodded, her eyes somber. "I heard."

He diverted his attention to finding a fork for his food. He didn't want to think about people talking about him. "She doesn't like my job."

"She must really hate it," his mother said.

The microwave beeped, but Dave didn't turn toward it. "I'm thinking of retiring."

His mother's surprise lifted her eyebrows. "Really? For Brooklynn?"

"No, for me," he said, turning to get his food. If he retired now, everyone would think he'd done it for Brooklynn.

So what? he asked himself. Is that so bad?

He loved her. He wanted to be with her. But if he retired before July, he'd lose a year of service. So he said nothing else. Just got his food out and sat beside his mother at the counter.

Eighty-one more days. He could wait eighty-one more days. Then he'd invite Brooklynn to his retirement ceremony and ask her to marry him.

Satisfied with his haphazard plan that had literally come to his mind as he ate beef and broccoli, he was able to relax with his mom and carry on a conversation about his brother, then the remodel.

His father came in the back door, and Dave gave him a hug too. To their credit, neither of his parents asked him how long he was going to stay, and he chilled on the couch with them as they watched their favorite game show.

When Dave felt only moments away from falling asleep, he got in his SUV and went home. Of course, once home, he was wide awake, and he laid in bed, staring at the ceiling and trying to find a way to get Brooklynn back before July.

22

Brooklynn dug in her flower garden, enjoying the scent of fresh earth and the way her pups romped through the grass with one another.

A few weeks had passed since the big storm, and the weather had cleared enough for all the weeds to grow. They were relentless in their pursuit to take over her flower beds and lawn, and Brooklynn found herself doing yard work every evening after grooming dogs.

Cinnamon, Cory, and Callie sure liked the time outside, but Brooklynn didn't like the mindless work. It meant she had plenty of time to stew about Dave. He'd texted for several days after she'd broken up with him, but she hadn't heard from him in a while now.

Her heart skipped a beat, but she acted like nothing had happened internally. Sometimes, out of nowhere, tears would choke her, and she'd have to try to remember what she'd been thinking about that had upset her.

The answer was always the same.

Dave.

She'd continued her therapy, but the conversations were now about Dave and not the ocean or the beach or her fears. She felt like she was living inside her greatest nightmare, and she couldn't wake up.

She'd declined her invitations to the family dinner, because she didn't want to face her parents. She'd briefly seen her father when he'd come to get his truck, but they hadn't spoken. Not really. She'd texted that she was fine, and her mother had tried to get her to come to dinner every day since.

Brooklynn wasn't seeing anyone these days. Just her clients and her dogs. So when the sound of an engine met her ears and didn't just drive by her house, she glanced up to see Laci had arrived.

She stood up and brushed her gloved hands together, though she still had half a flower bed to weed. "Hey," she said to her sister, wiping her bangs off her forehead.

She'd cut her hair since her evenings had become free. She'd taken up walking after dinner, something else the dogs really loved. She simply needed something to fill her time, some way to find herself again.

It was absolutely unbelievable that she'd lost herself all over again.

"Your yard looks amazing," Laci said, gazing around. "I haven't even started on mine."

"I hate spring," Brooklynn said, though she normally loved it. Loved the blossoms. Loved the scent in the air. Loved the thought of a rebirth after a long winter.

"Wondering if you wanted to go to lunch," Laci said.

"I don't want to go to town," Brooklynn said. "There's too much gossip. Too many people stare at me."

"So you're going to avoid Main Street forever?"

Yes, Brooklynn thought. "No," she said. "I still eat out plenty. Trust me."

Laci smiled and shook her head. "You love that Grub to Go."

Yes, she did. No, it wasn't a crime.

"You aren't working today?"

"We hired a new tech who can't work a few days during the week," Laci said. "So she's on every weekend now."

"Lucky," Brooklynn said.

"Yeah." Laci toed the ground, her tell that she had more to say and wasn't saying it.

Brooklynn didn't want to go to lunch, but she did want to hear her sister's news. She'd missed her family more than she wanted to admit. Same with Dave.

She peeled her gloves from her hands and tossed them on the sidewalk. "Let me wash up, and we can go to Bell Hill for lunch."

Laci perked up. "To the mac and cheese place?"

Brooklynn could definitely use some carbs, so she said, "Definitely. Be right back." She dashed inside, calling her dogs after her, and washed her hands. After a quick change of clothes, she got in the car with Laci.

They chatted about their siblings and parents on the way to Bell Hill, and Brooklynn really liked talking to another human adult. She told all kinds of things to her dog clients, but most of them still looked at her with doleful eyes, as if she was trying to harm them by giving them a bath.

"Dr. Paul asked me out," Laci finally said once she'd pulled into the parking lot at the restaurant.

"No," Brooklynn said, a gasp following. "What did you say?"

Laci looked at Brooklynn, something raw on her face. "I said yes. I'm...tired of pining over a man who's already moved on."

"But—have you—are you ready to move on?"

"I'm not getting any younger, and he's a good guy." She smiled, her eyes dancing with a light Brooklynn hadn't seen on her sister's face since her break-up. "We're going out tomorrow."

"Where are you going?"

Laci sobered. "Brunch up at the lodge."

Those tears flew into her eyes, and Brooklynn blinked so they wouldn't fall. "That's great," she said, but the words sounded false to her own ears.

"Dave's miserable without you," Laci said.

"How do you know?"

"He comes and gets a dog every weekend now. Before, it was just every once in a while."

Brooklynn wanted to believe her sister. She did. But Dave obviously didn't miss her that much, or he'd do something about it.

What do you want him to do? The question was harsh inside her mind. He'd sent her food, he'd texted her, he'd invited her over. She was the one who'd cut him out of her life.

All of that was great. Nice, even. But she wanted him to quit his job, which was one of the most selfish things on the planet, and she would not say it out loud.

"We're just not meant to be," she said softly. "We weren't as kids, and we aren't now." She sniffed, glad none of her tears had made it down her face. "He's always loved the ocean, and he's wanted to be in the Coast Guard for as long as I've known him."

"There was an article about the rescue in the paper," Laci said. "Did you see it?"

Brooklynn shook her head, her memories of Dave suddenly overwhelming her.

"They said good things about him," Laci said. "His commanding officer said he was the best captain the Coast Guard has had at this station in a long time."

Brooklynn didn't doubt that for a moment, but she wasn't sure what Laci's point was. "I'm starving," she said, getting out of the car and hoping the conversation would move to something else when they went inside.

Thankfully, it did, and Brooklynn asked Laci as many questions as she could about Dr. Paul. But her mind never strayed too far from Dave, the ocean, and why she couldn't answer his texts.

May faded into June, and Brooklynn's loneliness only increased. Julie had started coming over on Fridays after work, and that eased some of Brooklynn's talking to herself or her dogs. She went back to the family dinners, firmly telling her mother at the first one, "I don't want to talk about Dave. If you bring him up, I'm leaving."

Her mother had been on her best behavior, and so had everyone else. Aunt Mabel got engaged to her boyfriend, and that stole all the wind out of every other piece of gossip in Hawthorne Harbor. It was all anyone was talking about—even the canines.

Not really, but they might as well have been. Brooklynn supposed Aunt Mabel's engagement *was* a pretty big deal. After all, it wasn't every day that a couple that was almost ninety decided to start their lives together.

Brooklynn went to visit her great aunt the day after the announcement had been made, and she carried a loaf of her coconut lime bread she'd been perfecting over the weeks. She hadn't been up to the Magleby Mansion in a long time, nor to her aunt's cottage just down from it.

The summer breeze came off the ocean, and Brooklynn paused to drink in the sight of the beach below and the water beyond. It didn't hold the same fear it usually did, and she took a deep breath of the briny air, getting a hint of lavender in there too.

The Lavender Festival lay just a few weeks away, but Brooklynn wasn't volunteering for anything with this town event. Her grandmother had been asked to judge the cooking contest, as a Magleby was always involved with such things at the Lavender Festival.

She'd thought about trying her hand at a recipe with lavender in it, but it had never been one of her favorite flavors, and she'd decided against entering.

"Aunt Mabel," she called as she knocked on the door of the cottage.

"It's open," her great aunt called, and Brooklynn went inside to see nearly every flower in town had made its way inside the house. Another woman stood there, and Brooklynn recognized her as Gretchen Herrin.

"Oh, I didn't know you were busy."

"It's fine," Aunt Mabel said, getting up from the kitchen table. "Just fine. Fine." She hurried in her hobbled kind of way toward Brooklynn, adding, "Is that the coconut bread?"

Brooklynn chuckled and handed it to her. "Yep."

"Gretchen, we have to have this at the wedding."

"You aren't catering your own wedding?" Brooklynn asked.

"Heavens, no," Aunt Mabel said. "I've waited my whole life for this, and I'm not lifting a finger." She smiled so wide her face shone with happiness, and Gretchen sniffed as she wiped her eyes.

Aunt Mabel unwrapped the coconut lime bread and sliced several pieces before handing one to Gretchen. "You know Gretchen, don't you? She owns the flower shop across from the park."

"Of course," Brooklynn said, shaking the other woman's hand. "I think I've come out to the lavender farm for grooming."

"Sounds right," Gretchen said with a smile. She took a bite of the bread, a groan pulling through her throat. "Oh my goodness." She looked at the bread with wonder in her eyes. "This is fantastic." She met Aunt Mabel's eye. "You should hire her to cater the wedding."

Fear grabbed hold of Brooklynn's heart. "Uh, no," she said.

"Maybe we could just have it at the wedding shower," Aunt Mabel suggested, hope shining in her bright blue eyes.

"Now that I can do," Brooklynn said, feeding off the enthusiasm of her great aunt. "I can't believe you're doing this." She grinned and giggled, maybe the first rays of happiness she'd felt since walking out of Dave's house all those weeks ago.

"I was in love with Clyde when I was younger," Aunt Mabel said. "He was the one who got away. I'm not letting that happen again." She gazed off into memories only she could see. She startled and cleared her throat. "Sometimes second chances do happen, even when you're an old woman like me."

"Drew and I got a second chance," Gretchen said, something curious in her voice.

Brooklynn didn't like the energy in the cottage all of a sudden. "Well, I just came to say congratulations."

"Are you going to get back together with Dave?" Aunt Mabel asked. "If that's not a match made in heaven, I don't know what is."

Brooklynn felt like someone had poured liquid nitrogen down her throat. She couldn't move and breathing was quite difficult.

"I know a couple of women circling," Gretchen said, eyeing her. "But they're not sure it's a good time."

"When would be a good time?" Aunt Mabel snapped. "Don't be ridiculous. Even if they asked him, he'd say no. He's only had eyes for Brooklynn for years. While she was married even."

Brooklynn shook her head, tears splashing her face. She hadn't even realized they'd gathered in her eyes. "No, Dave and I...no."

"Okay, you tell her," Aunt Mabel said, sitting down at the table. "I'm old and tired of repeating myself."

Gretchen stepped away from the dozens of flowers she

had spread over the table. "Okay, so your great aunt told me once that I couldn't let Drew get away. That I'd regret it all my life if I let him walk out of my life." She smiled at Aunt Mabel, who sat at the table and ate her bread as if the conversation wasn't happening around her. "And she was right."

Brooklynn shook her head. "I just...."

"My husband died too," Gretchen said, reaching out and touching Brooklynn's shoulder. "I understand how scary it can be to open your heart up to love again."

Brooklynn just stared into the other woman's eyes, searching for an answer to life's greatest questions. She wasn't even sure what they were, but Gretchen seemed to have figured it all out already.

"So don't let him get away," Brooklynn said, her tongue thick in her mouth. "I think I *pushed* him away."

"Of course you did," Aunt Mabel said in her usual tactful way. "So go get him back."

"How?" Brooklynn asked, looking from Gretchen to Aunt Mabel and back.

"How should we know?" Aunt Mabel asked, sifting through the blooms on the table. "You two had a special relationship. What is at the core of it? Show up with that, and Dave will take you back." She tilted her head. "I think I like these pink ones, Gretchen. What do you think?"

Brooklynn stayed for a few minutes while they talked about flowers, and then she bent down to kiss her great aunt on the forehead. "I'll see you later, Aunt Mabel."

"Be brave, my girl," Aunt Mabel whispered, and Brooklynn left the cottage. She walked up the hill to the Mansion instead of going to her car, trying to find what was at the core of her and Dave's relationship.

Food.

The man loved to eat, and Brooklynn could think of a dozen things to take him right now.

Dogs.

The man loved dogs, and Brooklynn had three she could take over there right now—and access to dozens of others through Laci. Dave wanted a big dog, she knew that. One he could take running on the beach with him and throw a ball to. He'd brought home boxers and mixed breeds, and she wouldn't dare make a decision without consulting him first.

But that meant she'd have to talk to him.

"You *want* to talk to him," she told herself as she reached the top of the hill, out of breath. She gazed out over the town, the sense of home engulfing her.

There was a piece missing for her, though, and she knew exactly what it was.

Dave.

Always Dave.

23

Dave pushed into the station, already in a surly mood. He had two more weeks of making this drive, and it was getting harder and harder. Getting up at five o'clock to go running was hard. Heck, making coffee was hard.

Everything was hard without Brooklynn in his life.

He'd driven to Port Angeles with Audrey today, and she'd talked almost nonstop about his retirement party and dinner. The announcements had gone out last week, and she'd received hers in the mail.

Which meant Brooklynn had too.

"Can I see the RSVP list?" he asked his secretary, and he shuffled a few papers and folders on his desk before producing it.

"This is what we have so far, sir."

"Thanks, Rick." Dave scanned it, the one name he

wanted on the list not there. Had Brooklynn not received her invitation? Had she not realized what it meant?

His fingers itched to call her, but he wasn't sure he could handle the rejection if she didn't pick up. He'd been through everything over the past sixty-five days. He'd thought about getting a dog and making a grooming appointment with her. But she only serviced dogs less than forty pounds, and he wanted a bigger dog than that.

He'd considered getting a puppy, but he literally didn't have time. *After I retire* had become a mantra to him, and he'd been so busy helping Brian go through transfers and profiles to get a new captain before he left.

Calvin Wingman had arrived last week, and Dave didn't go home all week as he and Cal trained on the *Adelie* together for long hours.

"There's a lot of people already," Rick said, brining Dave back to the fact that he stood outside his office, throttling an innocent piece of paper.

"Yes," he said, handing it back. "Are you coming?"

"Of course, sir." He smoothed the paper on the desk.

"I didn't see your name on there. And you should bring Candice." Dave smiled, but he didn't have a happy cell in his body. "Let me know when Captain Wingman arrives."

"Yes, sir," Rick said, and Dave went in his office and closed the door. That right there should've been a dead giveaway to anyone walking by that he didn't want to be bothered.

But no one seemed to care, as his office became a revolving door for everyone who wanted to say congratulations. Didn't they know that was what the party and dinner were for? He hadn't wanted to do the event at all, but Brian had suggested it, and since he needed a reason to get Brooklynn in the same room as him, Dave had agreed.

And now the woman wouldn't RSVP.

"Sir, Captain Wingman is here," Rick finally said, and Dave sighed as he got up and stuffed his hat on this head.

"Thank you," he said to his secretary as he exited the office and saluted the other captain. He managed to put the RSVP list out of his mind while they ran the ferry lines to Victoria Island and back and did a patrol on recreational boaters. This summer seemed extraordinarily busy to Dave, but that could've just been because he couldn't wait to *not* be on this boat.

What an odd thought that was. He'd dedicated his whole life to the Coast Guard, moving wherever he was assigned and putting up with whatever new seaman he got on his crew.

"So what are you going to do once you retire?" Cal asked as they stood at the front of the boat.

"Oh, I don't know," Dave said with a sigh. He liked Cal well enough, and he was an excellent captain in his fifth year. "Probably get a dog and go hiking." He grinned, because that did sound like a great life—if he could get Brooklynn to do it with him.

Cal chuckled. "Sounds pretty amazing."

"How's the family settling in?" he asked, because he didn't want to talk about what he'd do once he was retired. He honestly had no idea, and a thread of fear pulled through him.

"Good," Cal said. "Chris got the kids enrolled in school for the fall, and she's slowly getting the house in shape."

Dave mm-hmm'ed in all the right places as Cal talked about the fixer upper they'd bought just outside of Port Angeles, about their two cats not liking the wide open space, and how great the beach was.

Cal had everything but the white picket fence, and he was a decade younger than Dave. It didn't seem fair.

He made Audrey wait five minutes while he checked the RSVP list on his way out, and still Brooklynn's name wasn't on it. Muttering to himself, he crossed the parking lot to find Audrey leaning against his SUV and looking at her phone.

She glanced up when he unlocked the doors and gave him a look that he ignored. Behind the wheel, he said, "Sorry I was late."

"What's with you?" she asked, buckling her seatbelt. Everyone knew Brooklynn had broken up with him. Did she really have to ask?

"Nothing," he said, practically jamming the key in the ignition.

"Bad day at sea?"

"Only nine more," he said. "Single digits now."

"Not that you're counting down or anything," she teased.

Oh, Dave had been counting down. For eighty-one long days, he'd been counting down. "Saw your name on the guest list," he said. "And it had a plus-one next to it."

"Yeah," she said, pulling her ponytail out and letting her hair fall over her shoulders.

"Oh, so you're going to make me work for it."

"Work for what?" she asked innocently, and Dave chuckled.

"Who are you bringing?"

"I'd rather not say," she said.

"Do I know him?"

"Maybe," she said, which meant yes.

"Is he military or civilian?"

"Is this Twenty Questions? I just said I didn't want to say who it was." She glared at him, and the look had enough sting in it for him to realize she really didn't want to say.

"All right," he said easily. "Sorry." He drove toward Hawthorne Harbor, his mood growing worse as the time for him to pull into his garage and spend the evening by himself approached.

"You want to get dinner?" he asked as they came to the outskirts of town.

"Are you asking me out?" Shock filled every word, and Dave flinched.

"No," he said slowly. "I just...we've gotten dinner before." He glanced at her. "Right?"

"If people see us eating dinner together, they'll talk," she said.

"They will not," he growled. "Mabel Magleby has the whole town in a snit over her wedding." He glanced left and right and turned toward Audrey's house instead of downtown where the restaurants were. "And we've eaten together before. People know we're friends."

"I don't want anything to come between you and Brooklynn," she said.

Dave hissed. "There is no me and Brooklynn, Audrey," he said, suddenly keen to get her out of the car.

"Yes, Dave, there is." She put her hand on his arm, and he wanted to jerk it away. He didn't, but he wanted to. "Just go talk to her."

"I've *tried* talking to her," he said, the words nearly exploding out of him. "I sent her food. She couldn't even say thank you."

Audrey removed her hand and settled back in her seat. "Ah, so she's what's eating you."

"Yes, all right?" He rounded the corner too fast, his emotions making his driving erratic. "She's what's eating me." Had been for weeks now. Months.

He pulled into her driveway, his jaw clenched. "See you tomorrow."

"Dave—"

"Audrey, I didn't press you about who you were

bringing to the party. Do not test me on this." He cut her a look out of the corner of his eye.

She held up both hands in a surrendering motion. "Yes, sir." She got out of the SUV, grabbed her duffle bag from the back, and went inside her house.

Dave sagged in his seat, the fight inside him dying.

He got food on the way home. Ate it alone on the couch. Stared at the little black box he'd placed on the bookcase. Helplessness filled him. If Brooklynn didn't come to his retirement party, he couldn't ask her to marry him.

Yes, you can, a little voice inside his mind whispered. She probably wouldn't like the public spectacle anyway.

But Dave wanted to do something big, something grand, to show her that yes, while he'd retired for him—he'd really done it for her. That he'd do anything to get her back into his life.

His bedtime came early due to his pre-dawn running schedule. He hadn't texted Brooklynn in a long time, and he flipped his phone over and over, trying to decide if he could now.

Finally deciding he wouldn't be able to sleep if he didn't, he sent off a quick message to her.

Just wondering if you got your invite to my retirement dinner and if you're coming. You need to RSVP to my secretary if you are.

So many if's. He hated them, and he placed his phone

face-down on the nightstand next to him and switched off the lamp.

The next morning, he woke before his alarm, hopeful as he reached for his phone. There were no new texts, and he almost stayed in bed. What was the point of running anymore? He didn't need to be in peak physical condition for retirement.

Still, he got himself up and dressed and out the door. The waves greeted him cheerily, as they always did. There was something soothing and wonderful about the ocean as it came ashore, and he went through his stretching routine with that music in his ears.

He set off jogging down the beach, the sun already lighting the day into twilight. It would be fully light in a half an hour, and Dave wondered if he'd still get up early to run when he didn't have to go to work afterward.

Nothing about retirement made sense to him, and without Brooklynn, how in the world could he fill his time?

A figure appeared on the beach ahead, but it didn't concern Dave. He'd seen dozens of people out walking or running at this time of morning, especially since summer had arrived a month or two ago.

This person didn't appear to be exercising, though.

They threw a ball, and a dog barked and ran into the waves after it, making Dave smile.

The woman sat at the picnic table, not looking at him as he approached. "Come on," she called to the dog, and he nearly fell down.

He stopped instantly and turned toward that oh-so-familiar voice. "Brooklynn?"

She'd stood and now faced him.

"It is you," he said, his breath heaving in his chest. His heartbeat continued to sprint around, and he couldn't seem to get enough blood flow to his brain to make it work.

She picked up a bag from the table where she'd been sitting. "Good morning, Dave." Her voice painted pictures in his soul, and he wanted to sink into her, hold on tight, and beg her to take him back.

She stepped toward him. Again, and then again, finally extending the bag. "I brought you breakfast." The dog came running up to her, and it wasn't one of hers. She bent down and scratched it behind the ears anyway. "I thought maybe you'd sit with me instead of completing your run."

Straightening, she looked him right in the eyes, and Dave could see all of her trepidation. "You're on the beach," he said.

"Because I knew that's where you'd be."

"You have a big dog."

"He's actually for you."

Dave didn't know what to do, or what to think. "What?" came out of his mouth, causing Brooklynn to smile.

Oh, that smile. It was devastatingly beautiful, and while hope pressed against his vocal chords, Dave didn't dare let it bleed through the rest of him.

Brooklynn stepped closer. Close enough to reach out and touch him, which she did. Just her palm flat against his chest, but still. It felt like a permanent brand, and he was definitely hers if she wanted him.

"This is my RSVP," she whispered just before stretching up to kiss him.

24

Brooklynn had anticipated Dave's confusion. She'd hoped he'd forgive her quickly. She'd prayed he'd let her kiss him.

So when he sighed, his hands immediately finding a place on her waist and pulling her right against him, all her dreams came true. He kissed her like she was the very air he needed to breathe, his mouth a bit rough at first. Then he slowed, and the kiss turned sweet.

"I'm so sorry," she said against his lips. "I've missed you so much."

He just kissed her again, eradicating any fears she'd had about coming here this morning. Yes, it had been hard to step onto the sand. Heck, even pulling into the parking lot had been hard. But she didn't want to let Dave get away, and if she had to come to the beach to prove it to him, she would.

In fact, she'd go to the ends of the earth so he'd know she loved him.

"I'm quitting the Coast Guard," he murmured, moving his lips along her jaw to her neck.

She leaned into his touch, her lungs trying to get enough air to speak. "I got the announcement," she said, holding onto his broad shoulders.

He pulled back slightly. "So you're coming to the party."

"Yes," she said. "I'll call your secretary today." She smiled at him, still feeling a bit timid. "Are you—I mean—did you quit because of me?"

"Yes," he said simply, his eyes open and honest. "I want—I need you in my life, Brooklynn."

Tears gathered in her eyes, and they were both happy and sad. "I'm scared," she whispered. "I don't want you to regret this decision and resent me for it."

"I've been thinking about retiring for months," he said, holding her close like he had in the past. "Before we started dating."

"Really?"

"Really," he said. "I needed to get to July to complete my twenty-second year."

"It's July."

"That it is." He grinned down at her. "I can't believe you came to the beach."

"I'm not as afraid of the ocean anymore," she said. "It's not my greatest fear."

"What is?"

"Losing you," she said.

"Sweetheart, you haven't lost me." He kissed her again, and Brooklynn marveled at his forgiving heart and generous spirit. Relief and love filled her, and she didn't remember Titan until the dog barked.

She giggled and pulled away from Dave. "So I got you this dog," she said. "He's still a puppy, but he loves to run, and he'll grow to be a big dog you take on your morning jogs."

"Yeah?" Dave crouched down in front of the dog. "What's your name, bud? Huh?"

"Laci and I named him Titan," Brooklynn said. "She's been keeping him with her. Getting him trained up for you. He's your retirement present."

"Thank you." Dave straightened, his emotions parading across his face. "He's great."

"He's a golden retriever," she said.

"I can see that," Dave said, glancing at the bag on the table behind her. "What's in the bag?"

"Breakfast."

"I suppose this is a retirement present too." His eyes twinkled, and oh, how Brooklynn had missed his playfulness.

"No," she said. "This was a safety net in case you wouldn't talk to me."

"Why wouldn't I talk to you?" he asked, sobering. "You're the one who went silent."

"I know," she said, her voice weak. "I just needed...I don't know what I needed."

"Have you figured it out?"

She shook her head. "Not really. But I don't think I need to. I want to be with you. So I came here to see if that was possible."

"I think I'm going to need to see what's in the bag first." He folded his arms as if it really mattered, and Brooklynn opened the bag and took out the wrapped sandwich.

If bacon and eggs between two doughnuts could be considered a sandwich. "It's the Sailor's Start," she said, handing it to him.

He took it, his eyes wide. A moment later, he burst out laughing. That glorious, wonderful laughter that filled the world with joy. It certainly filled Brooklynn with joy.

"This was a great back-up plan," he said, taking a bite. He chewed and swallowed, going quiet as he gazed at her. "But totally unnecessary. If you want me, Brooklynn, I'm yours, and I'll do everything I can to make you happy."

"I want you," she whispered.

"I love you," he whispered back, kissing her again and making her wonder what she was so worried about.

"THIS LOOKS OKAY?" SHE ASKED, TURNING AGAIN TO SEE THE back of the dress. "Laci, it has to be perfect."

"It's perfect," Julie said. The three of them were crammed into a single dressing room while Brooklynn tried on dress after dress.

"Everyone's going to be staring at me," she said, her nerves assaulting her again. "I mean, perfect."

"It fits like a glove," Laci said. "And the navy is nice with your hair. Are you wearing it up or down?"

"We're curling it," Julie said. "And she's letting me do her makeup." She grinned as if she'd been given the best job in the world. Really, Brooklynn had called her in a near panic and blurted, "I need all the help you can give me."

After all, she bathed and clipped dogs for a living. She didn't know how to walk in heels, and the last dress she'd bought was for her wedding, years ago. And she couldn't show up to Dave's retirement party in satin and lace.

The navy blue dress she wore now did have some lace across the bodice and up over her shoulders. In fact, the entire top above her chest was only lace, with her skin peeking through. The rest of the dress had an underlay that hugged her curves and flared to her knees.

"It's a pretty dress," she finally admitted.

"We're getting it," Laci said.

"How much is it?" Brooklynn asked, twisting to try to find a tag.

"You forget where you are," Julie said with a smile. "There are no tags here. I'll go ask Amanda." She slipped out of the dressing room, leaving Laci and Brooklynn alone.

"You're getting it," Laci said. "I'll pay for half if I have to."

"You're not paying for half," Brooklynn said. "And I am going to get it." Giddiness built up inside her. "I feel like I'm going to prom all over again."

"Same guy too."

Brooklynn smoothed her hands over her stomach and hips. "I'm a little rounder, but I think in a good way."

"Dave will think so." Laci said with a grin. "So get changed and let's get this. We still have to deal with shoes and jewelry, and I have to go to work this afternoon."

"You do? I thought that tech worked weekends." She turned her back on Laci so her sister could help with the zipper.

"Yeah, well, she's sick, and I told Paul I'd help out."

"Oh, I see how it is," Brooklynn said, stepping out of the dress. "You want to kiss your boyfriend and get paid for it."

Laci laughed, but she didn't try to refute the statement, which meant it was true.

"So you and Paul are getting along?"

"You realize who you sound like, right?" Laci asked, putting her hand on the doorknob. "Mom." She ducked out before Brooklynn could argue.

She didn't have an argument anyway. Horror hit her as

she realized her sister was right. "Oh, my heck," she whispered to her reflection. "I'm my mother."

Her doorbell rang five minutes before Dave had said he'd pick her up. Brooklynn was ready, and she grabbed her purse from the counter, said, "Be good, puppers," and opened the front door to the most spectacular sight on the planet.

Her boyfriend, the retiring Coast Guard captain, who wore his official blue uniform, buttoned and pinned properly.

Her breath caught in her throat, and she stilled under his gaze.

"Ready?" he asked.

Still, she couldn't move. "Ready." She couldn't believe she was the one he loved. That she got to spend her life with him.

He smiled at her gently. "Come on, then." He reached for her hand, and the moment her skin touched his, everything in the world was right.

He'd told her what the event would be like, so she expected to see various men and women wearing their Coast Guard uniforms. They wore either blue or white, and everyone seemed to know exactly how to make themselves look amazing with limited fashion choices. Brooklynn received several compliments on her dress, and she stayed close to Dave's side during the mingling portion of the party.

Dinner began, and she sat up at the head table with Dave, his commanding officer over the whole station, and the other captains. The food was delicious, and she was lucky enough to be placed next to another woman who knew how to make small talk look easy.

The commanding officer got up to say a few words about Dave, and the applause for him filled the whole building as if it were thunder.

He was clearly loved. And he loved the Coast Guard so much. Another twinge of guilt hit Brooklynn, something that had been plaguing her since Dave had told her he was retiring so they could be together.

Dave stepped to the microphone, and she managed to push away her guilt. He was a grown man. He could make his own decisions.

"Thank you for being here tonight," he said, filling the entire room with his charm and charisma. No wonder he could lead a crew into a terrible storm and come out victorious on the other side.

"To my parents, who always supported my military career." He spoke briefly about them, and how his mother would ask him questions about his various assignments as if she knew what life was like on a cutter, or how the icebreakers worked. It was a touching tribute to his family, and then he turned slightly to her.

"And that brings us to the last thing I'm going to say

tonight." He stepped away from the mic and a man stood from the table directly in front of them to hand him something.

Not just something.

A little black box.

Brooklynn's heart thrashed in her chest.

"I'm here tonight with my girlfriend," he said evenly into the microphone. He kept his eyes on the crowd. "She's the woman of my dreams, and someone I've had a crush on for over twenty years."

A few people in the crowd giggled, and his mother pressed her palm against her heart.

"And tonight, she'd do me the greatest honor of becoming my fiancée." He turned toward her and dropped to both knees. He wasn't in front of the mic anymore, but the place was so silent, he didn't need to be.

"Brooklynn Perrish, you're everything to me. Will you marry me?" He cracked the lid on the box as if the ring inside would be needed to sway her decision.

But she supposed she'd brought a sugary, bacony breakfast sandwich to the beach to do the same thing.

She nodded, her words stuck somewhere behind the lump in her throat.

"Yeah?" he asked.

Brooklynn looked out into the sea of military faces, and she felt brave and bold for just that moment. Long enough to stand up and say, "Yes, sir," in a loud, clear voice.

The room erupted into applause and whoops, and Dave swooped her into his arms, kissing her in front of everyone.

"You don't have to call me sir," he murmured into her ear before pulling back. He slipped the diamond on her finger and looked at her, his expression full of mischief. "But I sure like it."

25

Dave stood very still while he waited in line with the other groomsmen. Everyone else pulled at their collars or adjusted their cufflinks. Not Dave. He'd had plenty of experience wearing a uniform that rubbed and pinched in places, and this suit actually felt great.

Finally, the women came out of the bride's room, and Brooklynn stepped to his side, a beaming smile on her face.

"All ready?" he asked.

"Aunt Mabel's finishing up," she said, linking her arm through his. "Don't you dare let me fall in these ridiculous heels." She glanced at her feet. "I don't see why I have to wear them. You're not that much taller than me."

He was, but he wasn't going to argue with her. "You'll be okay," he said instead, tucking her arm tighter against him. "I've got you."

And he did have her. They'd been engaged for a couple of months now, with their wedding looming on the horizon. Before the new year, they'd be married, and Dave's greatest wish would be his reality.

He still couldn't believe it sometimes.

"I'm so excited for Aunt Mabel," Brooklynn said. "It's just so sweet she gets to have the wedding she's always wanted, all these years later."

"Hmm," he said, though he identified with Mabel Magleby a lot. As Brooklynn had been married before and claimed she'd already had her big affair, she and her mother were planning something a little more low-key.

They hadn't told him much, only that she wanted him to wear his uniform, and that it would be a simple affair. "Is that okay?" she'd asked.

Dave had kissed her until he couldn't breathe, and then he'd said, "Sweetheart, I'd marry you tomorrow at City Hall. Whatever you want is fine with me."

As a Magleby, she was part of the wedding party, and he'd agreed to be her groomsman. It would easily take ten minutes for all the Magleby's to march in with someone, and yet the line didn't move. Mabel didn't come out.

"I was married at the Mansion before," Brooklynn said, and Dave glanced at her.

"Is this where we're getting married?"

"No," she said.

"Where is that happening?" he asked. "It'll be December."

"I'm aware of when we're getting married," she said with a coy smile.

"So I don't get to know? How will I know where to show up?" He watched her, and she certainly didn't seem like she'd tell him. "You do want me to show up, don't you?"

"It's a surprise."

Plenty of surprise moved through Dave. "So when people ask me, what am I supposed to say?"

"What I just said."

"Brooklynn," he said, a hint of frustration in his voice. "I can't know?"

She considered him, her dark eyes searching his. "Fine," she said. "But remember you said you didn't care where we got married."

"That bad, huh?"

She shrugged and tried to hold back a smile. "I booked a ship."

"A ship?" He didn't mean to shout it, but several other members of the wedding party, including both of her sisters, looked his way. "You've got to be kidding," he said in a much quieter voice.

The door behind them opened, and Mabel came out. Several women gasped, and Dave had to admit that Mabel, even as many years as she had in her, glowed with a radiance only a bride could achieve.

"I'm not kidding," Brooklynn whispered as the line tidied up and got ready to enter the hall. "Brian said I could have the *Adelie*, and I booked it."

Before Dave could say a single word, the wedding party advanced, and he'd been given strict instructions to do two things: Smile and remain silent.

But the first chance he got, he was going to kiss Brooklynn until he couldn't see straight. He steadied her as they moved down the aisle, one painstaking step at a time. Then he moved to the right, while all the women went left.

Mabel came down the aisle with Brooklynn's father escorting her. They both wore smiles with as much luster as the sun, and Dave couldn't help the feeling of comfort and peace that flowed over him.

He caught Brooklynn's eye, and that same warm feeling expanded and grew. In just a few short months, he'd be waiting at that altar, watching her walk toward him on her father's arm.

Smiling, he mouthed *I love you*, and she pressed her fingertips to her lips and blew him a quick kiss.

The pastor at the front of the hall gave a nice speech about finding true love, even in hard times, or in unexpected places, or later in life. He cheered with everyone else when Mabel and Clyde finally kissed, and he was ready to dart forward and catch the older woman as she lifted her bouquet of pink and white flowers high above her head.

It seemed like the entire town of Hawthorne Harbor had crammed into the banquet hall at Magleby Mansion, which of course, they had. Mabel had been the matron of this town for a long time, and there were more wet eyes than dry ones.

Dave clapped along with everyone else, glad when the happy couple finally moved down the aisle so he could be reunited with Brooklynn.

"The *Adelie*?" he asked.

"Well, she was your ship for five years," Brooklynn said. "And I figured it was a good place for us to start our lives together."

He tucked a lock of fallen hair behind her ear. "And you're sure you want to wait until December? You know what the ocean is like in December, right?"

"I can handle it," she said. "And Brian said we could go below deck if it's raining."

"So how many people can I invite?" he asked, following the crowd out into the main part of the Mansion. The staff would get the chairs down and the tables up, and then the wedding luncheon would be served.

"We each get ten guests," she said, glancing up at him. "It's way harder for me than you. My family is *huge*."

He did some mental calculations. "Do kids count?"

"Brian would say yes."

"Oh, Brian will be fine," Dave said, guiding her to the door. "Want to walk outside while they set up?"

She nodded and picked up the hem of her bridesmaid dress to move down the steps.

"So I have five," he said. "With my parents and my brothers and Charlie's wife, if kids don't count."

"And I've got six with just my parents and siblings. My grandmother will freak if I don't invite her. And Julie. And Darcy." She started ticking up fingers, getting to ten and continuing. When she stopped, she looked at Dave with apprehension in her expression. Now that he was retired, he wanted to do everything in his power to never see that look in her eye again.

"Am I doing the right thing? Maybe we should just have it here, so everyone who wants to can come."

He took her effortlessly into his arms, enjoying the sunshine on his face and the way she fit right where he wanted her. "You wanted small. The ship is small." He kissed her ear, then her neck. "You can have my five extra."

"You don't have any friends you want to invite?"

"Well, the crew of the *Adelie* will be there, right?"

"Yeah."

"Those are my friends." He gazed down at her. "I just need *you* there, sweetheart." He kissed her, glad when some of her nervous tension bled away. "And you're sure you want to wait until December?"

She giggled and pushed on his chest, a futile effort to get him to step back. "Yes, now behave yourself. We're in public."

"I'm aware," he said dryly, glancing around though no

one paid any attention to them. "I just want you at home with me."

She smiled up at him, the softest, sweetest smile that showed how much she loved him. "Oh, that reminds me. We're going to look at that house next week. The one out on the south side of town."

"All right," he said. They'd decided to buy a new house together for their new lives. "You tell me when, and I'll check my schedule."

She laughed again, and Dave secured her hand in his. A bell rang, signaling that everyone could go back inside now and find their seats for the luncheon. Dave turned that way, but Brooklynn increased the pressure on his hand, making him face her again.

"What is it?" he asked, searching her face.

Instead of answering with words, she balanced in her heels and kissed him. "I love you, Dave."

He chuckled, kissed her again quickly, and said, "I love you too, sweetheart."

Hawthorne Harbor
SECOND CHANCE ROMANCE

the end

SNEAK PEEK! THE BILLIONAIRE'S ENEMY CHAPTER ONE

Stacey Stapleton replaced the phone in its fancy-pants cradle, casting it a glare as if it had done her a personal wrong. Everything about this room on the fifteenth floor screamed high-end, and there was no way for her to replicate it. Number one, she only had one floor, so she could never provide the bay view that this new hotel, Sweet Breeze, did.

Number two, she was currently saving every penny she had to replace the carpet in the five rooms she had available at her bed and breakfast, and she now had a huge charge sitting on her credit card for this little espionage escapade she'd indulged herself in.

She should've known coming to Sweet Breeze was a bad idea. The air here felt a little too sticky, the smiles on the staff's faces a little too sweet, and the service a little too slick.

"I don't need to replicate it," she said. People didn't come to Getaway Bay for the high-tech room phones or even the five-hundred thread count sheets on the king bed where she sat to wait for her room service order.

"Shoot." She dove for her phone, which she'd left on the clear glass top of the dresser. She started the timer on her phone, mentally telling herself to add a minute to the delivery time. No way this place could provide her a breakfast in the amount of time her cooks could down the beach at Aloha Hideaway.

Plus, while the view was nice for the first selfie or two, Stacey herself much preferred the privacy her bed and breakfast provided, the way the jungle grew right up to the building, almost like it was trying to erase the evidence of mankind's existence on the island, and the sound of waves from the nearby beach.

Here, she couldn't even open the window. The best she could do was press a button set into the wall near the bed to simulate the wave sounds. Lame.

With her timer going, and her stay coming to an end, Stacey gathered her personal hygiene items and got in the shower. The spray was hot and strong and perfectly fantastic. So this ritzy hotel that had been siphoning off customers for the ten months since it had opened had excellent showers.

Did people really choose a place to stay based on a shower review?

"Nope," she said into the spray. Then she turned and squirted some of the hibiscus-scented body wash out of the dispenser stuck to the wall. "And they're going to waste a ton of money with this thing." Just to prove her point, she sent a few squirts of the surely expensive soap directly onto the floor of the tub.

She scrubbed herself down, wondering why the owner of Sweet Breeze couldn't just provide those tiny bottles of bland body wash like every other hotel in the area. Her frustration frothed like the luxury bubbles still foaming on her loofa, and she turned to wash off, wishing her negative attitude and desperation would go down the drain too.

She slipped on the excess body wash she'd deliberately wasted, her arms splaying to the sides, searching for something to grab onto. But this shower was impossibly smooth on all sides, and she ended up grabbing onto the shower curtain. It wasn't even standard, as it didn't rip off the rod like hers would have.

Cursing herself for being spiteful, she found her feet and regained her balance, smoothing down the shower curtain like it was a cat. She almost expected it to start purring, not that she had any experience with a content cat.

Her feline friend was as grumpy as they came, and Malificent skulked around the bed and breakfast with a general disdain that applied to everything she came in contact with. If Stacey even tried to pet her, she was met with a hiss and the baring of claws. So she put out food and water and let the cat do what it wanted. No sense in poking the bear. Or in this case, the tabby.

She got out of the shower and dried off, pulling her reddish hair into a turban with a second towel. Heaven knew this place could afford to launder an extra towel, and she considered throwing a perfectly clean one on the floor too.

In the end, she remembered the fiasco with the body wash and left the unused towels on the rack. Plus, she wanted to do her part to use water wisely and a pin of guilt pushed into her heart that she'd used two towels when she could've done the job with one.

Back in the room, her phone had just ticked past the twelve-minute mark. "Seriously, how long does it take to make French toast?" she asked the spacious room. She'd booked their basic room, with one king bed, over a month ago, under a different name. She wasn't sure why. The owner of this swanky new monstrosity on Getaway Bay lived across the Pacific, probably in his equally ridiculous penthouse overlooking the city of Los Angeles.

No one from the Davenport Development Group would ever know who she was or when she'd stayed with them. They had supervisors and managers and assistants to handle everything for average guests like Jaida Moore, the name she'd registered under.

At Aloha Hideaway, Stacey managed everything. Sure, she had a small staff that were like family to her, but when the buck stopped, it was always in her wing of the house she'd inherited from her grandfather five years ago.

She started to dress, leaving her wet towel pooled at her feet. A loud, hollow noise came from the window, causing her to jolt with shock and fear. Her heart pounded up into her throat, and she hurried over to the pane she couldn't open to find a smudge of...something. A feather drifted down on the other side of the glass, time slowing as it wafted back and forth, back and forth.

A bird had just flown into the hotel. Probably a pigeon, which in Stacey's opinion, were the rats of the bird world. But still. A living creature had died because of this towering building on the beach that totally did *not* belong. Even Hawaii's fowl knew Sweet Breeze shouldn't be here.

Something clicked behind her, and she spun, her pulse dancing from the front of her ribcage to the back.

"Room service," a deep voice said and a cart started to push open the door.

A squeak of surprise flew from Stacey's mouth and she tried to cover her bra with her bare arms as she half hopped, half tiptoed back around the corner.

"I'm not dressed," she managed to say, her voice trembling and weak, two things Stacey never allowed anyone to see. In front of her family, her staff, her friends in the Women's Beach Club, Stacey was calm, cool, controlled.

She cracked jokes and ordered extra fruity drinks for everyone. She gave people weekends off and brought pineapple cookie monster salad to family picnics.

And now she was currently wearing only her bra and panties, and apparently the man pushing the cart through the door hadn't heard her.

"I'm not dressed," she called again, and the squeaky wheels on the cart stopped.

"You ordered room service?"

"Yes, but I need a few minutes to put on some pants." Did this guy speak English? She hadn't seen him in her haste to conceal herself behind the wall, and she bent to grab the first article of clothing she could.

It was her bathing suit cover-up and she pulled it on. Her bra straps stuck out the top, but at least she was as covered as she would be on the beach.

The door slammed closed, but the edge of the cart remained. Stacey took a deep breath and dared to peek around the corner, finding the man gone and her food producing the delicious aroma of bacon and sweet maple syrup.

"Impossible," she muttered as she looked at her phone. With all the commotion, she decided to subtract the minute she'd been planning to add on and saw her phone said the food had been delivered in thirteen minutes and twenty-four seconds.

"Ridiculous." She wasn't sure if she was talking about

herself or the room service. She also wasn't sure if she could produce food as quickly.

She lifted the cloche and found condensation on the inside of it. This food was still hot.

"Unbelievable." Stacey wondered if she'd ever speak in full sentences again. It seemed her whole vocabulary was made of single words. She looked at the cloche in disgust. They were probably ordered from somewhere secret, like the Cloche Underground or something. The metal looked like brushed nickel, far superior to anything Stacey had ever gotten from the restaurant supply store on the other side of the island.

Knocking sounded on the door. "Are you dressed now?"

He probably wanted a tip. And delivering a piping hot, smells-so-good-her-stomach-rumbled breakfast in only thirteen minutes, he deserved one.

Stacey shimmied out of the cover-up and pulled on a maxi dress in dark purple, the color of the hibiscus flowers that could only be found in the gardens at Aloha Hideaway. Her grandfather had cultivated them, cross-breeding the flowers to produce the unique color, the blooms fringed with white, and then he'd patented it. Now Stacey had three workers who dedicated full-time hours to the gardens, and she made a nice profit from selling them to locals, other hotels, cab companies, travel agents, and anyone who wanted to provide a special

Hawaiian experience to the tourists arriving on the big island.

After squeezing past the cart, she pulled open the door, ready to chew the man out for entering her room without knocking first. She opened her mouth as her voice lost its ability to form sound.

The man standing in the hall didn't look like the serving type. He had strong, broad, powerful shoulders that spanned nearly the width of the doorway. His body narrowed to his waist, where he'd tied a long, black apron. He wore a black pair of slacks beneath that, with a black shirt that strained across the chest and biceps.

His blue eyes, almost the same beautiful ocean blue as the bay beyond the window, pierced hers, and went well with his military-style haircut and clean-shaven face. He was tall, tan, and muscular, perfect for a pair of board shorts for early morning surfing, or the board room for an afternoon meeting.

"Sorry about that," he said, and his bass voice caused vibrations to tumble through Stacey's chest. They also got her heart going again, which sent blood to her brain, which told her voice to *say something!*

"It's fine."

Not that!

He rubbed his thumb across his right eyebrow, drawing her attention to the slice through the middle of it, like he'd been in a knife fight and lost. But he was too clean-cut for a knife fight, and Stacey's mind ran rampant with possibilities for that scar on his face.

"How's the food?" He nodded behind her, obviously seeing that she'd removed the cloche while he stood in the hall.

"I haven't actually tried it. But it's hot, so that's good." Why she was speaking at all, she didn't know. This server didn't need her critique of the food. "And delivered fast. Thirteen—I mean, less than fifteen minutes. Wow."

A smile pulled across his strong mouth, rendering Stacey weak in the wrong places and staring at such a gorgeous grin. Men as good-looking as him didn't seem fair. She wondered what his life had been like. Did he get special treatment in school? Did anyone ever tell him no? When he got pulled over for speeding, did he walk away with a ticket the way she did?

"Thank you." She held out a twenty-dollar bill. A ridiculous tip, but probably one that was expected for a hotel-resort such as Sweet Breeze.

He waved the money away without even glancing at it. There was something...not quite right about him. What room service attendant turned down money?

"Sorry about barging in. I thought...." The grin appeared again, and Stacey almost leaned against the wall so he wouldn't see how he affected her. "Sorry."

She nodded since her voice had gone on vacation again, and he turned and walked away. Wow, the view from the back was just as spectacular as the front, and Stacey pulled herself back into the room before he reached the corner just in case he turned back from the weight of her stare.

She leaned against the closed door and pressed one hand over her heart. She felt stupid for a lot of reasons, the biggest one being that she'd felt a spark of attraction for the handsome stranger who'd almost seen her naked.

SNEAK PEEK! THE BILLIONAIRE'S ENEMY CHAPTER TWO

Fisher DuPont practically punched open the black plastic door that led into the kitchens.

Keep it together, he told himself again. He'd been reciting it the whole way down from the fifteenth floor. He'd donned these ill-fitting clothes and practically shaved his head in an attempt to keep his identity hidden from the staff. He wanted to operate on the ground floor of Sweet Breeze, find out how the systems worked—if they were even working—and what the staff thought needed to be improved.

"Do we really just go into rooms with the orders?" he asked the head concierge, Kepa, on room service, only a slight growl to his words.

Kepa, much shorter than Fisher's six-foot-five frame, stared up at him. "Who told you that?"

Fisher pressed his lips together. He didn't want to say,

because Kepa likely had the power to fire anyone on his staff. "No one."

"Did you do that? Enter a guest's room without knocking and announcing yourself?"

Fisher considered the man, who's dark eyes felt like coal filled with fire. "Yes."

Kepa's nostrils flared and he held out his hand as if Fisher would put something in it.

"What?" he asked, not connecting the dots. And he'd made a living out of drawing his own dots and connecting them into pictures no one else had imagined before.

"Your apron. You're fired." Kepa wore sympathy in his eyes, but Fisher didn't detect any leeway in his decision.

So he untied the apron he'd only been wearing for an hour and handed it to the room service supervisor.

"What room?" Kepa asked.

"Fifteen-twenty-one." Fisher had an amazing memory with numbers, but he kept some facts about himself close to the vest. This was one such thing.

"I'll send someone to apologize. You should go." He flicked two fingers toward someone behind Fisher. "Please see this man off the premises."

Fisher allowed himself to be led out of the hotel he owned, getting in the car he'd rented down the street and driving away as if he had an island home to go to. In reality, he'd gone to work in his hotel that morning from the penthouse that took up the entire twenty-eighth floor. It swayed when the wind coming off the bay was really bad, but after ten months of living there, Fisher had gotten used to it. Kind of.

He pulled over at a gas station and went inside. "Restroom?"

The guy behind the counter looked him up and down, apparently decided he wasn't going to vandalize the bathroom, and handed Fisher a tiny brass key attached to a two-foot-long piece of piping that had been painted bright purple and had the state flower of Hawaii doodled in black marker all over it.

Fisher would never tire of the beautiful flowers in this island paradise. He'd needed a fresh start after a disastrous business venture with his father, and he'd taken it here in Getaway Bay. He no longer wanted to get away from his own life, so that was a definite improvement.

In the bathroom, he stripped out of the bad clothes and pulled his midnight-colored suit from his small satchel. Properly dressed, he could now return to the hotel, figure out who was staying in room fifteen-twenty-one, and make sure she understood that his staff did not barge into rooms just because they had a room service cart.

He handed the pipe-key back to the clerk. "Thanks." He needed coffee, stat, but he wasn't going to get it from a gas station. He'd had plenty of such brew in the past, and it was never quite up to his taste standard. No, there'd be much better coffee at the hotel, and he decided he could wait.

The man stared at him, and Fisher was sure his suit had cost as much as the clerk made in a year. He used to feel bad about his wealth, but he contributed to so many charities now, and he considered himself a pretty nice guy, so he didn't let the guilt pin him down for long. Plus, he'd worked too hard for too long to have a bleeding heart because he could afford the suits, the leather shoes, the fancy cars, the jets.

After returning the nondescript sedan to the rental company and getting behind the wheel of his convertible, he returned to Sweet Breeze, taking full advantage of the valet.

"Good morning, Mister DuPont," Sterling said as he opened the door. "Nice haircut."

Fisher stood and smiled, the haircut courtesy of Marshall Robison. Marshall could wield a pair of clippers as well as he ran his generational pineapple plantations, but Fisher's best friend and fellow founder of the Hawaii Nine-0 club had gone a little crazy with the blades.

He ran his hand along his nearly bald scalp, hoping his hair would grow back quickly. He'd have to slather sunscreen everywhere up top to make sure he didn't get a nasty burn in spots usually covered by his hair.

"Thanks. Is Owen in?"

"Arrived an hour ago, sir. I believe he said he had business in the gardens this morning." Sterling smiled and saluted before sliding behind the wheel of Fisher's car.

He took an extra moment to pull his jacket closed and

button it before he entered his hotel. He walked differently in the suit than he had in the servant clothes, and he made a note of it. Why did it matter what he wore? Was it because every eye swiveled to him when he wore suits like this? Every back straightened? Every employee brightened, smiled, and then got back to work?

Fisher wasn't sure, but he did know he didn't like the attention. He craved the anonymity the room service staff enjoyed, just like he'd basked in being able to walk around his hotel without scrutiny while he pushed a laundry cart in front of him.

That had been an interesting day, as he'd had no idea the enormity of linens, towels, cloth napkins from the four on-site restaurants, and other items the laundry staff took care of. He didn't know his hotel received bonuses for being under a certain limit for water usage, and he'd really learned a lot from the small army of people he employed—and who'd embraced him as one of their fellow laundromatters—in only an eight-hour shift.

Still, when the time was right, he wore the suits and played the part. Mostly because it was better than any of the alternatives he'd tried, and the show gave him something to fill his day with.

He bypassed the front desk and the guest elevators. Holding his thumb against a pad, he opened the lock to his private hallway and let the door snick closed behind him. His elevator would take him to any floor, and he pressed the fifteen, hoping a personal visit from the hotel owner would be enough to convince the curvy woman in room fifteen-twenty-one not to write a damaging review about his wait staff. About *him*.

The elevator spit him out with a ding, and he plucked a pair of thick, black-framed glasses from his breast pocket, sliding them into place on his face. Women claimed that they would've known Superman was Clark Kent, that Lois Lane was *so stupid*, but he found the glasses disguised him as well as a ball cap and the wrong clothes. It was almost like the glasses simply threw people off, and they spent so much time trying to make the three-thousand-dollar suit line up with the cheap, plastic frames that he was gone before they put the pieces together.

Plus, they covered up that slight scar in his eyebrow.

Fisher strode toward the door where he'd delivered breakfast only thirty minutes ago. He knocked this time, when every instinct had told him to last time. He'd have to have a talk with Peni about telling new-hires to enter rooms without knocking. Of course that wasn't how they did things at Sweet Breeze, and Fisher should've known better.

The same woman pulled open the door, her striking green eyes somehow penetrating right past his expensive defenses. Her hair tumbled and curled, falling below her shoulders in the most delicious shade of red he'd ever seen. He had a thing for redheads, though he'd never dated one.

And you're not here to ask for her number.

"Good morning," he said, his voice perfectly professional and crisp. "I understand there was a slight mishap here this morning."

"I already got an apology," she said, her eyes narrowing.

Fisher could practically see the wheels turning in her head. She looked vaguely familiar, though he couldn't place where he would've seen her before. He rarely interacted with the guests, and he'd only just begun making the rounds through his undercover operations to work in all the departments of his hotel. He went around town, but usually to reserved private rooms where he was ushered in and out without making a fuss. Heaven knew the presence of his hotel on this island alone had made enough turbulence for a while.

"Yes, my room service supervisor is fantastic." He put his CEO smile on his face. It had guided him successfully through many board meetings and swayed construction foremen—tough, stubborn men—toward his side of certain issues in critical moments.

"I wanted to come personally assure you that our room service attendants always knock and announce themselves before entering."

"Clearly, not always." She leaned her hip into the doorjamb and kept one handful of fingers curled around the door, barely letting him see inside. The smile on her face could only be described as...satisfied.

"Yes, well, from now on. Can I gift you a free night

here at Sweet Breeze for the misunderstanding?" Heck, she could ask for a week and Fisher would give it to her. Something itched along his collar, but he kept his hands pleasantly at his sides. The urge to smooth down the eyebrow that seemed to constantly want to go the wrong direction tugged, pulled, yanked at his resolve. He couldn't do it; he'd done it in front of her as the attendant. Such a gesture was too identifying.

"Yeah," the woman said, a smile that felt flirty stealing across her face and making her twice as beautiful. "I'll take a free night."

Fisher's heart was doing something weird in his chest, but he managed to nod and say, "I'll have my guest concierge have the certificate ready for you when you check out." He extended his hand for her to shake.

The moment she touched him, an earthquake that could've registered on the Richter scale shook his body. Her smile stayed hitched in place, and Fisher added his to the conversation.

"Thank you, Miss…."

"Sta—Moore. Jaida Moore." Her smile turned false, and Fisher hadn't built himself into a billionaire real estate mogul by not being able to detect a lie. He'd worked with enough carpenters, electricians, plumbers, and brick masons to know when corners were being cut. He'd seen everything from upright, honest men doing good work and making a good living to sleazy, sloppy work that tried to get passed off as adequate.

He certainly knew when he was being lied to, and Miss Jaida Moore wasn't very good at it.

"Very well, Miss Moore," he said, keeping his voice smooth, non-emotional. "Stop by the concierge desk before you go to get your certificate."

"Most people call them coupons," she said, her left eyebrow quirking in a way that felt challenging to Fisher. Slightly condescending too.

"Yes, well, Sweet Breeze doesn't offer coupons." He buttoned his jacket and gave an authoritative nod. "Have a great day, Miss Moore."

"You too, Mister Davenport."

Fisher froze as he turned, his muscles turning hard at the name. How had she known it? And why would she use it? His stare lasted long enough for her to bring back the grin, a little cockier and more sure of herself than before.

She lifted one shoulder into a sexy shrug that made Fisher wish he'd met this woman after a morning spent in the surf instead of while he was "Mister Davenport."

"I can Google, you know."

"Ah." He ducked his head, something inside him telling him to get out of there before the conversation turned too dangerous. "Until next time."

He walked away, glad for the first time that he'd registered the hotel under his father's conglomerate. She didn't need to know that Fisher had given up his slime ball father's name twenty-five years ago, when the man had walked out on him and his mother. She didn't need to know he'd gotten the scar in his eyebrow on one of his father's job sites, because the man cut corners as easily as he breathed. Hardly anyone knew those things, and Fisher was going to keep it that way, even if Jaida-whose-name-wasn't-Jaida stirred something in him he'd thought long dormant.

SNEAK PEEK! THE BILLIONAIRE'S ENEMY CHAPTER THREE

Stacey arrived at Aloha Hideaway, a sense of peace descending on her that she'd missed during her overnight stay just down the beach. There were several smaller hotels along the main drag that ran the length of Getaway Bay, as well as three bed and breakfasts dotting the area. Hers was tucked away between palm trees and a few acres of wild forest, with so much greenery, flowers, and four water features, the online pictures almost didn't look real.

But they were real, and Stacey had people to maintain all the amenities of her business. She needed to, because there was no way she could refurnish the rooms with luxury beds like the one she'd slept in last night. She didn't have funds for bigger flatscreen TVs. She almost had enough for new carpet, and she could refresh the rooms with paint once the summer season died off.

Breakfast had ended an hour ago, and Stacey's all-female staff was in full swing as the hour of check-out approached. Then they'd have a few hours of seemingly calm, where they all worked feverishly before check-in began.

Stacey's busiest days were Thursdays and Sundays with people coming to the Bay for the weekend. Sometimes Monday could be hairy too, if she had families staying with her, as they tended to tack on an extra day just to go to the beach.

The beach called to Stacey now, and she knew only the warm sand, bright sunshine, and rhythmic lapping of the waves would truly erase that tall, delicious man from her mind. He needled her thoughts, and not only because he was as handsome and polished as the day was long. There was something...not quite right about him.

If she'd had the opportunity, she'd put the classy, sophisticated Davenport who'd come to apologize in a police line-up—right next to the room service attendant. Perhaps they were brothers, though none of her online digging had produced evidence of more than one Davenport heir.

"How'd breakfast go?" she asked Betty as she stepped into the kitchen. Though Betty came in a short, petite package, she had a whip-like personality with a loud voice to match. Everyone listened to her, Stacey included, because Betty had more experience in the bed and breakfast industry than anyone else on the Aloha Hideaway staff.

She'd attended culinary school on the mainland and opened four restaurants back in Hawaii by the age of thirty. Now fifty-five, her hair had turned completely gray, but her steel-colored eyes had not lost a single ounce of their edge.

"Excellent," she said as she scrubbed steel wool across the flattop. "All five rooms came to eat. There was plenty. We're set for Kalua pork for dinner tonight."

The scent of sugar and smoke hung in the air as Stacey nodded. Betty arrived at the B&B at five o'clock every morning, hit the ground running, and had breakfast on the table at eight, as promised, seven days a week.

Aloha Hideaway never served lunch, though they would make picnic lunches upon special request. Dinner was served seven nights a week as well, and Betty usually did most of the prep and then left the rest for the night cook, Dillan.

"Mm, I love Thursdays." Stacey flashed Betty a smile as she walked through the kitchen toward the door on the other side. The kitchen was the hub of the sprawling house, with the main living room in front of it. Stacey had converted that into an airy, natural-light lobby by widening the front doors of what used to be a house and introducing more wild plants and a fountain.

Her bed and breakfast might not have all the bells and whistles that Sweet Breeze did, but it offered a lot more.

More Hawaiian culture. More attention to detail. More charm. Feeling confident now that she'd stayed in the imposing building down the beach, she reached the door that led to the east wing of the house. Her private wing. Her employee's quarters.

"I've never heard you say you like Thursdays before." Betty shook her head with a smile, her arms still pumping, pumping, pumping to get the flattop clean. The woman worked hard, and the kitchen ran without a speed bump, exactly how Stacey needed it to.

"Well, there's a first time for everything," Stacey said, pulling open the door and stepping through it. A long, cobbled hallway ran down the middle of this wing, the same way it did on the west side. There were five bedrooms over here, and five in the west wing. Stacey had chosen the largest bedroom, which was also the farthest from the center of the house, as her own.

The rooms on this side of the home didn't have their own bathrooms, but she'd renovated the west wing to include that. Guests didn't like sharing a bathroom or coordinating shower schedules with strangers.

Stacey had her own bathroom, and there were two more in this wing. Marge, her architectural landscaper that kept the grounds interesting and beautiful, lived in the bed and breakfast with Stacey. She had her own room and bathroom.

The other two rooms were furnished like guest rooms, but Stacey didn't rent them out. Her staff used them as break rooms, as places of refuge from the service industry that could get tiresome and heavy at times. The third room was used for storage, for little bars of soap, and fresh towels, and the rows and rows of shelves in that room actually soothed Stacey.

Her evening manager slept in the first bedroom for a few hours each night. Her maids took siestas while they waited for guests to check-out and leave rooms to be cleaned.

She heard chatter up ahead and stopped in the doorway to poke her head into the last bedroom on the left. Her four youngest employees, all in their late twenties or early thirties sat around a table, mugs of hot liquid in front of them.

Stacey knew Ashley only drank tea. She worked exclusively in the hibiscus gardens with the girl on her right, Bailey. Lizzie and Tayla were dressed in their maid uniforms, one sipping hot chocolate if the marshmallows were any indication, and the other nursing what looked like black coffee.

"Morning, ladies," Stacey said. Her staff didn't jump to attention the way she'd seen the employees at Sweet Breeze.

"Morning," the all chorused back. Stacey enjoyed the more casual relationship she had with her employees, and she wondered if dark, dangerous Davenport even knew how to be casual. What would that look like on him? Jeans? A T-shirt? Swim trunks? She couldn't imagine the imposing man who'd shown up at her door wearing that expensive suit in anything but crisp, white shirts and pressed designer slacks.

"Anything to report?" Stacey asked.

"Nope," Ashley said while the other girls shook their heads.

"All right. Complete the checklists and let me know our needs." Stacey gave them a smile and continued toward her suite. She put in an order for supplies and food on Thursdays, which also added to the general busyness. But she'd found it to be the best day to do an order, because then she was never short-supplied for her busiest times.

She depended on her support staff to turn in their checklists, so she could order the right items at the right time. But it would be another couple of hours before they'd be slid under her door and her gardeners went outside and her maids moved into the laundry facilities.

A couple of hours.

Stacey could really use a couple of hours on the beach to decompress and talk through her stay at Sweet Breeze. She sighed as she reached into her oversized purse for her phone. It sang out a snappy notification—literally three, sharp snaps as if someone was trying to get her attention—before she could touch it. The screen brightened, which helped her find the device, and she checked to see who'd texted.

Esther: *Beach in ten?*

"Already on my way," Stacey dictated as she thumbed out the message. She pulled off her maxi dress and changed into her bathing suit, covering it with the white, flowy shift she'd pulled on in desperation at the hotel.

She traded out the pajamas and toiletries she'd taken for her overnight stay and replaced them with sunscreen, her sunglasses, a huge, wide-brimmed hat, and her e-reader. Not that she was planning on reading. Oh, no. She had a very busy conversation ahead of her with her best friend, and the center of all the talk would be Mister Fisher Davenport himself.

Esther didn't arrive at their spot on the beach for twenty minutes. Usually right on time, Esther dropped her bag in a great, flustered show. "Have you seen the traffic in and out of that place?"

She didn't have to name Sweet Breeze for Stacey to know to what she was referencing. She adjusted the purple hibiscus behind her left ear and said, "It's bad right now?"

"Apparently lunchtime around here has turned into a bloodbath for parking. I couldn't find a space to save my life. I'm all the way down by the blasted Spam Hut." She unfolded her beach chair and sank into it, righting her bag at her side and pulling out a bottle of guava lemonade. She took a long drink, as if it would somehow calm her.

"I hear you. We've filed the complaint about the traffic with the city. There's a hearing next week."

"Hearing, schmearing." Esther shook her blonde head. "I'm telling you, no one on the City Council is going to do anything about that place." It was almost like Esther thought if she said Sweet Breeze, a pack of murderous wizards would appear, summoned by the very name of "that place."

"Probably not." Stacey reclined in her beach chair, extending her bare legs out in front of her to soak up the maximum amount of vitamin D and sunshine. She watched Esther from behind her shiny sunglasses, one of her favorite activities. There was nothing more entertaining that people-watching on the beach, and Stacey had mastered it a decade ago. She could tell which couples were happy, and who had come to Getaway Bay to well, get away. From each other or from their problems at home, Stacey didn't know.

She could detect wealth from a mile away, and find those who wanted everyone to look at them, and search out those who normally blended in. They were the most interesting, and Stacey loved watching people interact with others when they thought no one was looking.

Esther smeared sunscreen over her shoulders and down her arms. Petite and powerful, she owned a private car service in the Bay area, and she really despised the traffic Sweet Breeze had brought to their quaint corner of paradise.

"Your business isn't suffering, is it?" Stacey asked. She'd thought Esther was doing quite well with the new addition to their island. After all, a swanky hotel brought high rollers with loads of cash. And people like that never drove themselves around, not even to see the sights.

"Of course not," Esther snapped, lifting her eyes to meet Stacey's behind the mirrored shades. "But everything takes twice as long." She softened, her bad mood at having to park so far away and tromp through the hot sand melting into pure curiosity. "You stayed there last night. How was it?"

Her cerulean eyes took on a hungry glow, and Stacey laughed. "Honestly, Esther, you should go." She sat up straight. "I got a free night. You should use it."

"You got a free night? At Sweet Breeze? How?"

Stacey waved her hand like it was no big deal, though she'd be spilling the whole story in seconds. "Oh, there was a mishap with the room service, and I was offered a free room. I took it."

Esther positioned her own shades over her eyes. "We should have the Beach Club there next time we meet."

The thought of having their Women's Beach Club—a secret society of women on the island who'd been burned by men, had their husbands leave them for younger, prettier women, or who had simply decided not to pursue romance—inside Sweet Breeze made Stacey burst into laughter.

"That's perfect," she said, thinking of the perfectly romantic atmosphere Sweet Breeze worked so hard to create. "Ironic, but perfect."

"We can totally order room service. Maybe we'll get more free rooms."

Somehow, Stacey didn't think so. Men like Fisher fixed problems like the one she'd had that morning. She switched her gaze to the undulating teal water of the bay, a measure of relaxation finally sighing through her. "It was a nice hotel."

"Of course it's nice," Esther said. "It cost two billion dollars to build."

"I met him, you know."

"Who?"

"The owner."

"You did?" Esther kicked sand onto Stacey's feet as she launched herself forward. "How? What was he like?"

Before Stacey could answer, another bag got dropped on the sand beside Esther. "Watch out," Tawny Loveless, the third part of their little boyfriend-less triangle, said. "There's a god walking this way."

She was part of the Women's Beach Club and claimed she didn't want or need a man in her life. But she seemed to know who all the available men on the island were, and her radar for a good-looking man was unmatched.

Stacey didn't want to look, but she found her head

swiveling back the way Tawny had come. There was indeed a god walking their way, and she'd seen that gait before. Seen him before, only a couple of hours ago.

A hiss leaked from her body as it went cold. Though it was the height of summer, and the sun was practically burning everything and everyone on the beach, Stacey shivered. The tall, nearly bald man wore a dark gray rash guard that rippled with the lines of his muscles, and a bright orange pair of swim trunks.

"That's him," she said in a voice she simply meant to be hushed but which came out with a sort of reverence she didn't understand.

"Who?" Even Esther's normally boisterous tone had softened.

"The owner of Sweet Breeze. Fisher Davenport." And he was headed directly toward Stacey herself.

BOOKS IN THE HAWTHORNE HARBOR ROMANCE SERIES

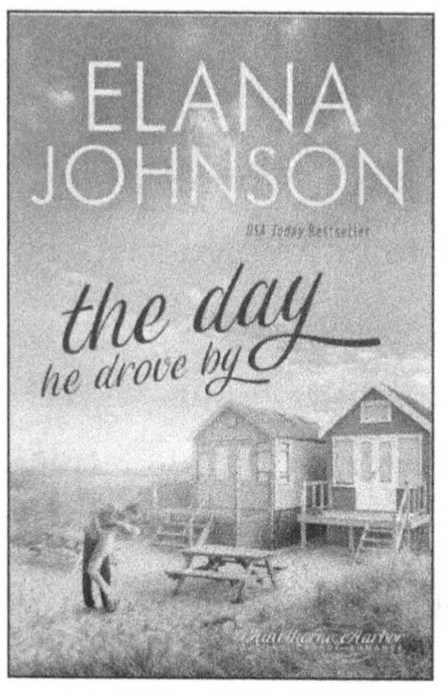

The Day He Drove By (Hawthorne Harbor Second Chance Romance, Book 1): A widowed florist, her ten-year-old daughter, and the paramedic who delivered the girl a decade earlier...

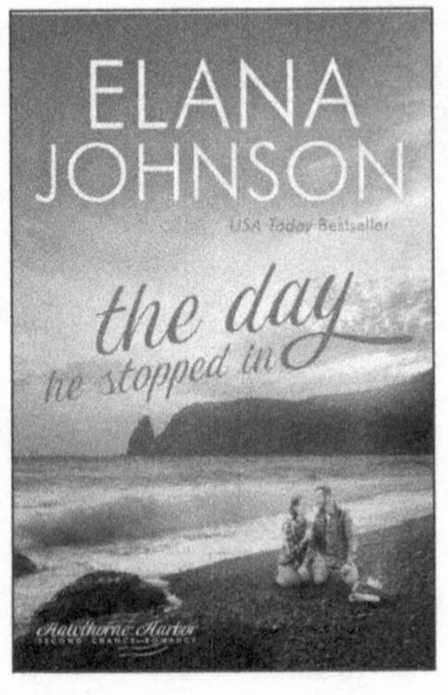

The Day He Stopped In (Hawthorne Harbor Second Chance Romance, Book 2): Janey Germaine is tired of entertaining tourists in Olympic National Park all day and trying to keep her twelve-year-old son occupied at night. When longtime friend and the Chief of Police, Adam Herrin, offers to take the boy on a ride-along one fall evening, Janey starts to see him in a different light. Do they have the courage to take their relationship out of the friend zone?

The Day He Said Hello (Hawthorne Harbor Second Chance Romance, Book 3): Bennett Patterson is content with his boring firefighting job and his big great dane...until he comes face-toface with his high school girlfriend, Jennie Zimmerman, who swore she'd never return to Hawthorne Harbor. Can they rekindle their old flame? Or will their opposite personalities keep them apart?

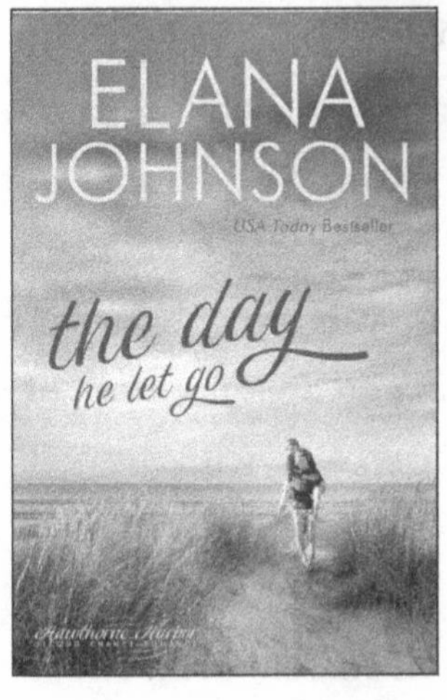

The Day He Let Go (Hawthorne Harbor Second Chance Romance, Book 4): Trent Baker is ready for another relationship, and he's hopeful he can find someone who wants him and to be a mother to his son. Lauren Michaels runs her own general contract company, and she's never thought she has a maternal bone in her body. But when she gets a second chance with the handsome K9 cop who blew her off when she first came to town, she can't say no... Can Trent and Lauren make their differences into strengths and build a family?

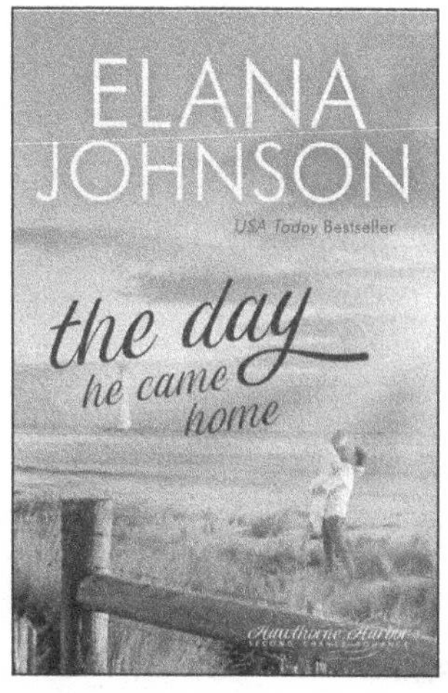

The Day He Came Home (Hawthorne Harbor Second Chance Romance, Book 5): A wounded Marine returns to Hawthorne Harbor years after the woman he was married to for exactly one week before she got an annulment...and then a baby nine months later. Can Hunter and Alice make a family out of past heartache?

The Day He Asked Again (Hawthorne Harbor Second Chance Romance, Book 6): A Coast Guard captain would rather spend his time on the sea...unless he's with the woman he's been crushing on for months. Can Brooklynn and Dave make their second chance stick?

BOOKS IN THE GETAWAY BAY BILLIONAIRE ROMANCE SERIES

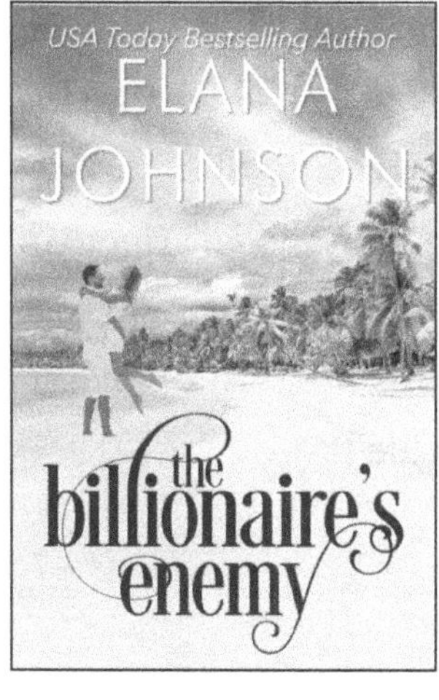

The Billionaire's Enemy (Book 1): A local island B&B owner hates the swanky high-rise hotel down the beach...but not the billionaire who owns it. Can she deal with strange summer weather, tourists, and falling in love?

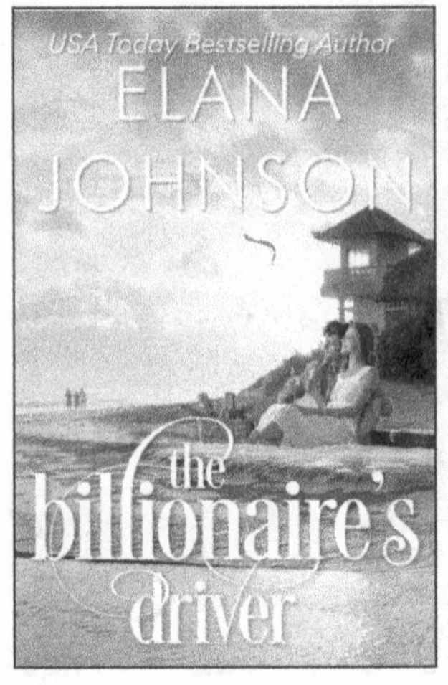

The Billionaire's Driver (Book 2): A car service owner who's been driving the billionaire pineapple plantation owner for years finally gives him a birthday gift that opens his eyes to see her, the woman who's literally been right in front of him all this time. Can he open his heart to the possibility of true love?

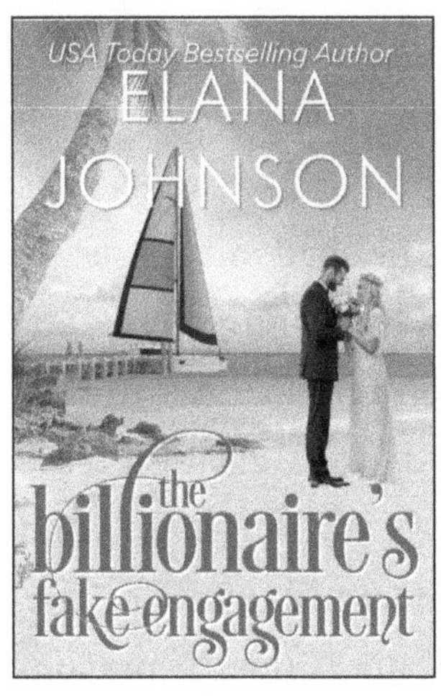

The Billionaire's Fake Engagement (Book 3): A former poker player turned beach bum billionaire needs a date to a hospital gala, so he asks the beach yoga instructor his dog can't seem to stay away from. At the event, they get "engaged" to deter her former boyfriend from pursuing her. Can he move his fake fiancée into a real relationship?

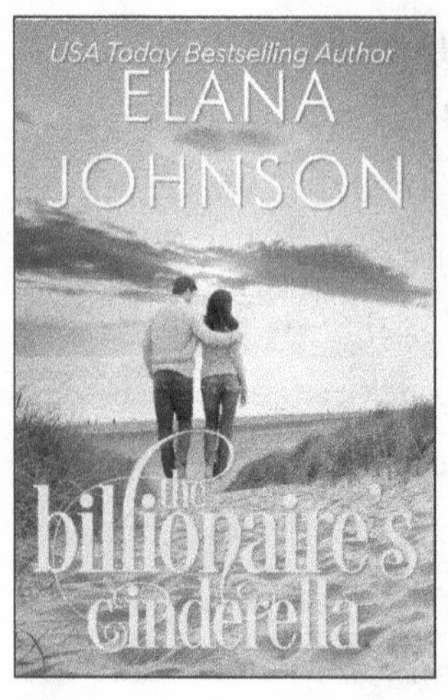

The Billionaire's Cinderella (Book 4): The owner of a beach-side drink stand has taken more bad advice from rich men than humanly possible, which requires her to take a second job cleaning the home of a billionaire and global diamond mine owner. Can she put aside her preconceptions about rich men and make a relationship with him work?

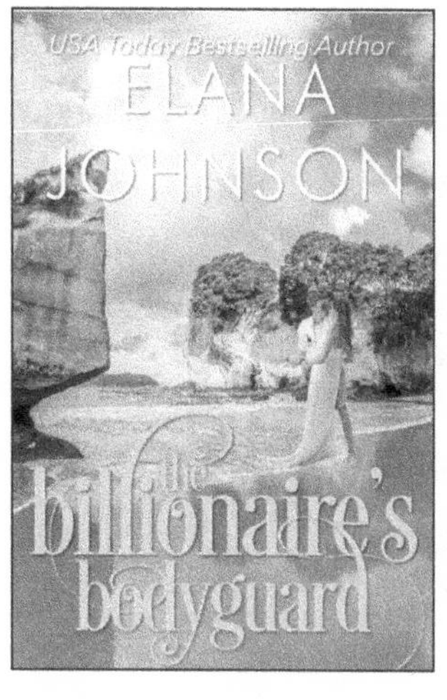

The Billionaire's Bodyguard (Book 5): Women can be rich too...and this female billionaire can usually take care of herself just fine, thank you very much. But she has no defense against her past...or the gorgeous man she hires to protect her from it. He's her bodyguard, not her boyfriend. Will she be able to keep those two B-words separate or will she take her second chance to get her tropical happily-ever-after?

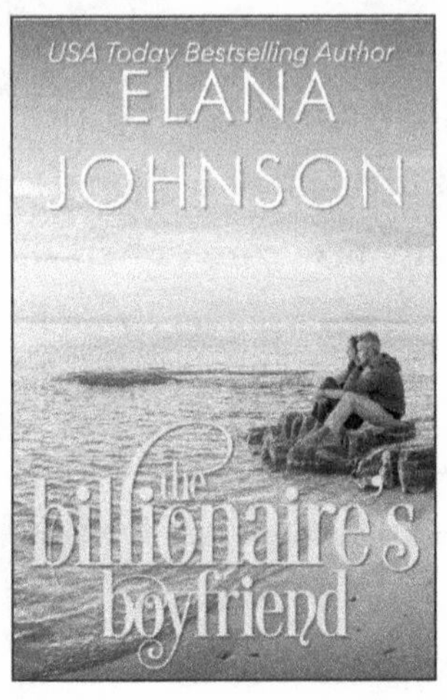

The Billionaire's Boyfriend (Book 6): Can a closet organizer fit herself into a single father's hectic life? Or will this female billionaire choose work over love...again?

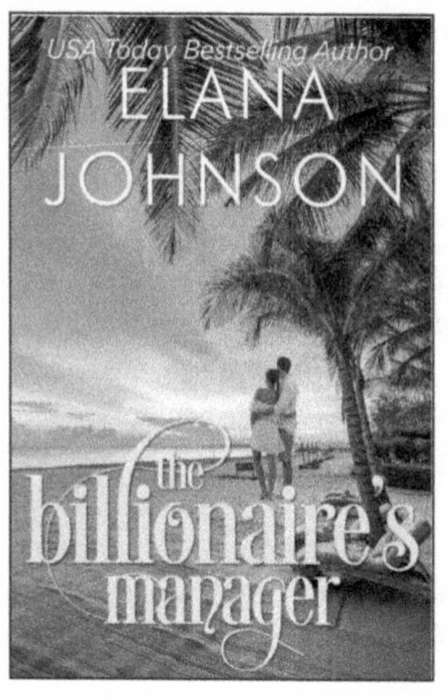

The Billionaire's Manager (Book 7): A billionaire who has a love affair with his job, his new bank manager, and how they bravely navigate the island of Getaway Bay...and their own ideas about each other.

The Billionaire's Ex-Wife (Book 8): A silver fox, a dating app, and the mistaken identity that brings this billionaire faceto-face with his ex-wife...

BOOKS IN THE BRIDES & BEACHES ROMANCE SERIES

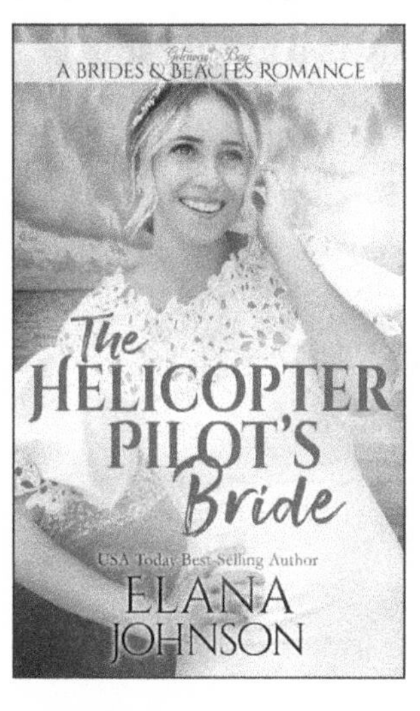

The Helicopter Pilot's Bride (Book 1): Charlotte Madsen's whole world came crashing down six months ago with the words, "I met someone else." Her marriage of eleven years dissolved, and she left one island on the east coast for the island of Getaway Bay. She was not expecting a tall, handsome man to be flat on his back under the kitchen sink when she arrives at the supposedly abandoned house. But former Air Force pilot, Dawson Dane, has a charming devil-may-care personality, and Charlotte could use some happiness in her life.

Can Charlotte navigate the healing process to find love again?

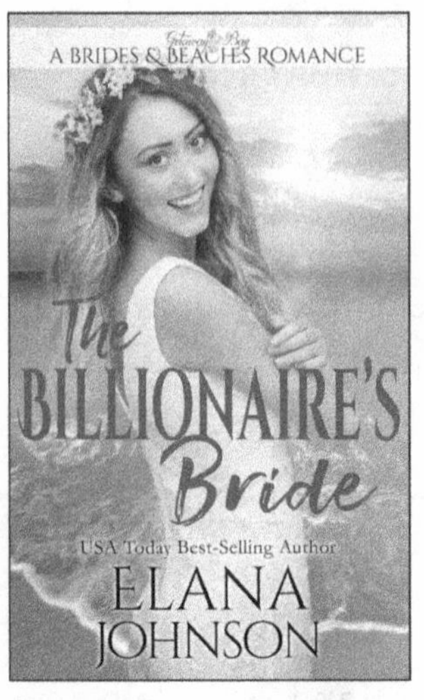

The Billionaire's Bride (Book 2): Two best friends, their hasty agreement, and the fake engagement that has the island of Getaway Bay in a tailspin...

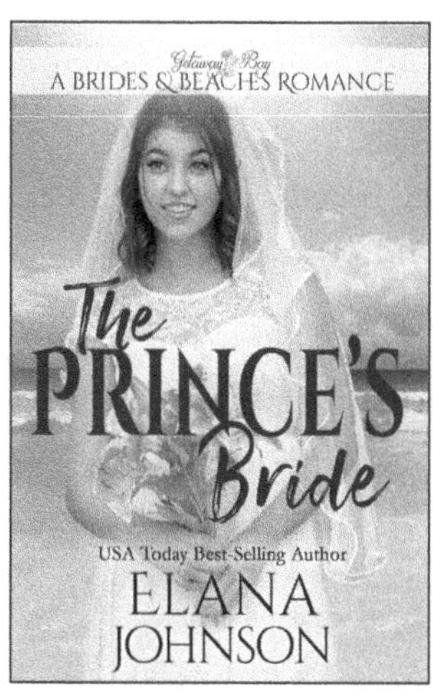

The Prince's Bride (Book 3): She's a synchronized swimmer looking to make some extra cash. He's a prince in hiding. When they meet in the "empty" mansion she's supposed to be housesitting, sparks fly. Can Noah and Zara stop arguing long enough to realize their feelings for each other might be romantic?

The Doctor's Bride (Book 4): A doctor, a wedding planner, and a flat tire... Can Shannon and Jeremiah make a love connection when they work next door to each other?

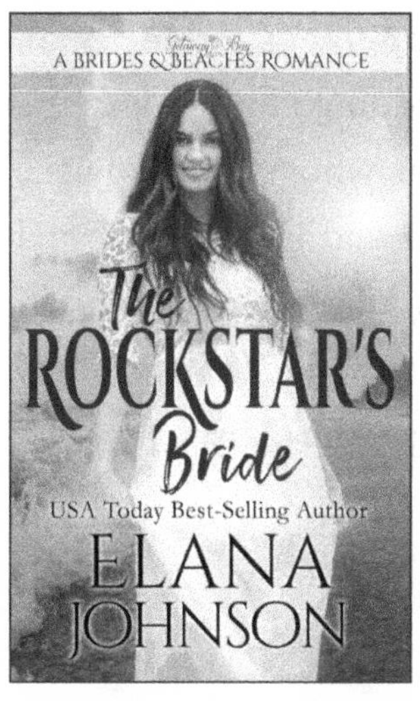

The Rockstar's Bride (Book 5): Riley finds a watch and contacts the owner, only to learn he's the lead singer and guitarist for a hugely popular band. Evan is only on the island of Getaway Bay for a friend's wedding, but he's intrigued by the gorgeous woman who returns his watch. Can they make a relationship work when they're from two different worlds?

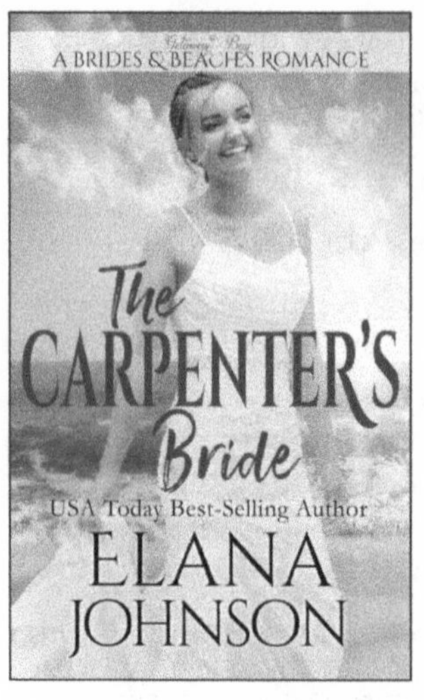

The Carpenter's Bride (Book 6): A wedding planner and the carpenter who's lost his wife... Can Lisa and Cal navigate the mishaps of a relationship in order to find themselves standing at the altar?

The Police Chief's Bride (Book 7): The Chief of Police and a woman with a restraining order against her... Can Wyatt and Deirdre try for their second chance at love? Or will their pasts keep them apart forever?

BOOKS IN THE STRANDED IN GETAWAY BAY ROMANCE SERIES

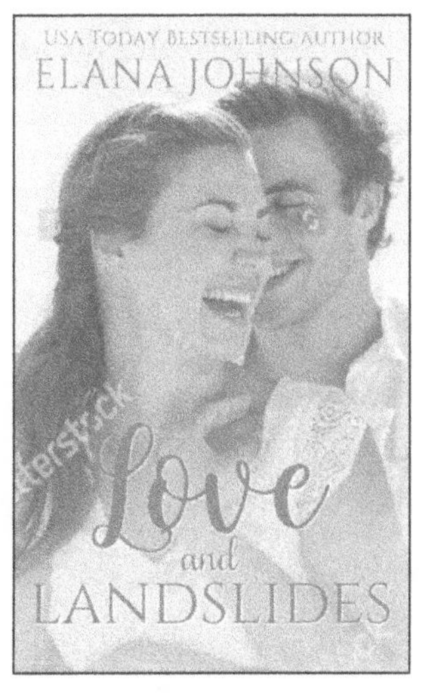

Love and Landslides (Book 1): A freak storm has her sliding down the mountain...right into the arms of her ex. As Eden and Holden spend time out in the wilds of Hawaii trying to survive, their old flame is rekindled. But with secrets and old feelings in the way, will Holden be able to take all the broken pieces of his life and put them back together in a way that makes sense? Or will he lose his heart and the reputation of his company because of a single landslide?

Kisses and Killer Whales (Book 2): Friends who ditch her. A pod of killer whales. A limping cruise ship. All reasons Iris finds herself stranded on an deserted island with the handsome Navy SEAL...

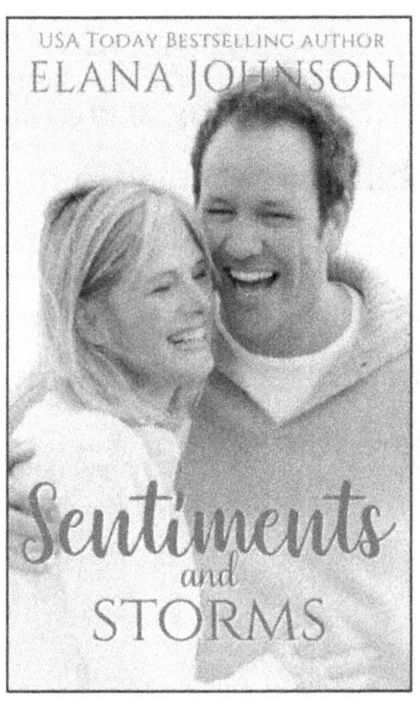

Storms and Sentiments (Book 3): He can throw a precision pass, but he's dead in the water in matters of the heart...

Crushes and Cowboys (Book 4): Tired of the dating scene, a cowboy billionaire puts up an Internet ad to find a woman to come out to a deserted island with him to see if they can make a love connection...

ABOUT ELANA

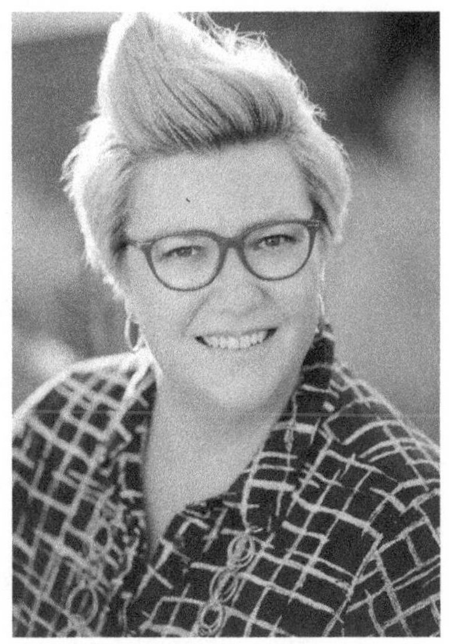

Elana Johnson is the USA Today bestselling author of dozens of clean and wholesome contemporary romance novels. She lives in Utah, where she mothers two fur babies, taxis her daughter to theater several times a week, and eats a lot of Ferrero Rocher while writing. Find her on her website at elanajohnson.com.

CPSIA information can be obtained
at www.ICGtesting.com
Printed in the USA
LVHW040332100623
749337LV00001B/71

9 781953 506115